Between You and Me

Sir Harry Lauder

Contents

BETWEEN YOU AND ME

BY

Sir Harry Lauder

*This book is dedicated
to the Fathers and Mothers
of the Boys who went
and those who prepared to go.*

"ONE OF THE BOYS WHO WENT"

Say, Mate, don't you figure it's great
  To think, when the war is all over,
And we're thro' with the mud--
And the spilling of blood,
  And we're shipped back again to old Dover;
When they've paid us our tin
And we've blown the lot in,
  And our very last penny is spent,
We'll still have a thought, if that's all we've got:
  Well, I'm one of the boys who went.

Perhaps, later on, when the wild days are gone
  And you're settling down for life--
You've a girl in your eye, you'll ask bye and bye
  To share up with you as your wife--
Then, when a few years have flown
And you've got "chicks" of your own
  And you're happy, and snug, and content,
Man, it will make your heart glad
When they boast of their Dad--
  My Dad--He was one of the boys who went.

CHAPTER I

It's a bonny world, I'm tellin' ye! It was worth saving, and saved it's been, if only you and I and the rest of us that's alive and fit to work and play and do our part will do as we should. I went around the world in yon days when there was war. I saw all manner of men. I saw them live, and fight, and dee. And now I'm back from the other side of the world again. And I'm tellin' ye again that it's a bonny world I've seen, but no so bonny a world as we maun make it--you and I. So let us speer a wee, and I'll be trying to tell you what I think, and what I've seen.

There'll be those going up and doon the land preaching against everything that is, and talking of all that should be. There'll be others who'll say that all is well, and that the man that wants to make a change is no better than Trotzky or a Hun. There'll be those who'll be wantin' me to let a Soviet tell me what songs to sing to ye, and what the pattern of my kilts should be. But what have such folk to say to you and me, plain folk that we are, with our work to do, and the wife and the bairns to be thinkin' of when it comes time to tak' our ease and rest? Nothin', I say, and I'll e'en say it again and again before I'm done.

The day of the plain man has come again. The world belongs to us. We made it. It was plain men who fought the war--who deed and bled and suffered in France, and Gallipoli and everywhere where men went about the business of the war. And it's plain men who have come home to Britain, and America, to Australia and Canada and all the other places that sent their sons out to fight for humanity. They maun fight for humanity still, for that fight is not won,--deed, and it's no more than made a fair beginning.

Your profiteer is no plain man. Nor is your agitator. They are set up against you and me, and all the other plain men and women who maun make a living and tak' care of those that are near and dear to them. Some of us plain folk have more than others of us, maybe, but there'll be no envy among us for a' that. We maun stand together, and we shall. I'm as sure of that as I'm sure that God has charged himself with the care of this world and all who dwell in it.

I maun talk more about myself than I richt like to do if I'm to make you see how I'm feeling and thinking aboot all the things that are loose wi' the world to-day. For, after all, it's himself a man knows better than anyone else, and if I've ideas about life and the world it's from the way life's dealt with me that I've learned them. I've no done so badly for myself and my ain, if I do say it. And that's why, maybe, I've small patience with them that's busy always saying the plain man has no chance these days.

Do you ken how I made my start? Are ye thinkin', maybe, that I'd a faither to send me to college and gie me masters to teach me to sing my songs, and to play the piano? Man, ye'd be wrong, an' ye thought so! My faither deed, puir man, when I was but a bairn of eleven--he was but thirty-twa himself. And my mither was left with me and six other bairns to care for. 'Twas but little schoolin' I had.

After my faither deed I went to work. The law would not let me gie up my schoolin' altogether. But three days a week I learned to read and write and cipher, and the other three I worked in a flax mill in the wee Forfarshire town of Arboath. Do ye ken what I was paid? Twa shillin' the week. That's less than fifty cents in American money. And that was in 1881, thirty eight years ago. I've my bit siller the noo. I've my wee hoose amang the heather at Dunoon. I've my war loan stock, and my Liberty and Victory bonds. But what I've got I've worked for and I've earned, and you've done the same for what you've got, man, and so can any other man if he but wull.

I do not believe God ever intended men to get too rich and prosperous. When they do lots of little things that go to make up the real man have to be left out, or be dropped out. And men think too much of things. For a lang time now things have been riding over men, and mankind has ceased riding over things. But now we plain folk are going again to make things subservient to life, to human life, to the needs and interests of the plain man. That is what I want to talk of always, of late--the need of plain living, plain speaking, plain, useful thinking.

For me the great discovery of the war was that humanity was the greatest thing in the world. I had to learn that no man could live for and by himself alone. I had to learn that I must think all the time of others. A great grief came to me when my son was killed. But I was not able to think and act for myself alone. I was minded to tak' a gun in my hand, and go out to seek to kill twa Huns for my bairn. But it was his mither who stopped me.

"Vengeance is Mine, saith the Lord. I will repay." She reminded me of those words. And I was ashamed, for that I had been minded to forget.

And when I would have hidden myself away from a' the world, and nursed my grief, I was reminded, again, that I must not. My boy had died for humanity. He had not been there in France aboot his own affairs. Was it for me, his father, to be selfish when he had been unselfish? Had I done as I planned, had I said I could not carry on because of my ain grief, I should have brought sorrow and trouble to others, and I should have failed to do my duty, since there were those who, in a time of sore trouble and distress, found living easier because I made them laugh and wink back the tears that were too near to dropping.

Oh, aye, I've had my share of trouble. So when I'm tellin' ye this is a bonny world do not be thinkin' it's a man who's lived easily always and whose lines have been cast only in pleasant places who is talking with ye. I've as little patience as any man with those fat, sleek folk who fold their hands and roll their een and speak without knowledge of grief and pain when those who have known both rebel. But I know that God brings help and I know this much more--that he will not bring it to the man who has not begun to try to help himself, and never fails to bring it to the man who has.

Weel, as I've told ye, it was for twa shillin' a week that I first worked. I was a strappin' lout of a boy then, fit to work harder than I did, and earn more, and ever and again I'd tell them at some new mill I was past fourteen, and they'd put me to work at full time. But I could no hide myself awa' from the inspector when he came around, and each time he'd send me back to school and to half time.

It was hard work, and hard living in yon days. But it was a grand time I had. I mind the sea, and the friends I had. And it was there, in Arboath, when I was no more than a laddie, I first sang before an audience. A travelling concert company had come to Oddfellows' Hall, and to help to draw the crowd there was a song competition for amateurs, with a watch for a prize. I won the prize, and I was as conceited as you please, with all the other mill boys envying me, and seein', at last, some use in the way I was always singing. A bit later there was another contest, and I won that, too, with a six-bladed knife for a prize. But I did not keep the knife, for, for all my mither could do to stop me, I'd begun even in those days to be a great pipe smoker, and I sold the knife for threepence, which bought me an ounce of thick black--a tobacco I still like, though I can afford a better now, could I but find it.

It was but twa years we stayed at Arboath. From there we went to Hamilton, on the west coast, since my uncle told of the plenty work there was to be found there at the coal mines. I went on at the pitheads, and, after a week or so, a miner gave me a chance to go below with him. He was to pay me ten shillings for a week's work as his helper, and it was proud I was the morn when I went doon into the blackness for the first time.

But I was no so old, ye'll be mindin', and I won't say I was not fearsome, too. It's a queer feelin' ye have when ye first go doon into a pit. The sun's gone, and the light, and it seems like the air's gone from your lungs with them. I carried a gauze lamp, but the bit flicker of it was worse than useless--it made it harder for me to see, instead of easier. The pressure's what ye feel; it's like to be chokin' ye until you're used to it. And then the black, damp walls, pressin' in, as if they were great hands aching to be at your throat! Oh, I'm tellin' ye there's lots of things pleasanter than goin' doon into a coal pit for the first time.

I mind, since then, I've gone doon far deeper than ever we did at Hamilton. At Butte, in Montana, in America, I went doon three thousand feet--more than half a mile, mind ye! There they find copper, and good copper, at that depth. But they took me doon there in an express elevator. I had no time to be afeared before we were doon, walkin' along a broad, dry gallery, as well lighted as Broadway or the Strand, with electric lights, and great fans to keep the air cool and dry. It's different, minin' so, to what it was when I was a boy at Hamilton.

But I'm minded, when I think of Butte, and the great copper mines there, of the thing I'm chiefly thinking of in writing this book.

I was in Butte during the war--after America had come in. 'Deed, and it was just before the Huns made their last bid, and thought to break the British line. Ye mind yon days in the spring of 1918? Anxious days, sad days. And in the war we all were fighting, copper counted for nigh as much as men. The miners there in Butte were fighting the Hun as surely as if they'd been at Cantigny or Chateau-Thierry.

Never had there been such pay in Butte as in yon time. I sang at a great theatre one of the greatest in all the western country. It was crowded at every performance. The folk sat on the stage, so deep packed, so close together, there was scarce room for my walk around. Ye mind how I fool ye, when I'm singin', by walkin' round and round the stage after a verse? It's my way of givin' short measure--save that folk seem to like to see me do it!

Weel, there was that great mining city, where the copper that was so needed for munitions was being mined. The men were well paid. Yet there was discontent. Agitators were at work among them, stirring up trouble, seeking to take their minds off their work and hurt the production of the copper that was needed to save the lives of men like those who were digging it out of the ground. They were thinkin', there, in yon days, that men could live for themselves and by themselves.

But, thank God, it was only a few who thought so. The great lot of the men were sound, and they did grand work. And they found their reward, too--as men always do when they do their work well and think of what it means.

There were others in Butte, too, who were thinking only of themselves. Some of them hung one of the agitators, whiles before I was there. They had not thought, any more than had the foolish men among the workers, how each of us is dependent upon others, of the debts that every day brings us, that we owe to all humanity.

Ye'll e'en forgie me if I wander so, sometimes, in this book? Ye'll ken how it is when you'll be talkin' with a friend? Ye'll begin about the bit land or the cow one of you means to sell to the other. Ye'll ha' promised the wife, maybe, when ye slipped oot, that ye'd come richt back, so soon as ye had finished wi' Sandy. And then, after ye'd sat ye doon together in a corner of the bar, why one bit word would lead to another, and ye'd be wanderin' from the subject afore ye knew it? It's so wi' me. I'm no writin' a book so much as I'm sittin' doon wi' ye all for a chat, as I micht do gi'en you came into my dressing room some nicht when I was singin' in your toon.

It's a far cry that last bit o' wandering meant--from Hamilton in my ain Scotland to Butte in the Rocky Mountains of America! And yet, for what I'm thinkin' it's no so far a cry. There were men I knew in Hamilton who'd have found themselves richt at hame among the agitators in Butte. I'm minded to be tellin' ye a tale of one such lad.

CHAPTER II

The lad I've in mind I'll call Andy McTavish, which'll no be his richt name, ye'll ken. He could ha' been the best miner in the pit. He could ha' been the best liked lad in a' those parts. But he was not. Nothin' was ever good enough for Andy. I'm tellin' ye, had he found a golden sovereign along the road, whiles he went to his work, he'd have come to us at the pit moanin' and complainin' because it was not a five pound note he'd turned up with his toe!

Never was Andy satisfied. Gi'en there were thirty shillin' for him to draw at the pit head, come Saturday night, he'd growl that for the hard work he'd done he should ha' had thirty-five. Mind ye, I'm not sayin' he was wrong, only he was no worse off than the rest, and better than some, and he was always feeling that it was he who was badly used, just he, not everyone. He'd curse the gaffer if the vein of coal he had to work on wasn't to his liking; he knew nothing of the secret of happiness, which is to take what comes and always remember that for every bit of bad there's nearly always a bit o' good waitin' around the corner.

Yet, with it all, there wasn't a keener, brighter lad than Andy in all Lanarkshire. He had always a good story to crack. He was handy with his fists; he could play well at football or any other game he tried. He wasn't educated; had he been, we all used to think, he micht ha' made a name for himself. I didn't see, in those days, that we were all wrong. If Andy'd been a good miner, if he'd started by doing well, at least, as well as he could, the thing he had the chance to do, then we'd have been right to think that all he needed to be famous and successful was to have the chance.

But, as it was, Andy was always too busy greetin' over his bad luck. It was bad luck that he had to work below ground, when he loved the sunshine. It was bad luck that the wee toon was sae dull for a man of his spirit. Andy seemed to think that some one should come around and make him happy and comfortable and rich-

-not that the only soul alive to whom he had a right to look for such blessings was himself.

I'll no say we weren't liking Andy all richt. But, ye ken, he was that sort of man we'd always say, when we were talking of him: "Oh, aye-- there's Andy. A braw laddie--but what he micht be!"

Andy thought he was better than the rest of us. There was that, for ane thing. He'd no be doing the things the rest of us were glad enough to do. It was naught to him to walk along the Quarry Road wi' a lassie, and buss her in a dark spot, maybe. And just because he'd no een for them, the wee lassies were ready to come, would he but lift his finger! Is it no always the way? There'd be a dozen decent, hard working miners who could no get a lassie to look their way, try as they micht--men who wanted nothing better than to settle doon in a wee hoose somewhere, and stay at home with the wife, and, a bit later, with the bairns.

Ye'd never be seein' Andy on a Saturday afternoon along the ropes, watchin' a football game. Or, if ye did, there'd be a sneer curling his lips. He was a braw looking lad, was Andy, but that sneer came too easily.

"Where did they learn the game" he'd say, turning up his nose. "If they'd gie me a crack I'd show them----"

And, sure enough, if anyone got up a game, Andy'd be the first to take off his coat. And he was a good player, but no sae good as he thought himself. 'Twas so wi' all the man did; he was handy enough, but there were aye others better. But he was all for having a hand in whatever was going on himself; he'd no the patience to watch others and learn, maybe, from the way they did.

Andy was a solitary man; he'd no wife nor bairn, and he lived by his lane, save for a dog and a bantam cock. Them he loved dearly and nought was too good for them. The dog, I'm thinkin', he had odd uses for; Andy was no above seekin' a hare now and then that was no his by rights. And he'd be out before dawn, sometimes, with old Dick, who could help him with his poaching. 'Twas so he lost Dick at last; a farmer caught the pair of them in a field of his, and the farmer's dog took Dick by the throat and killed him.

Andy was fair disconsolate; he was so sad the farmer, even, was sorry for him, and would no have him arrested, as he micht well have done, since he'd caught man and dog red handed, as the saying is. He buried the dog come the next evening, and was no fit to speak to for days. And then, richt on top of that, he lost his bird; it was killed in a main wi' another bantam, and Andy lost his champion bantam, and forty shillin' beside, That settled him. Wi' his two friends gone frae him, he had no more use for the pit and the countryside. He disappeared, and the next we heard was that he'd gone for a soldier. Those were the days, long, long gone, before the great war. We heard Andy's regiment was ordered to India, and then we heard no more of him.

Gi'en I had stayed a miner, I doubt I'd ever ha' laid een on Andy again, or heard of him, since he came no more to Hamilton, and I'd, most like, ha' stayed there, savin' a trip to Glasga noo and then, all the days of my life. But, as ye ken, I didna stay there. I'll be tellin', ye ken, hoo it was I came to gang on the stage and become the Harry you're all so good to when he sings to ye. But the noo I'll just say that it was years later, and I was singing in London, in four or five halls the same nicht, when I met Andy one day. I was fair glad to see him; I'm always glad to see a face from hame. And Andy was looking fine and braw. He'd good clothes on his back, and he was sleek and well fed and prosperous looking. We made our way to a hotel; and there we sat ourselves doon and chatted for three hours.

"Aye, and I'll ha' seen most of the world since I last clapped my een on you, Harry," he said. "I've heard much about you, and it's glad I am to be seein' you."

He told me his story. He'd gone for a soldier, richt enough, and been sent to India. He'd had trouble from the start; he was always fighting, and while that's a soldier's trade, he's no supposed to practice it with his fellows, ye ken, but to save his anger for the enemy. But, for once in a way, Andy's quarrelsome ways did him good. He was punished once for fighting wi' his corporal, and when his captain came to look into things he found the trouble started because the corporal called him, the captain, out of his name. So he made Andy his servant, and Andy served wi' him till he was killed in South Africa.

Andy was wounded there, and invalided home. He was discharged, and said he'd ha' no more of the army--he'd liked that job no better than any other he'd ever had. His captain, in his will, left Andy twa hunder pounds sterlin'--more siller than Andy's ever thought to finger in his life.

"So it was that siller gave you your start, Andy, man?" I said.

He laughed.

"Oh, aye!" he said. "And came near to givin' me my finish, too, Harry. I put the siller into a business down Portsmouth way--I set up for a contractor. I was doin' fine, too, but a touring company came along, and there was a lassie wi' 'em so braw and bonnie I'd like to have deed for love of her, man, Harry."

It was a sad little story, that, but what you'd expect. Andy, the lady killer, had ne'er had een for the lassies up home, who'd ha' asked nothin' better than to ha' him notice them. But this bit lass, whom he knew was no better than she should be, could ha' her will o' him from the start. He followed her aboot; he spent his siller on her. His business went to the dogs, and when she'd milked him dry she laughed and slipped awa', and he never saw her again. I'm thinkin', at that, Andy was lucky; had he had more siller she'd maybe ha' married him for it.

'Twas after that Andy shipped before the mast. He saw Australia and America, but he was never content to settle doon anywhere, though there were times when he had more siller than he'd lost at Portsmouth. Once he was robbed; twa or three times he just threw his siller away. It was always the same story; no matter how much he was earning it was never enough; he should always ha' had more.

But Andy learned his lesson at last. He fell in love once more; this time with a decent, bonnie lass who'd have no dealings wi' him until he proved to her that she could trust him. He went to work again for a contractor, and saved his siller. If he thought he should ha' more, he said nothing, only waited. It was no so long before he saved enough to buy a partnership wi' his gaffer.

"I'm happy the noo, Harry," he said. "I've found out that what I make depends on me, not on anyone else. The wife's there waiting for me when I gang hame at nicht. There's the ane bairn, and another coming, God bless him."

Weel, Andy'd learned nothing he hadn't been told a million times by his parents and his friends. But he was one of those who maun learn for themselves to mak siccar. Can ye no see how like he was to some of them that's makin' a great name for themselves the noo, goin' up and doon the land tellin' us what we should do? I'm no the one to say that it should be every man for himself; far from it. We've all to think of others beside ourselves. But when it comes to winning or losing in this battle of life we've all got to learn the same lesson that cost poor Andy so dear. We maun stand on our ain feet. Neither God nor man can help us until we've begun to help ourselves.

CHAPTER III

In the beginnin' I was no a miner, ye ken, in the pit at Hamilton. I went doon first as a miner's helper, but that was for but the one week. And at its end my gaffer just went away. He was to pay me ten shillings, but never a three-penny bit of all that siller did I see! It was cruel hard, and it hurt me sore, to think I'd worked sae long and so hard and got nothing for it, but there was no use greetin'. And on Monday I went doon into the pit again, but this time as a trapper.

In a mine, ye ken, there are great air-tight gates. Without them there'd be more fires and explosions than there are. And by each one there's a trapper, who's to open and close them as the pony drivers with their lurches that carry the mined coal to the hoists go in and out. Easy work, ye'll say. Aye--if a trapper did only what he was paid for doing. He's not supposed to do ought else than open and close gates, and his orders are that he must never leave them. But trappers are boys, as a rule, and the pony drivers strong men, and they manage to make the trappers do a deal of their work as well as their ain. They can manage well enough, for they're no slow to gie a kick or a cuff if the trapper bids them attend to their own affairs and leave him be.

I learned that soon enough. And many was the blow I got; many the time a driver warmed me with his belt, when I was warm enough already. But, for a' that, we had good times in the pit. I got to know the men I worked with, and to like them fine. You do that at work, and especially underground, I'm thinking. There, you ken, there's always some danger, and men who may dee together any day are like to be friendly while they have the chance.

I've known worse days, tak' them all in all, than those in Eddlewood Colliery. We'd a bit cabin at the top of the brae, and there we'd keep our oil for our lamps, and leave our good coats. We'd carry wi' us, too, our piece--bread and cheese, and cold tea, that served for the meal we ate at midday.

'Twas in the pit, I'm thinkin', I made my real start. For 'twas there I first began to tak' heed of men and see how various they were. Ever since then, in the days when I began to sing, and when my friends in the audiences decided that I should spend my life so instead of working mair with my twa hands, it's been what I knew of men and women that's been of service to me. When I come upon the idea for a new song 'tis less often a bit of verse or a comic idea I think of first--mair like it's some odd bit of humanity, some man a wee bit different from others. He'll be a bit saft, perhaps, or mean, or generous--I'm not carin', so long as he's but different.

And there, in the pit, men showed themselves to one another, and my een and my ears were aye open in those days. I'd try to be imitating this queer character or that, sometimes, but I'd do it only for my ain pleasure. I was no thinkin', in yon days, of ever singing on the stage. How should I ha' done so? I was but Harry Lauder, strugglin' hard to mak siller enough to help at home.

But, whiles I was at my work, I'd sing a bit song now and again, when I thought no one was by to hear. Sometimes I was wrong, and there's be one nearer than I thought. And so it got aboot in the pit that I could sing a bit. I had a good voice enough, though I knew nothing, then, of how to sing--I've learned much of music since I went on the stage. Then, though, I was just a boy, singing because he liked to hear himself sing. I knew few and I'd never seen a bit o' printed music. As for reading notes on paper I scarcely knew such could be done.

The miners liked to have me sing. It was in the cabin in the brae, where we'd gather to fill our lamps and eat our bread and cheese, that they asked me, as a rule. We were great ones for being entertained. And we never lacked entertainers. If a man could do card tricks, or dance a bit, he was sure to be popular. One man was a fairish piper, and sometimes the skirl of some old Hieland melody would sound weird enough, as I made my way to the cabin through a grey mist.

I was called upon oftener than anyone else, I think.

"Gie's a bit sang, Harry," they'd say. Maybe ye'll not be believing me, but I was timid at the first of it, and slow to do as they asked. But later I got over that, and those first audiences of mine did much for me. They taught me not to be afraid, so long as I was doing my best, and they taught me, too, to study my hearers and learn to decide what folk liked, and why they liked it.

I had no songs of my own then, ye'll understand; I just sang such bits as I'd picked up of the popular songs of the day, that the famous "comics" of the music halls were singing--or that they'd been singing a year before--aye, that'll be nearer the truth of it!

I had one rival I didn't like, though, as I look back the noo, I can see I was'na too kind to feel as I did aboot puir Jock. Jock coul no stand it to have anyone else applauded, or to see them getting attention he craved for himself. He could no sing, but he was a great story teller. Had he just said, out and out, that he was making up tales, 'twould have been all richt enough. But, no--Jock must pretend he'd been everywhere he told about, and that he'd been an actor in every yarn he spun. He was a great boaster, too--he'd tell us, without a blush, of the most desperate things he'd done, and of how brave he'd been. He was the bravest man alive, to hear him tell it.

They were askin' me to sing one day, and I was ready to oblige, when Jock started.

"Bide a wee, Harry, man," he said, "while I'll be tellin' ye of a thing that happened to me on the veldt in America once."

"The veldt's in South Africa, Jock," someone said, slyly.

"No, no--it's the Rocky Mountains you're meaning. They're in South Africa--I climbed three of them there in a day, once. Weel, I was going to tell ye of this time when we were hunting gold----"

And he went on, to spin a yarn that would have made Ananias himself blush. When he was done it was time to gang back to work, and my song not sung! I'd a new chorus I was wanting them to hear, too, and I was angry with puir Jock--more shame to me! And so I resolved to see if he was as brave as he was always saying. I'm ashamed of this, mind ye-- I'm admitting it.

So, next day, at piece time, I didn't join the crowd that went to the auld cabin. Instead I did without my bread and cheese and my cold tea-- and, man, I'm tellin' ye it means a lot for Harry to forego his victuals!--and went quickly along to the face where Jock was working. It happened that he was at work there alone that day, so I was able to make my plans against his coming back, and be sure it wouldna be spoiled. I had a mask and an old white sheet. On the mask I'd painted eyes with phosphorus, and I put it on, and draped the sheet over my shoulders. When Jock came along I rose up, slowly, and made some very dreadful noises, that micht well ha' frightened a man as brave even as Jock was always saying to us he was!

Ye should ha' seen him run along that stoop! He didna wait a second; he never touched me, or tried to. He cried out once, nearly dropped his lamp, and then turned tail and went as if the dell were after him. I'd told some of the miners what I meant to do, so they were waiting for him, and when he came along they saw how frightened he was. They had to support him; he was that near to collapse. As for me, there was so much excitement I had no trouble in getting to the stable unseen, and then back to my ain gate, where I belonged.

Jock would no go back to work that day.

"I'll no work in a haunted seam!" he declared, vehemently. "It was a ghost nine feet high, and strong like a giant! If I'd no been so brave and kept my head I'd be lying there dead the noo. I surprised him, ye ken, by putting up a fight--likes he'd never known mortal man to do so much before! Next time, he'd not be surprised, and brave though a man may be, he canna ficht with one so much bigger and stronger than himself."

He made a great tale of it before the day was done. As we waited at the foot of the shaft to be run up in the bucket he was still talking. He was boasting again, as I'd known he would. And that was the chance I'd been waiting for a' the time.

"Man, Jock," I said, "ye should ha' had that pistol wi' ye--the one with which ye killed all the outlaws on the American veldt. Then ye could ha' shot him."

"That shows how much you know, young Harry Lauder!" he said, scornfully. "Would a pistol bullet hurt a ghost? Talk of what ye ha' some knowledge of----"

"Aye," I said. "That's good advice, Jock. I suppose I'm not knowing so much as you do about ghosts. But tell me, man--would a ghost be making a noise like this?"

And I made the self-same noise I'd made before, when I was playing the ghost for Jock's benefit. He turned purple; he was clever enough to see the joke I'd played on him at once. And the other miners--they were all in the secret began to roar with laughter. They weren't sorry to see puir Jock shown up for the liar and boaster he was. But I was a little sorry, when I saw how hard he took it, and how angry he was.

He aimed a blow at me that would have made me the sorry one if it had landed fair, but I put up my jukes and warded it off, and he was ashamed, after than, wi' the others laughing at him so, to try again to punish me. He was very sensitive, and he never came back to the Eddlewood Colliery; the very next day he found a job in another pit. He was a good miner, was Jock, so that was no matter to him. But I've often wondered if I really taught him a lesson, or if he always kept on telling his twisters in his new place!

I stayed on, though, after Jock had gone, and after a time I drove a pony instead of tending a gate. That was better work, and meant a few shillings a week more in wages, too, which counted heavily just then.

I handled a number of bonnie wee Shetland ponies in the three years I drove the hutches to and from the pitshaft. One likable little fellow was a real pet. He followed me all about. It was great to see him play one trick I taught him. He would trot to the little cabin and forage among all the pockets till he found one where a man had left a bit of bread and cheese at piece time. He'd eat that, and then he would go after a flask of cold tea. He'd fasten it between his forefeet and pull the cork with his teeth--and then he'd tip the flask up between his teeth and drink his tea like a Christian. Aye, Captain was a droll, clever yin. And once, when I beat him for stopping short before a drift, he was saving my life. There was a crash just after I hit him, and the whole drift caved in. Captain knew it before I did. If he had gone on, as I wanted him to do, we would both ha' been killed.

CHAPTER IV

After I'd been in the mine a few years my brother Matt got old enough to help me to support the family, and so, one by one, did my still younger brothers. Things were a wee bit easier for me then; I could keep a bit o' the siller I earned, and I could think about singing once in a while. There were concerts, at times, when a contest was put on to draw the crowd, and whenever I competed at one of these I usually won a prize. Sometimes it would be a cheap medal; it usually was. I shall never forget how proud I was the night a manager handed me real money for the first time. It was only a five shilling piece, but it meant as much to me as five pounds.

That same nicht one of the other singers gave me a bit of advice.

"Gae to Glasga, Harry," he said. "There's the Harmonic Competition. Ye're dead certain to win a prize."

I took his advice, and entered, and I was one of those to win a medal. That was the first time I had ever sung before total strangers. I'd always had folk I knew well, friends of mine, for my audience before, and it was a nerve racking experience. I dressed in character, and the song I sang was an old one I doubt yell ha' heard-"Tooralladdie" it was called. Here's a verse that will show you what a silly song it was:

> "Twig auld Tooralladdie,
> Don't he look immense? His
>   watch and chain are no his ain
> His claes cost eighteenpence;
> Wi' cuffs and collar shabby,
> 0' mashers he's the daddy;

Hats off, stand aside and let
Past Tooralladdie!"

My success at Glasgow made a great impression among the miners. Everyone shook hands with me and congratulated me, and I think my head was turned a bit. But I'd been thinking for some time of doing a rash thing. I was newly married then, d'ye ken, and I was thinkin' it was time I made something of myself for the sake of her who'd risked her life wi' me. So that night I went home to her wi' a stern face.

"Nance!" I said. "I'm going to chuck the mine and go in for the stage. My mind's made up."

Now, Nance liked my singin' well enough, and she thought, as I did, that I could do better than some we'd heard on the stage. But I think what she thought chiefly was that if my mind was made `up to try it she'd not stand in my way. I wish more wives were like her, bless her! Then there'd be fewer men moaning of their lost chances to win fame and fortune. Many a time my wife's saved me from a mistake, but she's never stood in the way when I felt it was safe to risk something, and she's never laughed at me, and said, "I told ye so, Harry," when things ha' gone wrong--even when her advice was against what I was minded to try.

We talked it all over that nicht--'twas late, I'm tellin' ye, before we quit and crept into bed, and even then we talked on a bit, in the dark.

"Ye maun please yersel', Harry," Nance said. "We've thought of every thing, and it can do no harm to try. If things don't go well, ye can always go back to the pit and mak' a living."

That was so, ye ken. I had my trade to fall back upon. So I read all the advertisements, and at last I saw one put in by the manager of a concert party that was about to mak' a Scottish tour. He wanted a comic, and, after we'd exchanged two or three letters we had an interview. I sang some songs for him, and he engaged me, at thirty- five shillings a week--about eight dollars, in American money--a little more.

That seemed like a great sum to me in those days. It was no so bad. Money went farther then, and in Scotland especially, than it does the noo! And for me it was a fortune. I'd been doing well, in the mine, if I earned fifteen in a week. And this was for doing what I would rather do than anything in the wide, wide world! No wonder I went back to Hamilton and hugged my wife till she thought I'd gone crazy.

I had been engaged as a comic singer, but I had to do much more than sing on that tour, which was to last fourteen weeks--it started, I mind, at Beith, in Ayrshire. First, when we arrived in a town, I had to see that all the trunks and bags were taken from the station to the hall. Then I would set out with a pile of leaflets, describing the entertainment, and distribute them where it seemed to me they would do the most good in drawing a crowd. That was my morning's work.

In the afternoon I was a stage carpenter, and devoted myself to seeing that every thing at the hall was ready for the performance in the evening. Sometimes that was easy; sometimes, in badly equipped halls, the task called for more ingenuity than I had ever before supposed that I possessed. But there was no rest for me, even then; I had to be back at the hall after tea and check up part of the house. And then all I had to do was what I had at first fondly supposed I had been engaged to do-- sing my songs! I sang six songs regularly every night, and if the audience was good to me and liberal in its applause I threw in two or three encores.

I had never been so happy in my life. I had always been a great yin for the open air and the sunshine, and here, for years, I had spent all my days underground. I welcomed the work that went with the engagement, for it kept me much out of doors, and even when I was busy in the halls, it was no so bad--I could see the sunlight through the windows, at any rate. And then I could lie abed in the morning!

I had been used so long to early rising that I woke up each day at five o'clock, no matter how late I'd gone to bed the nicht before. And what a glorious thing it was to roll right over and go to sleep again! Then there was the travelling, too. I had always wanted to see Scotland, and now, in these fourteen weeks, I saw more of my native land than, as a miner, I might have hoped to do in fourteen years--or forty. Little did I think, though, then, of the real travelling I was to do later in my life, in the career that was then just beginning!

I made many friends on that first tour. And to this day nothin' delights me more than to have some in an audience seek me out and tell me that he or she heard me sing during those fourteen weeks. There is a story that actually happened to me that delights me, in connection with that.

It was years after that first tour. I was singing in Glasgow one week, and the hall was crowded at every performance--though the management had raised the prices, for which I was sorry. I heard two women speaking. Said one:

"Ha' ye heard Harry sing the week?"

The other answered:

"That I ha' not!"

"And will ye no'?"

"I will no'! I heard him lang ago, when he was better than he is the noo, for twapence! Why should I be payin' twa shillin' the noo?"

And, do you ken, I'm no sure she was'na richt! But do not be tellin' I said so!

That first tour had to end. Fourteen weeks seemed a long time then, though, the last few days rushed by terribly fast. I was nervous when the end came. I wondered if I would ever get another engagement. It seemed a venturesome thing I had done. Who was I, Harry Lauder, the untrained miner, to expect folk to pay their gude siller to hear me sing?

There was an offer for an engagement waiting for me when I got home. I had saved twelve pounds of my earnings, and it was proud I was as I put the money in my wife's lap. As for her, she behaved as if she thought her husband had come hame a millionaire. The new engagement was for only one night, but the fee was a guinea and a half--twice what I'd made for a week's work in the pit, and nearly what I'd earned in a week on tour.

But then came bad days. I was no well posted on how to go aboot getting engagements. I could only read all the advertisements, and answer everyone that looked as if it might come to anything. And then I'd sit and wait for the postie to come, but the letters he brought were not for me. It looked as though I had had all my luck.

But I still had my twelve pounds, and I would not use them while I was earning no more. So I decided to go back to the pit while I waited. It was as easy--aye, it was easier!--to work while I waited, since wait I must. I hauled down my old greasy working clothes, and went off to the pithead. They were glad enough to take me on--gladder, I'm thinkin', than I was to be taken. But it was sair hard to hear the other miners laughing at me.

"There he gaes--the stickit comic," I heard one man say, as I passed. And another, who had never liked me, was at pains to let me hear ***his*** opinion, which was that I had "had the conceit knocked oot o' me, and was glad tae tak' up the pick again."

But he was wrong, If it was conceit I had felt, I was as full of it as ever--fuller, indeed. I had twelve pounds to slow for what it had brought me, which was more than any of those who sneered at me could say for themselves. And I was surer than ever that I had it in me to make my mark as a singer of comic songs. I had listened to other singers now, and I was certain that I had a new way of delivering a song. My audiences had made me feel that I was going about the task of pleasing them in the right way. All I wanted was the chance to prove what was so plain to me to others, and I knew then, what I have found so often, since then, to be true, that the chance always comes to the man who is sure he can make use of it.

So I plied my pick cheerfully enough all day, and went hame to my wife at nicht with a clear conscience and a hopeful heart. I always looked for a letter, but for a long time I was disappointed each evening. Then, finally, the letter I had been looking for came. It was from J. C. MacDonald, and he wanted to know if I could accept an engagement at the Greenock Town Hall in New Year week, for ten performances. He offered me three pounds--the biggest salary anyone had named to me yet. I jumped at the chance, as you may well believe.

Oh, and did I no feel that I was an actor then? I did so, surely, and that very nicht I went out and bought me some astrachan fur for the collar of my coat! Do ye ken what that meant to me in yon days? Then every actor wore a coat with a fur trimmed collar--it was almost like a badge of rank. And I maun be as braw as any of them. The wife smiled quietly as she sewed it on for me, and I was a proud wee man when I strolled into the Greenock Town Hall. Three pounds a week! There was a salary for a man to be proud of. Ye'd ha' thought I was sure already of making three pounds every week all my life, instead of havin' just the one engagement.

Pride goeth before a fall ever, and after that, once more, I had to wait for an engagement, and once more I went back to the pit. I folded the astrachan coat and put it awa' under the bed, but I would'na tak' off the fur.

"I'll be needin' you again before sae lang," I told the coat as I folded it. "See if I don't."

And it was even so, for J. C. MacDonald had liked my singing, and I had been successful with my audiences. He used his influence and recommended me on all sides, and finally, and, this time, after a shorter time than before in the pit, Moss and Thornton offered me a tour of six weeks.

"Nance," I said to the wife, when the offer came and I had written to accept it, "I'm thinkin' it'll be sink or swim this time. I'll no be goin' back to the pit, come weal, come woe."

She looked at me.

"It's bad for the laddies there to be havin' the chance to crack their jokes at me," I went on. "I'll stick to it this time and see whether I can mak' a living for us by singin'. And I think that if I can't I'll e'en find other work than in the mine."

Again she proved herself. For again she said: "It's yersel' ye must please, Harry. I'm wi' ye, whatever ye do."

That tour was verra gude for me. If I'd conceit left in me, as my friend in the pit had said, it was knocked out. I was first or last on every bill, and ye ken what it means to an artist to open or close a bill? If ye're to open ye have to start before anyone's in the theatre; if ye close, ye sing to the backs of people crowdin' one another to get out. It's discouraging to have to do so, I'm tellin' ye, but it's what makes you grit your teeth, too, and determine to gon, if ye've any of the richt stuff in ye.

I sang in bigger places on that tour, and the last two weeks were in Glasgow, at the old Scotia and Gayety Music Halls. It was at the Scotia that a man shouted at me one of the hardest things I ever had to hear. I had just come on, and was doing the walk around before I sang my first song, when I heard him, from the gallery.

"Awa' back tae the pit, man!" he bellowed.

I was so angry I could scarce go on. It was no fair, for I had not sung a note. But we maun learn, on the stage, not to be disconcerted by anything an audience says or does, and, somehow, I managed to go on. They weren't afraid, ever, in yon days, to speak their minds in the gallery--they'd soon let ye know if they'd had enough of ye and yer turn. I was discouraged by that week in old Glasgow. I was sure they'd had enough of me, and that the career of Harry Lauder as a comedian was about to come to an inglorious end.

But Moss and Thornton were better pleased than I was, it seemed, for no sooner was that tour over than they booked me for another. They increased my salary to four pounds a week--ten shillings more than before. And this time my position on the bill was much better; I neither closed nor opened the show, and so got more applause. It did me a world of good to have the hard experience first, but it did me even more to find that my confidence in myself had some justification, too.

That second Moss and Thornton tour was a real turning point for me. I felt assured of a certain success then; I knew, at least, that I could always mak' a living in the halls. But mark what a little success does to a man!

I'd scarce dared, a year or so before, even to smile at those who told me, half joking, that I might be getting my five pound a week before I died. I'd been afraid they'd think I was taking them seriously, and call me stuck up and conceited. But now I was getting near that great sum, and was sure to get all of it before so long. And I felt that it was no great thing to look ahead to--I, who'd been glad to work hard all week in a coal mine for fifteen shillings!

The more we ha' the more we want. It's always the way wi' all o' us, I'm thinkin'. I was no satisfied at all wi' my prospects and I set out to do all I could, wi' the help of concerts, to better conditions.

CHAPTER V

There was more siller to be made from concerts in yon days than from a regular tour that took me to the music halls. The halls meant steady work, and I was surer of regular earnings, but I liked the concerts. I have never had a happier time in my work than in those days when I was building up my reputation as a concert comedian. There was an uncertainty about it that pleased me, too; there was something exciting about wondering just how things were going.

Now my bookings are made years ahead. I ha' been trying to retire--it will no be so lang, noo, before I do, and settle doon for good in my wee hoose amang the heather at Dunoon on the Clyde. But there is no excitement about an engagement now; I could fill five times as many as I do, if there were but some way of being in twa or three places at once, and of adding a few hours to the days and nichts.

I think one of the proudest times of my life was the first Saturday nicht when I could look back on a week when I had had a concert engagement each night in a different town. It was after that, too, that for the first time I flatly refused an engagement. I had the offer of a guinea, but I had fixed a guinea and a half as my minimum fee, and I would'na tak' less, though, after I'd sent the laddie awa' who offered me the guinea, I could ha' kicked myself.

There were some amusing experiences during those concert days. I often appeared with singers who had won considerable fame--artists who rendered classical numbers and opertic selections. I sometimes envied them for their musical gifts, but not seriously--my efforts were in a different field. As a rule I got along extremely well with my fellow performers, but sometimes they were inclined to look down on a mere comedian. Yell ken that I was making a name for myself then, and that I engaged for some concerts at which, as a rule, no comic singer would have been heard.

One night a concert had been arranged by a musical society in a town near Glasgow--a suburb of the city. I was to appear with a quartet soprano, contralto, tenor and bass. The two ladies and the tenor greeted me cheerfully enough, and seemed glad to see me--the contralto, indeed, was very friendly, and said she always went to hear me when she had the chance. But the bass was very distant. He glared at me when I came in, and did not return my greeting. He sat and scowled, and grew angrier and angrier.

"Well!" he said, suddenly. "The rest of you can do as you please, but I shall not sing to-night! I'm an artist, and I value my professional reputation too highly to appear with a vulgarian like this comic singer!"

"Oh, I say, old chap!" said the tenor, looking uncomfortable. "That's a bit thick! Harry's a good sort--I've heard him----"

"I'm not concerned with his personality!" said the bass. "I resent being associated with a man who makes a mountebank, a clown, of himself!"

I listened and said nothing. But I'll no be sayin' I did no wink at my friend, the contralto.

The other singers tried to soothe the bass down, but they couldn't. He looked like a great pouter pigeon, strutting about the room, and then he got red, and I thought he looked like an angry turkey cock. The secretary of the society came in, and the basso attacked him at once.

"I say, Mr. Smith!" he cried. "There's something wrong here, what! Fancy expecting me to appear on the same platform with this--this person in petticoats!"

The secretary looked surprised, as well he micht!!

"I'll not do it!" said the basso, getting angrier each second. "You can keep him or me--both you can't have!"

I was not much concerned. I was angry; I'll admit that. But I didna let him fash me. I just made up my mind that if I was no allowed to sing I'd have something to say to that basso before the evening was oot. And I looked at him, and listened to him bluster, and thought maybe I'd have a bit to do wi' him as well. I'm a wee man and a', but I'm awfu' strong from the work I did in the pit, and I'm never afraid of a bully.

I need ha' gie'n myself no concern as to the secretary. He smiled, and let the basso talk. And I'll swear he winked at me.

"I really can't decide such a matter, Mr. Roberts," he said, at last. "You're engaged to sing; so is Mr. Lauder. Mr. Lauder is ready to fulfill his engagement--if you are not I don't see how I can force you to do so. But you will do yourself no good if you leave us in the lurch--I'm afraid people who are arranging concerts will feel that you are a little unreliable."

The other singers argued with him, too, but it was no use. He would no demean himself by singing with Harry Lauder. And so we went on without him, and the concert was a great success. I had to give a dozen encores, I mind. And puir Roberts! He got no more engagements, and a little later became a chorus man with a touring opera company. I'm minded of him the noo because, not so lang syne, he met me face to face in London, and greeted me like an old friend.

"I remember very well knowing you, years ago, before you were so famous, Mr. Lauder," he said. "I don't just recall the circumstances-- I think we appeared together at some concerts--that was before I unfortunately lost my voice----"

Aweel, I minded the circumstances, if he did not, but I had no the heart to remind him! And I "lent" him the twa shillin' he asked. Frae such an auld friend as him I was lucky not to be touched for half a sovereign!

I've found some men are so. Let you succeed, let you mak' your bit siller, and they remember that they knew you well when you were no so well off and famous. And it's always the same way. If they've not succeeded, it's always someone else's fault, never their own. They dislike you because you've done well when they've done ill. But it's easy to forgie them--it's aye hard to bear a grudge in this world, and to be thinkin' always of punishin' those who use us despite-fully. I've had my share of knocks from folk. And sometimes I've dreamed of being able to even an auld score. But always, when the time's come for me to do it, I've nae had the heart.

It was rare fun to sing in those concerts. And in the autumn of 1896 I made a new venture. I might have gone on another tour among the music halls in the north, but Donald Munro was getting up a concert tour, and I accepted his offer instead. It was a bit new for a singer like myself to sing at such concerts, but I had been doing well, and Mr. Munro wanted me, and offered me good terms.

That tour brought me one of my best friends and one of my happiest associations. It was on it that I met Mackenzie Murdoch. I'll always swear by Murdoch as the best violinist Scotland ever produced. Maybe Ysaye and some of the boys with the unpronounceable Russian names can play better than he. I'll no be saying as to that. But I know that he could win the tears from your een when he played the old Scots melodies; I know that his bow was dipped in magic before he drew it across the strings, and that he played on the strings of your heart the while he scraped that old fiddle of his.

Weel, there was Murdoch, and me, and the third of our party on that tour was Miss Jessie MacLachlan, a bonnie lassie with a glorious voice, the best of our Scottish prima donnas then. We wandered all over the north and the midlands of Scotland on that tour, and it was a grand success. Our audiences were large, and they were generous wi' their applause, too, which Scottish audiences sometimes are not. Your Scot is a canny yin; he'll aye tak' his pleasures seriously. He'll let ye ken it, richt enough, and fast enough, if ye do not please him. But if ye do he's like to reckon that he paid you to do so, and so why should he applaud ye as weel?

But so well did we do on the tour that I began to do some thinkin'. Here were we, Murdoch and I, especially, drawing the audiences. What was Munro doing for rakin' in the best part o' the siller folk paid to hear us? Why, nothin' at all that we could no do our twa selves--so I figured. And it hurt me sair to see Munro gettin' siller it seemed to me Murdoch and I micht just as weel be sharing between us. Not that I didna like Munro fine, ye'll ken; he was a gude manager, and a fair man. But it was just the way I was feeling, and I told Murdoch so.

"Ye hae richt, Harry," he said. "There's sense in your head, man, wee though you are. What'll we do?"

"Why, be our ain managers!" I said. "We'll take out a concert party of our own next season."

At the end of the tour of twelve weeks Mac and I were more determined than ever to do just that. For the time we'd spent we had a hundred pounds apiece to put in the bank, after we'd paid all our expenses-- more money than I'd dreamed of being able to save in many years. And so we made our plans.

But we were no sae sure, afterward, that we'd been richt. We planned our tour carefully. First we went all aboot, to the towns we planned to visit, distributing bills that announced our coming. Shopkeepers were glad to display them for us for a ticket or so, and it seemed that folk were interested, and looking forward to having us come. But if they were they did not show it in the only practical way--the only way that gladdens a manager's heart. They did not come to our concerts in great numbers; indeed, an' they scarcely came at a'. When it was all over and we came to cast up the reckoning we found we'd lost a hundred and fifty pounds sterling--no small loss for two young and ambitious artists to have to pocket.

"Aye, an' I can see where the manager has his uses," I said to Mac. "He takes the big profits--but he takes the big risks, too."

"Are ye discouraged, man Harry!" Mac asked me.

"Not a bit of it!" said I. "If you're not, I'm not. I'll try it again. What do you say, Mac?"

We felt the same way. But I learned a lesson then that has always made me cautious in criticizing the capitalist who sits back and rakes in the siller while others do the work. The man has his uses, I'm tellin' ye. I found it oot then; they're findin' it oot in Russia now, since the Bolsheviki have been so busy. I'm that when the world's gone along for so many years, and worked out a way of doing things, there must be some good in it. I'm not sayin' all's richt and perfect in this world --and, between you and me, would it be muckle fun to live in it if it were? But there's something reasonable and something good about anything that's grown up to be an institution, even if it needs changing and reforming frae time to time. Or so I think.

Weel, e'en though I could see, noo, the reason for Munro to be gettin' his big share o' the siller Mac and I made, I was no minded not to ha' another try for it myself. Next season Mac and I made our plans even more carefully. We went to most of the same towns where business had been bad before, and this time it was good. And I learned something a manager could ha' told me, had he liked. Often and often it's necessary to tak' a loss on an artist's first tour that'll be more than made up for later. Some folk go to hear him, or see him, even that first time. An' they tell ithers what they've missed. It was so wi' us when we tried again. Our best audiences and our biggest success came where we'd been most disappointed the time before. This tour was a grand success, and once more, for less than three months of work, Mac and I banked more than a hundred pounds apiece.

But there was more than siller to count in the profits of the tours Mac and I made together. He became and has always remained one of my best and dearest friends--man never had a better. And a jollier companion I can never hope to find.

We always lived together; it was easier and cheaper, too, for us to share lodgings. And we liked to walk together for exercise, and to tak' our amusement as well as our work in common.

I loved to hear Mac practice. He was a true artist and a real musician, and when he played for the sheer love of playing he was even better, I always thought, than when he was thinking of his audience, though he always gave an audience his best. It was just, I think, that when there was only me to hear him he knew he could depend upon a sympathetic listener, and he had not to worry aboot the effect his playing was to have.

We were like a pair of boys on a holiday when we went touring together in those days, Mac and I. We were always playing jokes on one another, or on any other victims we could find usually on one another because there was always something one of us wanted to get even for. But the commonest trick was one of mine. Mac and I would come down to breakfast, say, at a hotel, and when everyone was seated I'd start, in a very low voice, to sing. Rather, I didn't really sing, I said, in a low, rhythmical tone, with a sort of half tune to it, this old verse:

> "And the old cow crossed the road,
> The old cow crossed the road,
> And the reason why it crossed the road
> Was to get to the other side."

I would repeat that, over and over again, tapping my foot to keep time as I did so. Then Mac would join in, and perhaps another of our company. And before long everyone at the table would catch the infection, and either be humming the absurd words or keeping time with his feet, while the others did so. Sometimes people didn't care for my song; I remember one old Englishman, with a white moustache and a very red face, who looked as if he might be a retired army officer. I think he thought we were all mad, and he jumped up at last and rushed from the table, leaving his breakfast unfinished. But the roar of laughter that followed him made him realize that it was all a joke, and at teatime he helped us to trap some newcomers who'd never heard of the game.

Mac and I were both inclined to be a wee bit boastful. We hated to admit, both of us, that there was anything we couldna do; I'm a wee bit that way inclined still. I mind that in Montrose, when we woke up one morning after the most success-ful concert we had ever given, and so were feeling very extra special, we found a couple o' gowf balls lyin' around in our diggings.

"What do ye say tae a game, Mac?" I asked him.

"I'm no sae glide a player, Harry," he said, a bit dubiously.

For once in a way I was honest, and admitted that I'd never played at all. We hesitated, but our landlady, a decent body, came in, and made light of our doots.

"Hoots, lads," she said. "A'body plays gowf nooadays. I'll gie ye the lend of some of our Jamie's clubs, and it's no way at a' to the links,"

Secretly I had nae doot o' my bein' able to hit a little wee ball like them we'd found so far as was needful. I thought the gowf wad be easier than digging for coal wi' a pick. So oot we set, carryin' our sticks, and ready to mak' a name for ourselves in a new way.

Syne Mac had said he could play a little, I told him he must take the honor and drive off. He did no look sae grateful as he should ha' done, but he agreed, at last.

"Noo, Harry, stand weel back, man, and watch where this ball lichts. Keep your een well doon the coorse, man."

He began to swing as if he meant to murder the wee ba', and I strained my een. I heard him strike, and I looked awa' doon the coorse, as he had bid me do. But never hide nor hair o' the ba' did I see. It was awesome.

"Hoots, Mac," I said, "ye must ha' hit it an awfu' swipe. I never saw it after you hit it."

He was smiling, but no as if he were amused.

"Aweel, ye wouldna--ye was looking the wrong way, man," he said. "I sort o' missed my swing that time. There's the ba'----"

He pointed, and sure enough, I saw the puir wee ba', over to right, not half a dozen yards from the tee, and lookin' as if it had been cut in twa. He made to lift it and put it back on the tee, but, e'en an' I had never played the game I knew a bit aboot the rules.

"Dinna gang so fast, Mac," I cried. "That counts a shot. It's my turn the noo."

And so I piled up a great double handfu' o' sand. It seemed to me that the higher I put the wee ba' to begin with the further I could send it when I hit it. But

I was wrong, for my attempt was worse than Mac's. I broke my club, and drove all the sand in his een, and the wee ba' moved no more than a foot!

"That's a shot, too!" cried Mac.

"Aye," I said, a bit ruefully. "I--I sort o' missed my swing, too, Mac."

We did a wee bit better after that, but I'm no thinkin' either Mac or I will ever play against the champion in the final round at Troon or St. Andrews.

CHAPTER VI

I maun e'en wander again from what I've been tellin' ye. Not that in this book there's any great plan; it's just as if we were speerin' together. But one thing puts me in mind o' another. And it so happened that that gay morn at Montrose when Mac and I tried our hands at the gowf brought me in touch with another and very different experience.

Ye'll mind I've talked a bit already of them that work and those they work for. I've been a laboring man myself; in those days I was close enough to the pit to mind only too well what it was like to be dependent on another man for all I earned and ate and drank. And I'd been oot on strike, too. There was some bit trouble over wages. In the beginning it was no great matter; five minutes of good give and tak' in talk wad ha' settled it, had masters and men got together as folk should do. But the masters wouldna listen, and the men were sair angry, and so there was the strike.

It was easy enough for me. I'd money in the savings bank. My brothers were a' at work in other pits where there was no strike called. I was able to see it through, and I cheered with a good will when the District Agents of the miners made speeches and urged us to stay oot till the masters gave in. But I could see, even then, that, there were men who did no feel sae easy in their minds over the strike. Jamie Lowden was one o' them. Jamie and I were good friends, though not sae close as some.

I could see that Jamie was taking the strike much more to heart than I. He'd come oot wi' the rest of us at the first, and he went to all the mass meetings, though I didna hear him, ever mak' a speech, as most of us did, one time or another. And so, one day, when I fell into step beside him, on the way hame frae a meetin', I made to see what he was thinking.

"Dinna look sae glum, Jamie, man," I said. "The strike won't last for aye. We've the richt on our side, and when we've that we're bound to win in the end."

"Aye, we may win!" he said, bitterly. "And what then, Harry? Strikes are for them that can afford them, Harry--they're no for workingman wi' a wife that's sick on his hands and a wean that's dyin' for lack o' the proper food. Gie'en my wife and my bairn should dee, what good would it be to me to ha' won this strike?"

"But we'll a' be better off if we win----"

"Better off?" he said, angrily. "Oh, aye--but what'll mak' up to' us for what we'll lose? Nine weeks I've been oot. All that pay I've lost. It would have kept the wean well fed and the wife could ha' had the medicine she needs. Much good it will do me to win the strike and the shillin' or twa extra a week we're striking for if I lose them!"

I'm ashamed to say I hadn't thought of the strike in that licht before. It had been a grand chance to be idle wi'oot havin' to reproach myself; to enjoy life a bit, and lie abed of a morn wi' a clear conscience. But I could see, the noo Jamie talked, how it was some of the older men did not seem to put much heart into it when they shouted wi' the rest of us: "We'll never gie in!"

It was weel enough for the boys; for them it was a time o' skylarkin' and irresponsibility. It was weel enough for me, and others like me, who'd been able to put by a bit siller, and could afford to do wi'oot our wages for a space. But it was black tragedy for Jamie and his wife and bairn.

Still ye'll be wonderin' how I was reminded of all this at Montrose, where Mac and I showed how bad we were at gowf! Weel, it was there I saw Jamie Lowden again, and heard how he had come through the time of the strike. I'll tell the tale myself; you may depend on't that I'm giving it to ye straight, as I had it from the man himself.

His wife, lying sick in her bed, always asked Jamie the same question when he came in from a meeting.

"Is there ony settlement yet, Jamie?" she would say.

"Not yet," he had to answer, time after time. "The masters are rich and proud. They say they can afford to keep the pits, closed. And we're telling them, after every meeting, that we'll een starve, if needs must, before we'll gie in to them. I'm thinkin' it's to starvin' we'll come, the way things look. Hoo are ye, Annie--better old girl?"

"I'm no that bad, Jamie," she answered, always, affectionately. He knew she was lying to spare his feelings; they loved one another very dearly, did those two. She looked down at the wee yin beside her in the bed. "It's the wean I'm thinkin' of, Jamie," she whispered. "He's asleep, at last, but he's nae richt, Jamie--he's far frae richt."

Jamie sighed, and turned to the stove. He put the kettle on, that he might make himself a cup of tea. Annie was not strong enough to get up and do any of the work, though it hurt her sair to see her man busy about the wee hoose. She could eat no solid food; the doctor had ordered milk for her, and beef tea, and jellies. Jamie could just manage the milk, but it was out of the question for him to buy the sick room delicacies she should have had every day of her life. The bairn was born but a week after the strike began; Jamie and Annie had been married little more than a year. It was hard enough for Annie to bring the wean into the world; it seemed that keeping him and herself there was going to be too much for her, with things going as they were.

"She was nae strong enough, Jamie, man," the doctor told him. "Ye'll ha' an invalid wife on your hands for months. Gie her gude food, and plenty on't, when she can eat again let her ha' plenty rest. She'll be richt then--she'll be better, indeed, than she's ever been. But not if things go badly--she can never stand that."

Jamie had aye been carefu' wi' his siller; when he knew the wife was going to present him wi' a bairn he'd done his part to mak' ready. So the few pound he had in the bank had served, at the start, weel enough. The strikers got a few shillings each week frae the union; just enough, it turned out, in Jamie's case, to pay the rent and buy the bare necessities of life. His own siller went fast to keep mither and wean alive when she was worst. And when they were gone, as they were before that day I talked wi' him, things looked black indeed for Jamie and the bit family he was tryin' to raise.

He could see no way oot. And then, one nicht, there came a knocking at the door. It was the doctor--a kindly, brusque man, who'd been in the army once. He was popular, but it was because he made his patients afraid of him, some said. They got well because they were afraid to disobey him. He had a very large practice, and, since he was a bachelor, with none but himself to care for, he was supposed to be almost wealthy--certainly he was rich for a country doctor.

"Weel, Jamie, man, and ho's the wife and the wean the day?" he asked.

"They're nane so braw, doctor," said Jamie, dolefully. "But yell see that for ye-rsel', I'm thinkin'."

The doctor went in, talked to Jamie's wife a spell, told her some things to do, and looked carefully at the sleeping bairn, which he would not have awakened. Then he took Jamie by the arm.

"Come ootside, Jamie," he said. "I want to hae a word wi' ye."

Jamie went oot, wondering. The doctor walked along wi' him in silence a wee bit; then spoke, straight oot, after his manner.

"Yon's a bonnie wean o' yours, Jamie," he said. "I've brought many a yin into the world, and I'm likin' him fine. But ye can no care for him, and he's like to dee on your hands. Yer wife's in the same case. She maun ha' nourishin' food, and plenty on't. Noo, I'm rich enough, and I'm a bachelor, with no wife nor bairn o' my ain. For reasons I'll not tell ye I'll dee, as I've lived, by my lain. I'll not be marryin' a wife, I mean by that.

"But I like that yin of yours. And here's what I'm offerin' ye. I'll adopt him, gi'en you'll let me ha' him for my ain. I'll save his life. I'll bring him up strong and healthy, as a gentleman and a gentleman's son. And I'll gie ye a hundred pounds to boot--a hundred pounds that'll be the saving of your wife's life, so that she can be made strong and healthy to bear ye other bairns when you're at work again."

"Gie up the wean?" cried Jamie, his face working. "The wean my Annie near died to gie me? Doctor, is it sense you're talking?"

"Aye, and gude, hard sense it is, too, Jamie, man. I know it sounds dour and hard. It's a sair thing to be giving up your ain flesh and blood. But think o' the bairn, man! Through no fault o' your ain, through misfortune that's come upon ye, ye can no gie him the care he needs to keep him alive. Wad ye rather see him dead or in my care? Think it ower, man. I'll gie ye two days to think and to talk it ower wi' the wife. And--I'm tellin' ye're a muckle ass and no the sensible man I've thought ye if ye do not say aye."

The doctor did no wait for Jamie to answer him. He was a wise man, that doctor; he knew how Jamie wad be feelin' just then, and he turned away. Sure enough, Jamie was ready to curse him and bid him keep his money. But when he was left alone, and walked home, slowly, thinking of the offer, he began to see that love for the wean urged him nigh as much to accept the offer as to reject it.

It was true, as the doctor had said, that it was better for the bairn to live and grow strong and well than to dee and be buried. Wad it no be selfish for Jamie, for the love he had for his first born, to insist on keeping him when to keep him wad mean his death? But there was Annie to think of, too. Wad she be willing? Jamie was sair beset. He didna ken how to think, much less what he should be doing.

It grieved him to bear such an offer to Annie, so wan and sick, puir body. He thought of not telling her. But when he went in she was sair afraid the doctor had told him the bairn could no live, and to reassure her he was obliged to tell just why the doctor had called him oot wi' him.

"Tak' him away for gude and a', Jamie?" she moaned, and looked down at the wailing mite beside her. "That's what he means? Oh, my bairn--my wean----!"

"Aye, but he shall not!" Jamie vowed, fiercely, dropping to his knees beside the bed, and putting his arms about her. "Dinna fash yersel', Annie, darling. Ye shall keep your wean--our wean."

"But it's true, what the doctor said, that it wad be better for our bairn, Jamie----"

"Oh, aye--no doot he meant it in kindness and weel enow, Annie. But how should he understand, that's never had bairn o' his own to twine its fingers around one o' his? Nor seen the licht in his wife's een as she laid them on her wean?"

Annie was comforted by the love in his voice, and fell asleep. But when the morn came the bairn was worse, and greetin' pitifully. And it was Annie herself who spoke, timidly, of what the doctor had offered. Jamie had told her nothing of the hundred pounds; he knew she would feel as he did, that if they gave up the bairn it wad be for his ain sake, and not for the siller.

"Oh, Jamie, my man, I've been thinkin'," said puir Annie. "The wean's sae sick! And if we let the doctor hae him he'd be well and strong. And it micht be we could see him sometimes. The doctor wad let us do sae, do ye nae think it?"

Lang they talked of it. But they could came tae nae ither thought than that it was better to lose the bairn and gie him his chance to live and to grow up than to lose him by havin' him dee. Lose him they must, it seemed, and Jamie cried out against God, at last, and swore that there was no help, even though a man was ready and willing to work his fingers to the bone for wife and bairn. And sae, wi' the heaviest of hearts, he made his way to the doctor's door and rang the bell.

"Weel, and ye and the wife are showing yer good sense," said the doctor, heart-ily, when he heard what Jamie had to say. "We'll pull the wean through. He's of gude stock on both sides--that's why I want to adopt him. I'll bring a nurse round wi' me tomorrow, come afternoon, and I'll hae the papers ready for ye to sign, that give me the richt to adopt him as my ain son. And when ye sign ye shall hae yer hundred pounds."

"Ye--ye can keep the siller, doctor," said Jamie, suppressing a wish to say some-thing violent. "'Tis no for the money we're letting ye hae the wean--'tis that ye may save his life and keep him in the world to hae his chance that I canna gie him, God help me!"

"A bargain's a bargain, Jamie, man," said the doctor, more gently than was his wont. "Ye shall e'en hae the hundred pounds, for you'll be needin' it for the puir wife. Puir lassie--dinna think I'm not sorry for you and her, as well."

Jamie shook his head and went off. He could no trust himself to speak again. And he went back to Annie wi' tears in his een, and the heart within him heavy as it were lead. Still, when he reached hame, and saw Annie looking at him wi' such grief in her moist een, he could no bear to tell her of the hundred pounds. He could no bear to let her think it was selling the bairn they were. And, in truth, whether he was to tak' the siller or not, it was no that had moved him.

It was a sair, dour nicht for Jamie and the wife. They lay awake, the twa of them. They listened to the breathing of the wean; whiles and again he'd rouse and greet a wee, and every sound he made tore at their heart strings. They were to say gude-bye to him the morrow, never to see him again; Annie was to hold him in her mither's arms for the last time. Oh, it was the sair nicht for those twa, yell ken withoot ma tellin' ye!

Come three o' the clock next afternoon and there was the sound o' wheels ootside the wee hoose. Jamie started and looked at Annie, and the tears sprang to their een as they turned to the wean. In came the doctor, and wi' him a nurse, all starched and clean.

"Weel, Jamie, an' hoo are the patients the day? None so braw, Annie, I'm fearin'. 'Tis a hard thing, my lassie, but the best in the end. We'll hae ye on yer feet again in no time the noo, and ye can gie yer man a bonnier bairn next time! It's glad I am ye'll let me tak' the wean and care for him."

Annie could not answer. She was clasping the bairn close to her, and the tears were running down her twa cheeks. She kissed him again and again. And the doctor, staring, grew uncomfortable. He beckoned to the nurse, and she stepped toward the bed to take the wean from its mither. Annie saw her, and held the bairn to Jamie.

"Puir wean--oh, oor puir wean!" she sighed. "Jamie, my man--kiss him-- kiss him for the last time----"

Jamie sobbed and caught the bairn in his great arms. He held it as tenderly as ever its mither could ha' done. And then, suddenly, still holding the wean, he turned on the doctor.

"We canna do it, Doctor!" he cried. "I cried out against God yesterday. But-- there is a God! I believe in Him, and I will put my trust in Him. If it is His will that oor wean shall dee--dee he must. But if he dees it shall be in his mither's arms."

His eyes were blazing, and the doctor, a little frightened, as if he thought Jamie had gone mad, gave ground. But Jamie went on in a gentler voice.

"I ken weel ye meant it a' for the best, and to be gude to us and the wean, doctor," he said, earnestly. "But we canna part with our bairn. Live or dee he must stay wi' his mither!"

He knelt down. He saw Annie's eyes, swimming with new tears, meeting his in a happiness such as he had never seen before. She held out her hungry arms, and Jamie put the bairn within them.

"I'm sorry, doctor," he said, simply.

But the doctor said nothing. Without ane word he turned, and went oot the door, wi' the nurse following him. And Jamie dropped to his knees beside his wife and bairn and prayed to the God in whom he had resolved to put his trust.

Ne'er tell me God does not hear or heed such prayers! Ne'er tell me that He betrays those who put their trust in Him, according to His word.

Frae that sair day of grief and fear mither and wean grew better. Next day a wee laddie brocht a great hamper to Jamie's door. Jamie thocht there was some mistake.

"Who sent ye, laddie?" he asked.

"I dinna ken, and what I do ken I maun not tell," the boy answered. "But there's no mistake. 'Tis for ye, Jamie Lowden."

And sae it was. There were all the things that Annie needed and Jamie had nae the siller to buy for her in that hamper. Beef tea, and fruit, and jellies--rare gude things! Jamie, his een full o' tears, had aye his suspicions of the doctor. But when he asked him, the doctor was said angry.

"Hamper? What hamper?" he asked gruffly. That was when he was making a professional call. "Ye're a sentimental fule, Jamie Lowden, and I'd hae no hand in helpin' ye! But if so be there was some beef extract in the hamper, 'tis so I'd hae ye mak' it--as I'm tellin' ye, mind, not as it says on the jar!"

He said nowt of what had come aboot the day before. But, just as he was aboot to go, he turned to Jamie.

"Oh, aye, Jamie, man, yell no haw been to the toon the day?" he asked. "I heard, as I was comin' up, that the strike was over and all the men were to go back to work the morn. Ye'll no be sorry to be earnin' money again, I'm thinkin'."

Jamie dropped to his knees again, beside his wife and bairn, when the doctor had left them alone. And this time it was to thank God, not to pray for favors, that he knelt.

Do ye ken why I hae set doon this tale for you to read? Is it no plain? The way we do--all of us! We think we may live our ain lives, and that what we do affects no one but ourselves? Was ever a falswer lee than that? Here was this strike, that was so quickly called because a few men quarreled among themselves. And yet it was only by a miracle that it did not bring death to Annie and her bairn and ruin to Jamie Lowden's whole life--a decent laddie that asked nowt but to work for his wife and his wean and be a good and useful citizen.

Canna men think twice before they bring such grief and trouble into the world? Canna they learn to get together and talk things over before the trouble, instead of afterward? Must we act amang ourselves as the Hun acted in the wide world? I'm thinking we need not, and shall not, much longer.

CHAPTER VII

The folks we met were awfu' good to Mackenzie Murdoch and me while we were on tour in yon old days. I've always liked to sit me doon, after a show, and talk to some of those in the audience, and then it was even easier than it is the noo. I mind the things we did! There was the time when we must be fishermen!

It was at Castle Douglas, in the Galloway district, that the landlord of our hotel asked us if we were fishermen. He said we should be, since, if we were, there was a loch nearby where the sport was grand.

"Eh, Mac?" I asked him. "Are ye as good a fisherman as ye are a gowfer?"

"Scarcely so good, Harry," he said, smiling.

"Aweel, ne'er mind that," I said. "We'll catch fish enough for our supper, for I'm a don with a rod, as you'll see."

Noo, I believed that I was strictly veracious when I said that, even though I think I had never held a rod in my hand. But I had seen many a man fishing, and it had always seemed to me the easiest thing in the world a man could do. So forth we fared together, and found the boat the landlord had promised us, and the tackle, and the bait. I'll no say whether we took ought else--'tis none of your affair, you'll ken! Nor am I making confession to the wife, syne she reads all I write, whether abody else does so or nicht.

The loch was verra beautiful. So were the fish, I'm never doubting, but for that yell hae to do e'en as did Mac and I--tak' the landlord's word for 't. For ne'er a one did we see, nor did we get a bite, all that day. But it was comfortable in the air, on the bonny blue water of the loch, and we were no sair grieved that the fish should play us false.

Mac sat there, dreamily.

"I mind a time when I was fishing, once," he said, and named a spot he knew I'd never seen. "Ah, man, Harry, but it was the grand day's sport we had that day! There was an old, great trout that every fisherman in those parts had been after for twa summers. Many had hooked him, but he'd got clean awa'. I had no thocht of seeing him, even. But by and by I felt a great pull on my line--and, sure enow, it was he, the big fellow!"

"That was rare luck, Mac," I said, wondering a little. Had Mac been overmodest, before, when he had said he was no great angler? Or was he----? Aweel, no matter. I'll let him tell his tale.

"Man, Harry," he went on, "can ye no see the ithers? They were excited. All offered me advice. But they never thocht that I could land him. I didna mysel'--he was a rare fish, that yin! Three hours I fought wi' him, Harry! But I brocht him ashore at last. And, Harry, wad ye guess what he weighed?"

I couldna, and said so. But I was verra thochtfu'.

"Thirty-one pounds," said Mac, impressively.

"Thirty-one pounds? Did he so?" I said, duly impressed. But I was still thochtfu', and Mac looked at me.

"Wasna he a whopper, Harry?" he asked. I think he was a wee bit disappointed, but he had no cause--I was just thinking.

"Aye," I said. "Deed an' he was, Mac. Ye were prood, the day, were ye no? I mind the biggest fish ever I caught. I wasna fit to speak to the Duke o' Argyle himsel' that day!"

"How big was yours?" asked Mac, and I could see he was angry wi' himself. Do ye mind the game the wee yins play, of noughts and crosses? Whoever draws three noughts or three crosses in a line wins, and sometimes it's for lettin' the other have last crack that ye lose. Weel, it was like a child who sees he's beaten himself in that game that Mac looked then.

"How big was mine, Mac?" I said. "Oh, no so big. Ye'd no be interested to know, I'm thinking."

"But I am," said Mac. "I always like to hear of the luck other fishermen ha' had."

"Aweel, yell be makin' me tell ye, I suppose," I said, as if verra reluctantly. "But--oh, no, Mac, dinna mak' me. I'm no wantin' to hurt yer feelings."

He laughed.

"Tell me, man," he said.

"Weel, then--twa thousand six hundred and fourteen pounds," I said.

Mac nearly fell oot o' the boat into the loch. He stared at me wi' een like saucers.

"What sort of a fish was that, ye muckle ass?" he roared.

"Oh, just a bit whale," I said, modestly. "Nowt to boast aboot. He gied me a battle, I'll admit, but he had nae chance frae the first----"

And then we both collapsed and began to roar wi' laughter. And we agreed that we'd tell no fish stories to one another after that, but only to others, and that we'd always mak' the other fellow tell the size of his fish before we gave the weighing of ours. That's the only safe rule for a fisherman who's telling of his catch, and there's a tip for ye if ye like.

Still and a' we caught us no fish, and whiles we talked we'd stopped rowing, until the boat drifted into the weeds and long grass that filled one end of the loch. We were caught as fine as ye please, and when we tried to push her free we lost an oar. Noo, we could not row hame wi'oot that oar, so I reached oot wi' my rod and tried to pull it in. I had nae sort of luck there, either, and broke the rod and fell head first into the loch as well!

It was no sae deep, but the grass and the weeds were verra thick, and they closed aboot me the way the arms of an octopus mich and it was scary work gettin' free. When I did my head and shoulders showed above the water, and that was all.

"Save me, Mac!" I cried, half in jest, half in earnest. But Mac couldna help me. The boat had got a strong push from me when I went over, and was ten or twelve feet awa'. Mac was tryin' to do all he could, but ye canna do muckle wi' a flat bottomed boat when ye're but the ane oar, and he gied up at last. Then he laughed.

"Man, Harry, but ye're a comical sicht!" he said. "Ye should appear so and write a song to go wi' yer looks! Noo, ye'll not droon, an', as ye're so wet already, why don't ye wade ower and get the oar while ye're there?"

He was richt, heartless though I thought him. So I waded over to where the oar rested on the surface of the water, as if it were grinning at me. It was tricksy work. I didna ken hoo deep the loch micht grow to be suddenly; sometimes there are deep holes in such places, that ye walk into when ye're the least expecting to find one.

I was glad enough when I got back to the boat wi' the oar. I started to climb in.

"Gie's the oar first," said Mac, cynically. "Ye micht fall in again, Harry, and I'll just be makin' siccar that ane of us twa gets hame the nicht!"

But I didna fall in again, and, verra wet and chilly, I was glad to do the rowing for a bit. We did no more fishing that day, and Mac laughed at me a good deal. But on the way hame we passed a field where some boys were playing football, and the ball came along, unbenknownst to either of us, and struck Mac on the nose. It set it to bleeding, and Mac lost his temper completely and gave chase, with the blood running down and covering his shirt.

It was my turn to laugh at him, and yell ken that I took full advantage o't! Mac ran fast, and he caught one of the youngsters who had kicked the ball at him and cuffed his ear. That came near to makin' trouble, too, for the boy's father came round and threatened to have Mac arrested. But a free seat for the show made him a friend instead of a foe.

Speakin' o' arrests, the wonder is to me that Mac and I ever stayed oot o' jail. Dear knows we had escapades enough that micht ha' landed us in the lock up! There was a time, soon after the day we went fishing, when we made friends wi' some folk who lived in a capital house with a big fruit garden attached to it. They let us lodgings, though it was not their habit to do so, and we were verra pleased wi' ourselves.

We sat in the sunshine in our room, having our tea. Ootside the birds were singing in the trees, and the air came in gently.

"Oh, it's good to be alive!" said Mac.

But I dinna ken whether it was the poetry of the day or the great biscuit he had just spread wi' jam that moved him! At any rate there was no doot at a' as to what moved a great wasp that flew in through the window just then. It wanted that jam biscuit, and Mac dropped it. But that enraged the wasp, and it stung Mac on the little finger. He yelled. The girl who was singing in the next room stopped; the birds, frightened, flew away. I leaped up--I wanted to help my suffering friend.

But I got up so quickly that I upset the teapot, and the scalding tea poured itself out all over poor Mac's legs. He screamed again, and went tearing about the room holding his finger. I followed him, and I had heard that one ought to do something at once if a man were scalded, so I seized the cream jug and poured that over his legs.

But, well as I meant, Mac was angrier than ever. I chased him round and round, seriously afraid that my friend was crazed by his sufferings.

"Are ye no better the noo, Mac?" I asked.

That was just as our landlady and her daughter came in. I'm afraid they heard language from Mac not fit for any woman's ears, but ye'll admit the man was not wi'oot provocation!

"Better?" he shouted. "Ye muckle fool, you--you've ruined a brand new pair of trousies cost me fifteen and six!"

It was amusing, but it had its serious side. We had no selections on the violin at that night's concert, nor for several nights after, for Mac's finger was badly swollen, and he could not use it. And for a long time I could make him as red as a beet and as angry as I pleased by just whispering in his ear, in the innocentest way: "Hoo's yer pinkie the noo, Mac?"

It was at Creetown, our next stopping place, that we had an adventure that micht weel ha' had serious results. We had a Sunday to spend, and decided to stay there and see some of the Galloway moorlands, of which we had all heard wondrous tales. And after our concert we were introduced to a man who asked us if we'd no like a little fun on the Sawbath nicht. It sounded harmless, as he put it so, and we thocht, syne it was to be on the Sunday, it could no be so verra boisterous. So we accepted his invitation gladly.

Next evening then, in the gloamin', he turned up at our lodgings, wi' two dogs at his heel, a greyhound and a lurcher--a lurcher is a coursing dog, a cross between a collie and a greyhound.

He wore dark clothes and a slouch hat. But, noo that I gied him a closer look, I saw a shifty look in his een that I didna like. He was a braw, big man, and fine looking enough, save for that look in his een. But it was too late to back oot then, so we went along.

I liked well enow to hear him talk. He knew his country, and spoke intelligently and well of the beauties of Galloway. Truly the scenery was superb. The hills in the west were all gold and purple in the last rays of the dying sun, and the heather was indescribably beautiful.

But by the time we reached the moorlands at the foot of the hills the sun and the licht were clean gone awa', and the darkness was closing down fast aboot us. We could hear the cry of the whaup, a mournful, plaintive note; our own voices were the only other sounds that broke the stillness. Then, suddenly, our host bent low and loosed his dogs, after whispering to them, and they were off as silently and as swiftly as ghosts in the heather.

We realized then what sort of fun it was we had been promised. And it was grand sport, that hunting in the darkness, wi' the wee dogs comin' back faithfully, noo and then, to their master, carrying a hare or a rabbit firmly in their mouths.

"Man, Mae, but this is grand sport!" I whispered.

"Aye!" he said, and turned to the owner of the dogs.

"I envy you," he said. "It must be grand to hae a moor like this, wi' dogs and guns."

"And the keepers," I suggested.

"Aye--there's keepers enow, and stern dells they are, too!"

Will ye no picture Mac and me, hangin' on to one anither's hands in the darkness, and feelin' the other tremble, each guilty one o' us? So it was poachin' we'd been, and never knowing it! I saw a licht across the moor.

"What's yon?" I asked our host, pointing to it.

"Oh, that's a keeper's hoose," he answered, indifferently. "I expect they'll be takin' a walk aroond verra soon, tae."

"Eh, then," I said, "would we no be doing well to be moving hameward? If anyone comes this way I'll be breaking the mile record between here and Creetown!"

The poacher laughed.

"Ay, maybe," he said. "But if it's old Adam Broom comes ye'll hae to be runnin' faster than the charge o' shot he'll be peppering your troosers wi' in the seat!"

"Eh, Harry," said Mac, "it's God's blessings ye did no put on yer kilt the nicht!"

He seemed to think there was something funny in the situation, but I did not, I'm telling ye.

And suddenly a grim, black figure loomed up nearby.

"We're pinched, for sure, Mac," I said.

"Eh, and if we are we are," he said, philosophically. "What's the fine for poaching, Harry?"

We stood clutching one anither, and waitin' for the gun to speak. But the poacher whispered.

"It's all richt," he said. "It's a farmer, and a gude friend o' mine."

So it proved. The farmer came up and greeted us, and said he'd been having a stroll through the heather before he went to bed. I gied him a cigar--the last I had, too, but I was too relieved to care for that. We walked along wi' him, and bade him gude nicht at the end of the road that led to his steading. But the poacher was not grateful, for he sent the dogs into one of the farmer's corn fields as soon as he was oot of our sicht.

"There's hares in there," he said, "and they're sure to come oot this gate. You watch and nail the hares as they show."

He went in after the dogs, and Mac got a couple of stones while I made ready to kick any animal that appeared. Soon two hares appeared, rustling through the corn. I kicked out. I missed them, but I caught Mac on the shins, and at the same moment he missed with his stones but hit me instead! We both fell doon, and thocht no mair of keeping still we were too sair hurt not to cry oot a bit and use some strong language as well, I'm fearing. We'd forgotten, d'ye ken, that it was the Sawbath eve!

Aweel, I staggered to my feet. Then oot came more hares and rabbits, and after them the twa dogs in full chase. One hit me as I was getting up and sent me rolling into the ditch full of stagnant water.

Oh, aye, it was a pleasant evening in its ending! Mac was as scared as I by that time, and when he'd helped me from the ditch we looked aroond for our poacher host. We were afraid to start hame alane. He showed presently, laughing at us for two puir loons, and awfu' well pleased with his nicht's work.

I canna say sae muckle for the twa loons! We were sorry looking wretches. An' we were awfu' remorsefu', too, when we minded the way we'd broken the Sawbath and a'--for a' we'd not known what was afoot when we set out.

But it was different in the morn! Oh, aye--as it sae often is! We woke wi' the sun streamin' in our window. Mac leaned on his hand and sniffed, and looked at me.

"Man, Harry," said he, "d'ye smell what I smell?"

And I sniffed too. Some pleasant odor came stealing up the stairs frae the kitchen. I leaped up.

"'Tis hare, Mac!" I cried. "Up wi' ye! Wad ye be late for the breakfast that came nigh to getting us shot?"

CHAPTER VIII

Could go on and on wi' tales of yon good days wi' Mac. We'd our times when we were no sae friendly, but they never lasted overnicht. There was much philosophy in Mac. He was a kindly man, for a' his quick temper; I never knew a kinder. And he taught me much that's been usefu' to me. He taught me to look for the gude in a' I saw and came in contact wi'. There's a bricht side to almost a' we meet, I've come to ken.

It was a strange thing, the way Mac drew comic things to himsel'. It seemed on our Galloway tour, in particular, that a' the funny, sidesplitting happenings saved themselves up till he was aboot to help to mak' them merrier. I was the comedian; he was the serious artist, the great violinist. But ye'd never ha' thocht our work was divided sae had ye been wi' us.

It was to me that fell one o' the few heart-rending episodes o' the whole tour. Again it's the story of a man who thocht the world owed him a living, and that his mission was but to collect it. Why it is that men like that never see that it' not the world that pays them, but puir individuals whom they leave worse off for knowing them, and trusting them, and seeking to help them?

I mind it was at Gatehouse-of-Fleet in Kircudbrightshire that, for once in a way, for some reason I do not bring to mind, Mac and I were separated for a nicht. I found a lodging for the night wi' an aged couple who had a wee cottage all covered wi' ivy, no sae far from the Solway Firth. I was glad o' that; I've aye loved the water.

It was nae mair than four o'clock o' the afternoon when I reached the cottage and found my landlady and her white-haired auld husband waitin' to greet me. They made me as welcome as though I'd been their ain son; ye'd ne'er ha' thocht they were just lettin' me a bit room and gie'n me bit and sup for siller. 'Deed, an' that's what I like fine about the Scots folk. They're a' full o' kindness o' that sort. There's something hamely aboot a Scots hotel ye'll no find south o' the border, and, as for a lodging, why there's nowt to compare wi' Scotland for that. Ye feel ye're ane o' the family so soon as ye set doon yer traps and settle doon for a crack wi' the gude woman o' the hoose.

This was a fine, quiet, pawky pair I found at Gatehouse-of-Fleet. I liked them fine frae the first, and it was a delight to think of them as a typical old Scottish couple, spending the twilight years of their lives at hame and in peace. They micht be alane, I thocht, but wi' loving sons and daughters supporting them and caring for them, even though their affairs called them to widely scattered places.

Aweel, I was wrong. We were doing fine wi' our talk, when a door burst open, and five beautiful children came running in.

"Gie's a piece, granny," they clamored. "Granny--is there no a piece for us? We're so hungry ye'd never ken----"

They stopped when they saw me, and drew awa', shyly.

But they need no' ha' minded me. Nor did their granny; she knew me by then. They got their piece--bread, thickly spread wi' gude, hame made jam. Then they were off again, scampering off toward the river. I couldna help wonderin' about the bairns; where was their mither? Hoo came it they were here wi' the auld folks? Aweel, it was not my affairs.

"They're fine bairns, yon," I said, for the sake of saying something.

"Oh, aye, gude enow," said the auld man. I noticed his gude wife was greetin' a bit; she wiped her een wi' the corner of her apron. I thocht I'd go for a bit walk; I had no mind to be preying into the business o' the hoose. So I did. But that nicht, after the bairns were safe in bed and sound asleep, we all sat aboot the kitchen fire. And then it seemed the auld lady was minded to talk, and I was glad enow to listen. For ane thing I've always liked to hear the stories folk ha' in their lives. And then, tae, I know from my ane experience, how it eases a sair heart, sometimes, to tell a stranger what's troublin' ye. Ye can talk to a stranger where ye wouldna and couldna to ane near and dear to ye. 'Tis a strange thing, that--I mind we often hurt those who love us best because we can talk to ithers and not to them. But so it is.

"I saw ye lookin' at the bairns the day," she said. "Aye, they're no mine, as ye can judge for yersel'. It was our dochter Lizzie bore them. A fine lassie, if I do say so. She's in service the noo at a big hoose not so far awa' but that she can slip over often to see them and us. As for her husband----"

Tears began to roll doon her cheeks as she spoke. I was glad the puir mither was no deed; it was hard enough, wi' such bonny bairns, to ha' to leave them to others, even her ane parents, to bring up.

"The father o' the bairns was a bad lot--is still, I've no doot, if he's still living. He was wild before they were wed, but no so bad, sae far as we knew then. We were no so awfu' pleased wi' her choice, but we knew nothing bad enough aboot him to forbid her tak' him. He was a handsome lad, and a clever yin. Everyone liked him fine, forbye they distrusted him, too. But he always said he'd never had a chance. He talked of how if one gie a dog a bad name one micht as well droon him and ha' done. And we believed in him enow to think he micht be richt, and that if he had the chance he'd settle doon and be a gude man enow."

He' ye no heard that tale before? The man who's never had a chance! I know a thousand men like that. And they've had chances you and I wad ha' gie'n whatever we had for and never had the manhood to tak' them! Eh, but I was sair angry, listening to her.

She told o' how she and her husband put their heads togither. They wanted their dochter to have a chance as gude as' any girl. And so what did they do but tak' all the savings of their lives, twa hundred pounds, and buy a bit schooner for him. He was a sailor lad, it seems, from the toon nearby, and used to the sea.

"'Twas but a wee boat we bought him, but gude for his use in journeying up and doon the coast wi' cargo. His first trip was fine; he made money, and we were all sae happy, syne it seemed we'd been richt in backing him, for a' the neighbors had called us fools. But then misfortune laid sair hands upon us a'. The wee schooner was wrecked on the rocks at Gairliestone. None was lost wi' her, sae it kicht ha' been worse--though I dinna ken, I dinna ken!

"We were a' sorry for the boy. It was no his fault the wee boat was lost; none blamed him for that. But, d'ye ken, he came and brocht himsel' and his wife and his bairns, as they came along, to live wi' us. We were old. We'd worked hard all our lives. We'd gie'n him a' we had. Wad ye no think he'd have gone to work and sought to pay us back? But no. Not he. He sat him doon, and was content to live upon us--faither and me, old and worn out though he knew we were.

"And that wasna the worst. He asked us for siller a' the time, and he beat Lizzie, and was cruel to the wee bairns when we wouldna or couldna find it for him. So it went on, for the years, till, in the end, we gied him twenty pounds more we'd put awa' for a rainy day that he micht tak' himself' off oot o' our sicht and leave us be in peace. He was aff tae Liverpool at once, and we've never clapped een upon him syne then.

"Puir Lizzie! She loves him still, for all he's done to her and to us. She says he'll come back yet, rich and well, and tak' her out o' service, and bring up the bairns like the sons and dochters of gentlefolk. And we--weel, we say nowt to shake her. She maybe happier thinking so, and it's a sair hard time she's had, puir lass. D'ye mind the wee lassie that was sae still till she began to know ye--the weest one of them a'? Aye? Weel, she was born six months after her faither went awa', and I think she's our favorite among them a'."

"And ye ha' the care and the feedin' and the clothin' o' all that brood?" I said. "Is it no cruel hard'?"

"Hard enow," said the auld man, breaking his silence. "But we'd no be wi'oot them. They brichten up the hoose it'd be dull' and drear wi'oot them. I'm hoping that daft lad never comes back, for all o' Lizzie's thinking on him!"

And I share his hope. Chance! Had ever man a greater chance than that sailor lad? He had gone wrong as a boy. Those old folk, because their daughter loved him, gave him the greatest chance a man can have--the chance to retrieve a bad start, to make up for a false step. How many men have that? How many men are there, handicapped as, no doubt, he was, who find those to put faith in them? If a man may not take advantage of sicca chance as that he needs no better chance again than a rope around his neck with a stone tied to it and a drop into the Firth o' Forth!

I've a reminder to this day of that wee hoose at Gatehouse-of-Fleet. There was an old fashioned wag-at-the-wa' in the bedroom where I slept. It had a very curiously shaped little china face, and it took my fancy greatly. Sae, next morning, I offered the old couple a good, stiff price for it mair than it was worth, maybe, but not mair than it was worth to me. They thought I was bidding far too much, and wanted to tak' half, but I would ha' my ain way, for sae I was sure neither of was being cheated. I carried it away wi' me, and the little clock wags awa' in my bedroom to this very day.

There's a bit story I micht as weel tell ye mesel', for ye'll hear it frae Mac in any case, if ever ye chance to come upon him. It's the tale o' Kirsty Lamont and her rent box. I played eavesdropper, or I wouldna know it to pass it on to ye, but it's tae gude tae lose, for a' that. I'll be saying, first, that I dinna know Kirsty Lamont, though I mak' sae free wi' her name, gude soul!

It was in Kirremuir, and there'd been a braw concert the nicht before. I was on my way to the post office, thinking there'd be maybe a bit letter from the wife--she wrote to me, sometimes, then, when I was frae hame, oor courtin' days not being so far behind us as they are noo. (Ah, she travels wi' me always the noo, ye ken, sae she has nae need to write to me!) Suddenly I heard my own name as I passed a bunch o' women gossiping.

"What thocht ye o' Harry Lauder?" one of them asked another.

And the one she asked was no slow to say! "I think this o' Harry Lauder, buddies!" she declared, vehemently. "I think it's a dirty trick he's played on me, the wee deeil. I'm not sayin' it was altogither his fault, though--he's not knowing he did it!"

"How was the way o' that, Kirsty Lamont?" asked another.

"I'm tellin' ye. Fan the lassies came in frae the mull last nicht they flang their working things frae them as though they were mad.

"'Fat's all the stushie?' I asked them. They just leuch at me, and said they were hurryin' so they could hear Harry Lauder sing. They said he was the comic frae Glasga, and they asked me was I no gang wi' them tae the Toon Ha' to hear his concert.

"'No,' I says. 'All the siller in the hoose maun gang for the rent, and it's due on Setterday. Fat wad the neighbors be sayin' if they saw Kirsty Lamont gang to a concert in a rent week--fashin' aboot like that!'"

"But Phem--that's my eldest dochter, ye ken--she wad ha' me gang alang. She bade me put on my bonnet and my dolman, and said she'd pay for me, so's to leave the siller for the rent. So I said I'd gang, since they were so keen like, and we set oot jist as John came hame for his tea. I roort at him that he could jist steer for himself for a nicht. And he asked why, and I said I was gang to hear Harry Lauder.

"'Damn Harry Lauder!' he answers, gey short. "Ye'll be sorry yet for this nicht's work, Kirsty Lamont. Leavin' yer auld man tae mak' his ain tea, and him workin' syne six o'clock o' the morn!'"

"I turn't at that, for John's a queer ane when he tak's it intil's head, but the lassies poo'd me oot th' door and in twa-three meenits we were at the ha'. Fat a crushin' a fechtin' the get in. The bobby at the door saw me--savin' that we'd no ha' got in. But the bobby kens me fine--I've bailed John oot twice, for a guinea ilka time, and they recognize steady customers there like anywheres else!

"The concert was fine till that wee man Harry came oot in his kilt. And then, losh, I startit to laugh till the watter ran doon my cheeks, and the lassies was that mortified they wushed they had nae brocht me. I'm no ane to laugh at a concert or a play, but that wee Harry made ithers laugh beside me, so I was no the only ane to disgrace mysel'.

"It was eleven and after when we got hame. And there was no sogn o' John. I lookit a' ower, and he wisna in the hoose. Richt then I knew what had happened. I went to the kist where I kep' the siller for the rent. Not a bawbee left! He'll be spendin' it in the pubs this meenit I'm talkie' to ye, and we'll no see him till he hasna a penny left to his name. So there's what I think of yer Harry Lauder. I wish I wis within half a mile o' him this meenit, and I'd tell him what I thocht o' him, instead o' you! It's three months rent yer fine Harry Lauder has costit me! Had he na been here in Kirrie last nicht de ye think I'd ever ha' left the rent box by its lane wi' a man like our Jock in the hoose?"

You may be sure I did not turn to let the good Kirsty see my face. She wasna sae angry as she pretended, maybe, but I'm thinkin' she'd maybe ha' scratched me a bit in the face o' me, just to get even wi' me, had she known I was so close!

I've heard such tales before and since the time I heard Kirsty say what she thocht o' me. Many's the man has had me for an explanation of why he was sae late. I'm sorry if I've made trouble t'wixt man and wife, but I'm flattered, too, and I may as well admit it!

Ye can guess hoo Mac took that story. I was sae unwise as tae tell it to him, and he told it to everyone else, and was always threatening me with Kirsty Lamont. He pretended that some one had pointed her oot to him, so that he knew her by sicht, and he wad say that he saw her in the audience. And sometimes he'd peep oot the stage door and say he saw her waiting for me.

And, the de'il! He worked up a great time with the wife, tellin' aboot this Kirsty

Lamont that was so eager to see me, till Nance was jealous, almost, and I had to tell her the whole yarn before she'd forgie me! Heard ye ever the like o' such foolishness? But that was Mac's way. He could distil humor from every situation.

CHAPTER IX

Yon were grand days, that I spent touring aboot wi' Mac, singing in concerts. It was an easy going life. The work was light. My audiences were comin' to know me, and to depend on me. I had no need, after a time, to be worrying; we were always sure of a good hoose, wherever we went. But I was no quite content. I was always being eaten, in yon time, wi' a lettle de'il o' ambition, that gnawed at me, and wadna gie me peace.

"Man, Harry," he'd say, "I ken weel ye're doin' fine! But, man canna ye do better? Ca' canny, they'll be tellin' ye, but not I! Ye maun do as well as ye can. There's the wife to think of, and the bairn John-- the wee laddie ye and the wife are so prood on!"

It was so, and I knew it. My son John was beginning to be the greatest joy to me. He was so bricht, sae full o' speerit. A likely laddie he was. His mither and I spent many a lang evening dreaming of his future and what micht be coming his way.

"He'll ne'er ha' to work as a laddie as his faither did before him," I used to say. "He shall gang to schule wi' the best in the land."

It was the wife had the grandest dream o' all.

"Could we no send him to the university?" she said. "I'd gie ma een teeth, Harry, to see him at Cambridge!"

I laughed at her, but it was with a twist in the corners o' ma mooth. There was money coming in regular by then, and there was siller piling up in the bank. I'd nowt to think of but the wee laddie, and there was time enow before it would be richt to be sending him off--time enow for me to earn as muckle siller as he micht need. Why should he no be a gentleman? His blood was gude on both sides, frae his mither and frae me. And, oh, I wish ye could ha' seen the bonnie laddie as his mither and I did! Ye'd ken, then, hoo it was I came to be sae ambitious that I paid no heed to them that thocht it next door to sinfu' for me to be aye thinkin' o' doing even better than I was!

There were plenty like that, ye'll ken. Some was a wee bit jealous. Some, who'd known me my life lang, couldna believe I could hope to do the things it was in my heart and mind to try. They believed they were giving me gude advice when they bade me be content and not tempt providence.

"Man, Harry, listen to me," said one old friend. "Ye've done fine. Ye're a braw laddie, and we're all prood o' ye the noo. Don't seek to be what ye can never be. Ye'll stand to lose all ye've got if ye let pride rule ye."

I never whispered my real ambition to anyone in yon days--saving the wife, and Mackenzie Murdoch. Indeed, and it was he who spoke first.

"Ye'll not be wasting all yer time in the north country, Harry," he said. "There's London calling to ye!"

"Aye--London!" I said, a bit wistfully, I'm thinking. For me, d'ye ken, a Scots comic, to think o' London was like an ordinary man thinkin' o' takin' a trip to the North Pole. "My time's no come for that, Mac."

"Maybe no," said Mac. "But it will come--mark my words, Harry. Ye've got what London'll be as mad to hear as these folk here. Ye've a way wi' ye, Harry, my wee man!"

'Deed, and I did believe that mysel'! It's hard for a man like me to know what he can do, and say so when the time comes, wi'oot making thoughtless folk think he's conceited. An artist's feeling aboot such things is a curious one, and hard for any but artists to understand. It's a grand presumption in a man, if ye look at it in one way, that leads him to think he's got the right to stand up on a stage and ask a thousand people, or five thousand, to listen to him--to laugh when he bids them laugh, greet when he would ha' them sad.

To bid an audience gather, gie up its plans and its pursuits, tak' an hoor or two of its time--that's a muckle thing to ask! And then to mak' them pay siller, too, for the chance to hear you! It's past belief, almost, how we can do it, in the beginning. I'm thinking, the noo, how gude a thing it was I did not know, when I first quit the pit and got J. C. MacDonald to send me oot, how much there was for me to learn. I ken it weel the noo--I ken how great a chance it was, in yon early days.

But when an artist's time has come, when he has come to know his audiences, and what they like, and why--then it is different. And by this time I was a veteran singer, as you micht say. I'd sung before all sorts of folk. They'd been quick enough to let me know the things they didn't like. In you days, if a man in a gallery didna like a song or the way I sang it, he'd call oot. Sometimes he'd get the crowd wi' him--sometimes they'd rally to me, and shout him doon.

"Go on, Harry--sing yer own way--gang yer ain gait!" I've heard encouraging cries like that many and many a time. But I've always learned from those that disapproved o' me. They're quieter the noo. I ha' to watch folk, and see, from the way they clap, and the way they look when they're listening, whether I'm doing richt or wrong.

It's a digression, maybe, but I micht tell ye hoo a new song gets into my list. I must add a new song every sae often, ye ken. An' I ha' always a dozen or mair ready to try. I help in the writing o' my ain songs, most often, and so I ken it frae the first. It's changed and changed, both in words and music, over and over again. Then, when I think it's finished, I begin to sing it to mysel'. I'll sing while I'm shaving, when I tak' my bath, as I wander aboot the hoose or sit still in a railway train. I try all sorts of different little tricks, shadings o' my voice, degrees of expression.

Sometimes a whole line maun be changed so as to get the right sort o' sound. It makes all the difference in the world if I can sing a long "oh" sound, sometimes, instead o' a clippit e or a short a. To be able to stand still, wi' ma moth open, big enow for a bird to fly in, will mak' an audience laugh o' itself.

Anyway, it's so I do wi' a new song. I'll ha' sung it maybe twa-three thousand times before ever I call it ready to try wi' an audience. And even then I'm just beginning to work on it. Until I know how the folk in front tak' it I can't be sure. It may strike them in a way quite different from my idea o' hoo it would. Then it may be I'll ha' to change ma business. My audiences always collaborate wi' me in my new songs--and in my old ones, too, bless 'em. Only they don't know it, and they don't realize how I'm cheating them by making them pay to hear me and then do a deal o' my work for me as well.

It's a great trick to get an audience to singing a chorus wi' ye. Not in Britain--it's no difficult there, or in a colony where there are many Britons in the hoose. But in America I must ha' been one o' the first to get an audience to singing. American audiences are the friendliest in the world, and the most liberal wi' applause ye could want to find. But they've always been a bit shy aboot singin' wi ye. They feel it's for ye to do that by yer lane.

But I've won them aroond noo, and they help me more than they ken. Ye'll see that when yer audience is singing wi' ye ye get a rare idea of hoo they tak' yer song. Sometimes, o' coorse, a song will be richt frae the first time I sing it on the stage; whiles it'll be a week or a month or mair before it suits me. There's nae end to the work if ye'd keep friends wi' those who come oot to hear ye, and it's just that some singers ha' never learned, so that they wonder why it is ithers are successfu' while they canna get an engagement to save them. They blame the managers, and say a man can't get a start unless he have friends at coort. But it's no so, and I can prove it by the way I won my way.

I had done most of my work in Scotland when Mac and I and the wife began first really to dream aloud aboot my gae'in to London. Oh, aye, I'd been on tours that had crossed the border; I'd been to Sunderland, and Newcastle on Tyne, but everywhere I'd been there was plenty Soots folk, and they knew the Scots talk and were used to the flutter o' ma kilts. Not that they were no sae in England, further south, too--'deed, and the trouble was they were used too well to Scotch comedians there.

There'd been a time when it was enow for a man to put on a kilt and a bit o' plaid and sing his song in anything he thocht was Scottish. There'd been a fair wave o' such false Scottish comics in the English halls, until everyone was sick and tired o' 'em. Sae it was the managers all laughed at the idea of anither, and the one or twa faint tries I made to get an engagement in or near London took me nowheres at a'.

Still and a' I was set upon goin' to the big village on the Thames before I deed, and I'm an awfu' determined wee man when ma mind's well made up. Times I'd whisper a word to a friend in the profession, but they all laughed at me.

"Stick to where they know ye and like ye, Harry," they said, one and a'. "Why tempt fortune when you're doin' so well here?"

It did seem foolish. I was successful now beyond any dreams I had had in the beginning. The days when a salary of thirty five shillings a week had looked enormous made me smile as I looked back upon them. And it would ha' been a bold manager the noo who'd dared to offer Harry Lauder a guinea to sing twa-three songs of a nicht at a concert.

Had the wife been like maist women, timid and sair afraid that things wad gang wrang, I'd be singing in Scotland yet, I do believe. But she was as bad as me. She was as sure as I was that I couldna fail if ever I got the chance to sing in London.

"There's the same sort of folks there as here, Harry," she said. "Folks are the same, here and there, the wide world ower. Tak' your chance if it comes--ye'll no be losin' owt ye've got the noo if ye fail. But ye'll not fail, laddie--I ken that weel."

Still, resolving to tak' a chance if it came was not ma way. It's no man's way who gets anywheres in this world, I've found. There are men who canna e'en do so much--to whom chances come they ha' neither the wit to see nor the energy to seize upon. Such men one can but pity; they are born wi' somethin' lacking in them that a man needs. But there is anither sort, that I do not pity--I despise. They are the men who are always waiting for a chance. They point to this man or to that, and how he seized a chance--or how, perhaps, he failed to do so.

"If ever an opportunity like that comes tae me," ye'll hear them say, "just watch me tak' it! Opportunity'll ne'er ha' to knock twice upon my door."

All well and good. But opportunity is no always oot seekin doors to knock upon. Whiles she'll be sittin' hame, snug as a bug in a rug, waitin' fer callers, her ear cocked for the sound o' the knock on *her* door. Whiles the knock comes she'll lep' up and open, and that man's fortune is made frae that day forth. Ye maun e'en go seekin' opportunity yersel, if so be she's slow in coming to ye. It's so at any rate, I've always felt. I've waited for my chance to come, whiles, but whiles I've made the chance mysel', as well.

It was after the most successful of the tours Mac and I got up together, one of those in Galloway, that I got a week in Birkenhead. Anither artist was ill, and they just wired wad I come? I was free at the time, and glad o' the siller to be made, for the offer was a gude one, so I just went. That was firther south than I'd been yet; the audiences were English to the backbone wi' no Scots to speak of amang them.

No Scots, I say! But what audience ha' I e'er seen that didna hae its sprinklin' o' gude Scots? I've sang in 'most every part o' the world, and always, frae somewhere i' the hoose, I'll hear a Scots voice callin' me by name. Scots ha' made their way to every part o' the world, I'm knowin' the noo, and I'm sure of at least ane friend in any audience, hoo'ever new it be to me.

So, o' coorse, there were some Scots in that audience at Birkenhead. But because in that Mersey town most of the crowd was sure to be English, wi' a sprinkling o' Irish, the management had suggested that I should leave out my Scottish favorites when I made up my list o' songs. So I began wi' a sentimental ballad, went on wi' an English comic song, and finished with "Calligan-Call-Again," the very successful Irish song I had just added to my list.

Ye'll ken, mebbe, if ye've heard me, that I can sing in English as good as the King's own when I've the mind to do it. I love my native land. I love Scots talk, Scots food, Scots--aweel, I was aboot to say something that would only sadden many of my friends in America. Hoots, though mebbe they'll no put me in jail if I say I liked a wee drappie o' Scottish liquor noo and again! But it was no a hard thing for me not to use my Scottish tongue when I was singing there in Birkenhead, though it went sair against ma judgment. And one nicht, at the start of ma engagement, they were clamorous as I'd ne'er seen them sae far south.

"Gi'es more, Harry," I heard a Scottish voice roar. I'd sung my three songs; I'd given encores; I was bowing acknowledgment of the continuing applause. But I couldna stop the applauding. In America they say an artist "stops" the show when the audience applauds him so hard that it will not let the next turn go on, and that was what had happened that nicht in Birkenhead. I didna want to sing any of ma three songs ower again, and I had no main that waur no Scottish.

So I stood there, bowing and scraping, wi' the cries of "Encore," "Sing again, Harry," "Give us another," rising in all directions from a packed house. I raised ma hand, and they were still.

"Wad ye like a little Scotch?" I asked,

There was a roar of laughter, and then one Scottish voice bawled oot an answer.

"Aye, thank ye kindly, man Harry," it roared. "I'll tak' a wee drappie o' Glenlivet----"

The house roared wi' laughter again, and learned doon and spoke to the orchestra leader. It happened that I'd the parts for some of my ain songs wi' me, so I could gie them "Tobermory" and then "The Lass o' Killiecrankie."

Weel, the Scots songs were far better received than ever the English ones or the Irish melody had been. I smiled to mysel' and went back to ma dressin' room to see what micht be coming. Sure enough 'twas but twa-three meenits when the manager came in.

"Harry," he said, "you knocked them dead with those Scotch songs. Now do you see I was right from the start when I said you ought to sing them?"

I looked at the man and just smiled. He richt frae the start! It was he had told me not to sing ma Scottish songs--that English audiences were tired o' everything that had to do wi' a kilt or a pair o' brogues! But I let it pass.

"Oh, aye," I said, "they liked them fine, didn't they? So ye're thinkin' I'd better sing more Scotch the rest o' the week?"

"Better?" he said, and he laughed. "You'll have no choice, man. What one audience has heard the next one knows about. They'll make you sing those songs again, whether or no."

I've found that that is so--'deed, I knew it before he did. I never appear but that I've requests for practically every song I've ever sung. Some one remembers hearing me before when I was including them, or they've heard someone speak. I've been asked within a year to sing "Torralladdie"--the song I won a medal wi' at Glasga while I was still workin' in the pit at Hamilton! No evening is lang enow to sing all my songs in--all those I've gi'en my friends in my audiences at one time and anither in all these nearly thirty years I've been upon the stage. Else I'd be tryin' it, for the gude fun it wad be.

Anyway, every nicht after that the audience wanted its wee drappie o' Scotch, and got it, in good measure, for I love to sing the Scottish songs. And when the week was at an end I was promptly re-engaged for a return visit the next season, at the biggest salary that had yet been offered to me. I was a prood man the day; I felt it was a great thing that had come to me, there on the banks o' the Mersey, sae far frae hame and a', in the England they'd a' tauld me was hae nane o' me and ma sangs!

And that week was a turning point in ma life, tae. It chanced that, what wi' ane thing and anither, I was free for the next twa-three weeks. I'd plenty of engagements I could get, ye'll ken, but I'd not closed ma time yet wi' anyone. Some plans I'd had had been changed. So there I was. I could gang hame, and write a letter or twa, and be off in a day or so, singing again in the same auld way. Or--I could do what a' my friends tauld me was madness and worse to attempt. What did I do? I bocht a ticket for London!

CHAPTER X

There was method in my madness, tho', ye'll ken. Here was I, nearer far to London, in Birkenhead than I was in Glasga. Gi'en I was gae'in there some time, I could save my siller by going then. So off I went-- resolved to go and look for opportunity where opportunity lived.

Ye'll ken I could see London was no comin' after me--didna like the long journey by train, maybe. So I was like Mahomet when the mountain wouldna gang to him. I needed London mair then than London needed me, and 'twas no for me to be prood and sit twiddlin' my thumbs till times changed.

I was nervous, I'll admit, when I reached the great toon. I was wrong to lash mysel', maybe, but it means a great deal to an artist to ha' the stamp o' London's approval upon him. 'Tis like the hall mark on a bit o' siller plate. Still and a' I could no see hoo they made oot I was sae foolish to be tryin' for London. Mebbe they were richt who said I could get no opening in a London hall. Mebbe the ithers were richt, too, who said that if I did the audience would howl me down and they'd ring doon the curtain on me. I didna believe that last, though, I'm tellin' ye--I was sure that I'd be as well received in London as I had been in Birkenhead, could I but mak' a manager risk giving me a turn.

Still I was nervous. The way it lookit to me, I had a' to gain and nothin' much tae lose. If I succeeded--ah, then there were no bounds to the future I saw before me! Success in London is like no success in the provinces. It means far more. I'd ha' sung for nothin'--'deed, and I'd ha' paid oot ma own good siller to get a turn at one of the big halls.

I had a London agent by that time, a mannie who booked engagements for me in the provinces. That was his specialty; he did little business in London itself. He was a decent body; he'd got me the week in Birkenhead, and I liked him fine. When

I went to his office he jumped up and shook hands with me.

"Glad to see you, Lauder," he said. "Wish more of you singers and performers from the provinces would run up to London for a visit from time to time."

"I'm no precisely here on a veesit," I said, rather dryly. "What's chances of finding a shop here?"

"Lord, Lord have you got that bee in your bonnet, too, Harry," he asked, with a sigh. "You all do. You're doing splendidly in the provinces, Harry. You're making more money than some that are doing their turns at the Pay. and the Tiv. Why can't you be content?"

"I'm just not, that's a'," I said. "You think there's nae a chance for me here, then?"

"Not a chance in the world," he said, promptly. "It's no good, Harry, my boy. They don't want Scotch comics here any more. No manager would give you a turn now. If he did he'd be a fool, because his audience wouldn't stand for you. Stay where you belong in Scotland and the north. They can understand you, there, and know what you're singing about."

I could see there was no use arguing wi' him. And I could see something else, too. He was a good agent, and it was to his interest to get me as many engagements, and as good ones, as he could, since he got a commission on all I earned through him. But if he did not believe I could win an audience, what sort of man was he to be persuading a manner to gang against his judgment and gie me a chance in his theatre?

So I determined that I must see the managers mysel'. For, as I've taul ye before, I'm an awfu' persistent wee man when my mind's made up, and no easily to be moved from a resolution I've once ta'en. I was shaken a bit by the agent, I'll not mind tellin' ye, for it seemed to me he must know better than I. Who was Harry Lauder, after a', to set his judgment against that o' a man whose business it was to ken all aboot such things? Still, I was sae sure that I went on.

Next morning I met Mr. Walter F. Munroe, and he was gude enow to promise to introduce me to several managers. He took me off wi' him then and there, and we made a round o' all the music hall offices, and saw the managers, richt enow. Yell mind they were all agreeable and pleasant tae me. They said they were glad tae see me, and wrote me passes for their halls, and did a' they could tae mak' me feel at hame. But they wouldna gie me the turn I was asking for!

I think Munroe hadna been verra hopefu' frae the first, but he did a' I wanted o' him--gie'd me the opportunity to talk to the managers mysel'. Still, they made me feel my agent had been richt. They didna want a Scot on any terms at a', and that was all to it.

I was feelin' blue enow when it came time for lunch, but I couldna do less than ask Munroe if he'd ha' bit and sup wi' me, after the kindness he'd shown me. We went into a restaurant in the Strand. I was no hungry; I was tae sair at heart, for it lookit as if I maun gang hame and tell the wife my first trip to London had been a failure.

"By George--there's a man we've not seen!" said Munroe, suddenly, as we sat, verra glum and silent.

"Who's that?" I asked.

"Tom Tinsley--the best fellow in London. You'll like him, whether he can do anything for you or not. I'll hail him----"

He did, and Mr. Tinsley came over toward our table. I liked his looks.

"He's the manager of Gatti's, in the Westminster Bridge Road," whispered Munroe. "Know it?"

I knew it as one of the smaller halls, but one with a decided reputation for originality and interesting bills, owing to the personality of its manager, who was never afraid to do a new thing that was out of the ordinary. I was glad I was going to meet him.

"Here's Harry Lauder wants to meet you, Tom," said Munroe. "Shake hands with him. You're both good fellows."

Tinsley was as cordial as he could be. We sat and chatted for a bit, and I managed to banish my depression, and keep up my end of the conversation in gude enow fashion, bad as I felt. But when, Munroe put in a word aboot ma business in London I saw a shadow come over Tinsley's face. I could guess how many times in a day he had to meet ambitious, struggling artists.

"So you're here looking for a shop, hey?" he said, turning to me. His manner was still pleasant enough, but much of his effusive cordiality had vanished. But I was not to be cast down. "What's your line?"

"Scotch comedian," I said. "I----"

He raised his hand, and laughed.

"Stop right there--that's done the trick! You've said enough. Now, look here, my dear boy, don't be angry, but there's no use. We've had Scotch comedians here in London before, and they're no good to us. I wish I could help you, but I really can't risk it."

"But you've not heard me sing," I said. "I'm different frae them ye talk of. Why not let me sing you a bit song and see if ye'll not think sae yersel?"

"I tell ye it's no use," he said, a little impatiently. "I know What my audiences like and what they don't. That's why I keep my hall going these days."

But Munroe spoke up in my favor, too; discouraging though he was we were getting more notice from Tinsley than we had had frae any o' the ithers! Ye can judge by that hoo they'd handled us.

"Oh, come, Tom," said Munroe. "It won't take much of your time to hear the man sing a song you do as much for all sorts of people every week. As a favor to me--come, now----"

"Well, if you put it like that," said Tinsley, reluctantly. He turned to me. "All right, Scotty," he said. "Drop around to my office at half past four and I'll see what's to be done for you. You can thank this nuisance of a Munroe for that--though it'll do you no good in the long run, you'll find, and just waste your time as well as mine!"

There was little enough incentive for me to keep that appointment. But I went, naturally. And, when I got there, I didn't sing for Tinsley. He was too busy to listen to me.

"You're in luck, just the same, Scotty," he said. "I'm a turn short, because some-one's got sick. Just for to-night. If you'll bring your traps down about ten o'clock you can have a show. But I don't expect you to catch on. Don't be too disappointed if you don't. London's tired of your line."

"Leave that to me, Mr. Tinsley," I said. "I've knocked 'em in the provinces and I'll be surprised if I don't get a hand here in London. Folks must be the same here as in Birkenhead or Glasga!"

"Don't you ever believe that, or it will steer you out of your way," he answered. "They're a different sort altogether. You've got one of the hardest audiences in the world to please, right in this hall. I don't blame you for wanting to try it, though. If you should happen to bring it off your fortune's made."

I knew that as well as he. And I knew that now it was all for me to settle. I didn't mean to blame the audience if I didn't catch on; I knew there would be no one to blame but myself. If I sang as well as I could, if I remembered all my business, if, in a word, I did here what I'd been doing richt along at hame and in the north of England, I needn't be afraid of the result, I was sure.

And then, I knew then, as I know noo, that when ye fail it's aye yer ain fault, one way or anither.

I wadna ha' been late that nicht for anything. 'Twas lang before ten o'clock when I was at Gatti's, waiting for it to be my turn. I was verra tired; I'd been going aboot since the early morn, and when it had come supper time I'd been sae nervous I'd had no thought o' food, nor could I ha' eaten any, I do believe, had it been set before me.

Weel, waitin' came to an end, and they called me on. I went oot upon the stage, laughin' fit to kill mysel', and did the walk aroond. I was used, by that time, to havin' the hoose break into laughter at the first wee waggle o' my kilt, but that nicht it was awfu' still. I keened in that moment what they'd all meant when they'd tauld me a London audience was different frae any ever I'd clapped een upon. Not that my een saw that one--the hoose micht ha' been ampty, for ought I knew! The stage went around and around me.

I began wi' "Tobermory," a great favorite among my songs in yon days. And at the middle o' the first verse I heard a sound that warmed me and cheered me--the beginnings of a great laugh. The sound was like wind rising in the trees. It came down from the gallery, leaped across the stalls from the pit--oh, but it was the bonny, bonny sound to ma ears! It reached my heart--it went into my feet as I danced, it raised my voice for me!

"Tobermory" settled it--when they sang the chorus wi' me on the second voice, in a great, roaring measure, I knew I was safe. I gave them "Calligan-Vall-Again" then, and ended with "The Lass o' Killicrankie." I'd been supposed to ha' but a short turn, but it was hard for me to get off the stage. I never had an audience treat me better. 'Tis a great memory to this day--I'll ne'er forget that night in Gatti's old hall, no matter hoo lang I live.

But I was glad when I heard the shootin' and the clappin' dee doon, and they let the next turn go on. I was weak----I was nigh to faintin' as I made my way to my dressing room. I had no the strength to be changin' ma clothes, just at first, and I was still sittin' still, tryin' to pull mysel' together, when Tinsley came rushing in. He clapped his hand on my shoulder.

"Lauder, my lad, you've done it!" he cried. "I never thought you could--you've proved every manager in London an ass to-night!"

"You think I'll do?" I asked.

He was a generous man, was Tinsley.

"Do!" he said. "You've made the greatest hit of the week when the news gets out, and you'll be having the managers from the West End halls camping on your doorstep. I've seen nothing like it in years. All London will be flocking here the rest in a long time."

I needn't say, I suppose, that I was immediately engaged for the rest of that week at Gatti's. And Tinsley's predictions were verified, for the managers from the west end came to me as soon as the news of the hit I had made reached them. I bore them no malice, though some of them had been ruder than they need ha' been when I went to see them. They'd had their chance; had they listened to me and recognized what I could do, they could ha' saved their siller. I'd ha' signed a contract at a pretty figure less the day after I reached London than I was willin' to consider the morning after I'd had my show at Gatti's.

I made verra profitable and happy arrangements wi' several halls, thanks to the London custom that's never spread much to America, that lets an artist appear at sometimes as many as five halls in a nicht. The managers were still surprised; so was my agent.

"There's something about you they take to, though I'm blowed if I see what it is!" said one manager, with extreme frankness.

Noo, I'm a modest man, and it's no for me to be tellin' them that feel as he did what it is, maybe, they don't see. 'Deed, and I'm no sure I know mysel'. But here's a bit o' talk I heard between two costers as I was leavin' Gatti's that first nicht.

"Hi, Alf, wot' jer fink o' that Scotch bloke?" one of them asked his mate.

The other began to laugh.

"Blow me, 'Ennery, d'ye twig what 'e meant? I didn't," he said. "Not 'arf! But, lu'mme, eyen't he funny?"

Weel, after a', a manager can no do mair than his best, puir chiel. They thocht they were richt when they would no give me a turn. They thocht they knew their audiences. But the two costers could ha' told them a thing or two. It was just sicca they my agent and the managers and a' had thocht would stand between me and winning a success in London. And as it's turned out it's the costers are my firmest friends in the great city!

Real folk know one anither, wherever they meet. If I just steppit oot upon the stage and sang a bit song or twa, I'd no be touring the world to-day. I'd be by hame in Scotland, belike I'd be workin' in the pit still. But whene'er I sing a character song I study that character. I know all aboot him. I ken hoo he feels and thinks, as weel as hoo he looks. Every character artist must do that, whether he is dealing with Scottish types or costers or whatever.

It was astonishin' to me hoo soon they came to ken me in London, so that I wad be recognized in the streets and wherever I went. I had an experience soon after I reached the big toon that was a bit scary at the first o' it.

I was oot in a fog. Noo, I'm a Scot, and I've seen fogs in my time, but that first "London Particular" had me fair puzzled. Try as I would I couldna find ma way down Holborn to the Strand. I was glad tae see a big policeman looming up in the mist.

"Here, ma chiel," I asked him, "can ye not put me in the road for the Strand?"

He looked at me, and then began to laugh. I was surprised.

"Has onything come ower you?" I asked him. I could no see it was a laughing matter that I should be lost in a London fog. I was beginning to feel angry, too. But he only laughed louder and louder, and I thocht the man was fou, so I made to jump away, and trust someone else to guide me. But he seized my arm, and pulled me back, and I decided, as he kept on peering at my face, that I must look like some criminal who was wanted by the police.

"Look here--leave me go!" I cried, thoroughly alarmed. "You've got the wrong man. I'm no the one you're after."

"Are ye no?" he asked me, laughing still. "Are ye no Harry Lauder? Ye look like him, ye talk like him! An' fancy meetin' ye here! Last time I saw ye was in New Cumnock--gie's a shak o' yer haund!"

I shook hands wi' him gladly enough, in my relief, even though he nearly shook the hand off of me. I told him where I was playing the nicht.

"Come and see me," I said. "Here's a bob to buy you a ticket wi'."

He took it, and thanked me. Then, when he had put it awa', he leaned forward.

"Can ye no gie me a free pass for the show, man Harry?" he whispered.

Oh, aye, there are true Scots on the police in London!

CHAPTER XI

Many a strange experience has come to me frae the way it's so easy for folk's that ha' seen me on the stage, or ha' nae mair than seen my picture, maybe, to recognize me. 'Tis an odd thing, too, the confidences that come to me--and to all like mysel', who are known to the public. Folks will come to me, and when I've the time to listen, they'll tell me their most private and sacred affairs. I dinna quite ken why--I know I've heard things told to me that ha' made me feel as a priest hearing confession must.

Some of the experiences are amusing; some ha' been close to being tragic--not for me, but for those who came to me. I'm always glad to help when I can, and it's a strange thing how often ye can help just by lendin' a fellow creature the use o' your ears for a wee space. I've a time or two in mind I'll be tellin' ye aboot.

But it's the queer way a crowd gathers it took me the longest to grow used to. It was mair sae in London than I'd ever known it before. In Scotland they'd no be followin' Harry Lauder aboot--a Scot like themselves! But in London, and in special when I wore ma kilt, it was different.

It wasna lang, after I'd once got ma start in London, before I was appearing regularly in the East End halls. I was a great favorite there; the Jews, especially, seemed to like me fine. One Sunday I was down Petticoat Lane, in Whitechapel, to see the sichts. I never thocht anyone there wad recognize me, and I stood quietly watching a young Jew selling clothes from a coster's barrow. But all at once another Jew came up to me, slapped me on the back, and cried oot: "Ach, Mr. Lauder, and how you vas to-day? I vish there vas a kilt in the Lane-- you would have it for nothing!"

In a minute they were flocking around me. They all pulled me this way, and that, slapped me on the back, embraced me. It was touching, but-- weel, I was glad to get awa', which I did so soon as I could wi'oot hurtin' the feelings of my gude friends the Hebrews.

The Hebrews are always very demonstrative. I'm as fond o' them as, thank fortune, they are o' me. They make up a fine and appreciative audience. They know weel what they like, and why they like it, and they let you ken hoo they feel. They are an artistic race; more so than most others, I think. They've had sair misfortunes to bear, and they've borne them weel.

One nicht I was at Shoreditch, playing in the old London Music Hall. The East Enders had gi'en me a fairly terrific reception that evening, and when it was time for me to be off to the Pavilion for my next turn they were so crowded round the stage door that I had to ficht ma way to ma brougham. It was a close call for me, onyway, that nicht, and I was far frae pleased when a young man clutched me by the hand.

"Let me get off, my lad!" I cried, sharply. "I'm late for the 'Pav.' the noo! Wait till anither nicht----"

"All right, 'Arry," he said, not a bit abashed. "I vas just so glad to know you vas doing so vell in business. You're a countryman of mine, and I'm proud o' you!"

Late though I was, I had to laugh at that. He was an unmistakable Jew, and a Londoner at that. But I asked him, as I got into my car, to what country he thought we both belonged.

"Vy! I'm from Glasgow!" he said, much offended. "Scotland forever!"

So far as I know the young man had no ulterior motive in claiming to be a fellow Scot. But to do that has aye been a favorite trick of cadgers and beggars. I mind weel a time when I was leaving a hall, and a rare looking bird collared me. He had a nose that showed only too plainly why he was in trouble, and a most unmistakably English voice. But he'd taken the trouble to learn some Scots words, though the accent was far ayant him.

"Eh, Harry, man," he said, jovially. "Here's the twa o' us, Scots far frae hame. Wull ye no lend me the loan o' a twopence?"

"Aye," I said, and gi'ed it him. "But you a Scot! No fear! A Scot wad ha' asked me for a tanner--and got it, tae!"

He looked very thoughtful as he stared at the two broad coppers I left on his itching palm. He was reflecting, I suppose, on the other fourpence he might ha' had o' me had he asked them! But doubtless he soon spent what he did get in a pub.

There were many times, though, and are still, when puir folk come to me wi' a real tale o' bad luck or misfortune to tell. It's they who deserve it the most are most backward aboot asking for a loan; that I've always found. It's a sair thing to decide against geevin' help; whiles, though, you maun feel that to do as a puir body asks is the worst thing for himsel'.

I mind one strange and terrible thing that came to me. It was in Liverpool, after I'd made my London success--long after. One day, while I was restin' in my dressing room, word was brocht to me that a bit lassie who looked as if she micht be in sair trouble wad ha' a word wi' me. I had her up, and saw that she was a pretty wee creature --no more than eighteen. Her cheeks were rosy, her eyes a deep blue, and very large, and she had lovely, curly hair. But it took no verra keen een to see she was in sair trouble indeed. She had been greetin' not sae lang syne, and her een were red and swollen frae her weeping.

"Eh, my, lassie," I said, "can I help ye, then? But I hope you're no in trouble."

"Oh, but I am, Mr. Lauder!" she cried. "I'm in the very greatest trouble. I can't tell you what it is--but--you can help me. It's about your cousin--if you can tell me where I can find him----"

"My cousin, lassie?" I said. "I've no cousin you'd be knowing. None of my cousins live in England--they're all beyond the Tweed."

"But--but--your cousin Henry--who worked here in Liverpool--who always stayed with you at the hotel when you were here?"

Oh, her story was too easy to read! Puir lassie--some scoundrel had deceived her and betrayed her. He'd won her confidence by pretending to be my cousin--why, God knows, nor why that should have made the lassie trust him. I had to break the truth to her, and it was terrible to see her grief.

"Oh!" she cried. "Then he has lied to me! And I trusted him utterly-- with everything I could!"

It was an awkward and painful position for me--the worst I can bring to mind. That the scoundrel should have used my name made matters worse, from my point of view. The puir lassie was in no condition to leave the theatre when it came time for my turn, so I sent for one o' the lady dressers and arranged for her to be cared for till later. Then, after my turn, I went back, and learned the whole story.

It was an old story enough. A villain had betrayed this mitherless lassie; used her as a plaything for months, and then, when the inevitable happened, deserted her, leaving her to face a stern father and a world that was not likely to be tender to her. The day she came to me her father had turned her oot--to think o' treatin' one's ain flesh and blood so!

There was little enow that I could do. She had no place to gae that nicht, so I arranged wi' the dresser, a gude, motherly body, to gie her a lodging for the nicht, and next day I went mysel' to see her faither--a respectable foreman he turned oot to be. I tault him hoo it came that I kenned aboot his dochter's affairs, and begged him would he no reconsider and gie her shelter? I tried to mak' him see that onyone micht be tempted once to do wrong, and still not be hopelessly lost, and asked him would he no stand by his dochter in her time o' sair trouble.

He said ne'er a word whiles I talked. He was too quiet, I knew. But then, when I had said all I could, he told me that the girl was no longer his dochter. He said she had brought disgrace upon him and upon a godly hoose, and that he could but hope to forget that she had ever lived. And he wished me good day and showed me the door.

I made such provision for the puir lassie as I could, and saw to it that she should have gude advice. But she could no stand her troubles. Had her faither stood by her--but, who kens, who kens? I only know that a few weeks later I learned that she had drowned herself. I would no ha' liked to be her faither when he learned that.

Thank God I ha' few such experiences as that to remember. But there's a many that were more pleasant. I've made some o' my best friends in my travels. And the noo, when the wife and I gang aboot the world, there's good folk in almost every toon we come to to mak' us feel at hame. I've ne'er been one to stand off and re-fuse to have ought to do wi' the public that made me and keeps me. They're a' my friends, that clap me in an audience, till they prove that they're no'--and sometimes it's my best friends that seem to be unkindest to me!

There's no way better calculated to get a crowd aboot than to be hurryin' through the streets o' London in a motor car and ha' a breakdoon! I've been lucky as to that; I've ne'er been held up more than ten minutes by such trouble, but it al-ways makes me nervous when onything o' the sort happens. I mind one time I was hurrying from the Tivoli to a hall in the suburbs, and on the Thames Embankment something went wrong.

I was worried for fear I'd be late, and I jumped oot to see what was wrang. I clean forgot I was in the costume for my first song at the new hall--it had been my last, tae, at the Tiv. I was wearin' kilt, glengarry, and all the costume for the swab germ' corporal o' Hielanders in "She's Ma Daisy." D'ye mind the song? Then ye'll ken hoo I lookit, oot there on the Embankment, wi' the lichts shinin' doon on me and a', and me dancin' aroond in a fever o' impatience to be off!

At once a crowd was aroond me--where those London crowds spring frae I've ne'er been able to guess. Ye'll be bowlin' alang a dark, empty street. Ye stop--and in a second they're all aboot ye. Sae it was that nicht, and in no time they were all singin', if ye please! They sang the choruses of my songs--each man, seemingly, picking a different yin! Aye, it was comical--so comical it took my mind frae the delay.

CHAPTER XII

I was crackin' yin or twa the noo aboot them that touch ye for a bawbee noo and then. I ken fine the way folks talk o' me and say I'm close fisted. Maybe I am a' that. I'm a Scot, ye ken, and the Scots are a close fisted people. I'm no sayin' yet whether yon's a fault or a virtue. I'd fain be talkin' a wee bit wi' ye aboot it first.

There's aye ither things they're fond o' saying aboot a Scot. Oh, aye, I've heard folk say that there was but the ane way to mak' a Scot see a joke, an' that was to bore a hole in his head first. They're sayin' the Scots are a folk wi'oot a sense o' humor. It may be so, but ye'll no be makin' me think so--not after all these years when they've been laughin' at me. Conceited, is that? Weel, ha' it yer ane way.

We Scots ha' aye lived in a bonny land, but a land that made us work hard for what it gie'd us. It was no smiling, easy going southern country like some. It was no land where it was easy to mak' a living, wi' bread growing on one tree, and milk in a cocoanut on another, and fruits and berries enow on all sides to keep life in the body of ye, whether ye worked or no.

There's no great wealth in Scotland. Her greatest riches are her braw sons and daughters, the Scots folk who've gone o'er a' the world. The land is full o' rocks and hills. The man who'd win a crop o' rye or oats maun e'en work for the same. And what a man works hard for he's like to value more than what comes easy to his hand. Sae it's aye been with the Scots, I'm thinking. We've had little, we Scottish folk, that's no cost us sweat and labor, o' one sort or anither. We've had to help ourselves, syne there was no one else had the time to gie us help.

Noo, tak' this close fisted Scot they're a' sae fond o' pokin' fun at. Let's consider ane o' the breed. Let's see what sort o' life has he been like to ha' led. Maybe so it wull mak' us see hoo it came aboot that he grew mean, as the English are like to be fond o' calling him.

Many and many the canny Scot who's made a great place for himsel' in the world was born and brocht up in a wee village in a glen. He'd see poverty all aboot him frae the day his een were opened. It's a hard life that's lived in many a Scottish village. A grand life, aye--ne'er think I'm not meaning that. I lived hard masel', when I was a bit laddie, but I'd no gie up those memories for ought I could ha' had as a rich man's son. But a hard life.

A laddie like the one I ha' in mind would be seein' the auld folk countin' every bawbee because they must. He'd see, when he was big enow, hoo the gude wife wad be shakin' her head when his faither wanted, maybe, an extra ounce or twa o' thick black.

"We maun think o' the bairn, Jock," she'd be saying. "Put the price of it in the kist, Jock--ye'll no be really needin' that."

He'd see the auld folk makin' auld clothes do; his mither patching and mending; his faither getting up when there was just licht to see by in the morn and working aboot the place to mak' it fit to stand the storms and snows and winds o' winter, before he went off to his long day's work. And he'd see all aboot him a hard working folk, winning from a barren soil that they loved because they had been born upon it.

Maybe it's meanness for folk like that to be canny, to be saving, to be putting the bawbees they micht be spending on pleasure in the kist on the mantel where the pennies drop in one by one, sae slow but sure. But your Scot's seen sickness come in the glen. He kens fine that sometimes there'll be those who couldna save, no matter how they tried. And he'll remember, aye, most Scots will be able to remember, how the kists on a dozen mantels ha' been broken into to gie help to a neighbor in distress wi'oot a thocht that there was ought else for a body to do but help when there was trouble and sorrow in a neighbor's hoose.

Aye, I've heard hard jokes cracked aboot the meanness o' the Scot. Your Scot, brocht up sae in a glen, will gang oot, maybe, and fare into strange lands to mak' his living when he's grown--England, or the colonies, or America. Where-over he gaes, there he'll tak' wi' him the canniness, the meanness if ye maun call it such, his childhood taught him. He'll be thrown amang them who've ne'er had to gie thocht to the morrow and the morrow's morrow; who, if ever they've known the pinch o' poverty, ha' clean forgotten.

But wull he care what they're thinkin' o' him, and saying, maybe, behind his back? Not he, if he be a true Scot. He'll gang his ain gait, satisfied if he but think he's doing richt as he sees and believes the richt to be. Your Scot wad be beholden to no man. The thocht of takin' charity is abhorrent to him, as to few ither folk on earth. I've told of hoo, in a village if trouble comes to a hame, there'll be a ready help frae ithers no so muckle better off. But that's no charity, ye ken! For ilka hoose micht be the next in trouble; it's one for a' and a' for one in a Scottish glen. Aye, we're a clannish folk, we Scots; we stand together.

I ken fine the way they're a' like to talk o' me. There's a tale they tell o' me in America, where they're sae fond o' joking me aboot ma Scotch closefistedness. They say, yell ken, that I was playing in a theatre once, and that when the engagement was ended I gie'd photographs o' masel to all the stage hands picture postcards. I called them a' together, ye ken, and tauld them I was gratefu' to them for the way they'd worked wi' me and for me, and wanted to gie 'em something they could ha' to remember me by.

"Sae here's my picture, laddies," I said, "and when I come again next year I'll sign them for you."

Weel, noo, that's true enough, nae doot--I've done just that, more than the ane time. Did I no gie them money, too? I'm no saying did I or did I no. But ha' I no the richt to crack a joke wi' friends o' mine like the stage hands I come to ken sae well when I'm in a theatre for a week's engagement?

I've a song I'm singing the noo. In it I'm an auld Scottish sailor. I'm pretendin', in the song, that I'm aboot to start on a lang voyage. And I'm tellin' my friends I'll send them a picture postcard noo and then frae foreign parts.

"Yell ken fine it's frae me," I tell my friends, "because there'll be no stamp on the card when it comes tae ye!"

Always the audience roars wi' laughter when I come to that line. I ken fine they're no laughin' at the wee joke sae much as at what they're thinkin' o' me and a' they've heard o' my tightness and closeness. Do they think any Scot wad care for the cost of a stamp? Maybe it would anger an Englishman did a postcard come tae him wi'oot a stamp. It wad but amuse a Scot; he'd no be carin' one way or anither for the bawbee the stamp wad cost. And here's a funny thing tae me. Do they no see I'm crackin' a joke against masel'? And do they think I'd be doing that if I were close the way they're thinkin' I am?

Aye, but there's a serious side tae all this talk o' ma being sae close. D'ye ken hoo many pleas for siller I get each and every day o' ma life? I could be handin' it out frae morn till nicht! The folk that come tae me that I've ne'er clapped een upon! The total strangers who think they've nowt to do but ask me for what they want! Men will ask me to lend them siller to set themselves up in business. Lassies tell me in a letter they can be gettin' married if I'll but gie them siller to buy a trousseau with. Parents ask me to lend them the money to educate their sons and send them to college.

And, noo, I'll be asking you--why should they come tae me? Because I'm before the public--because they think they know I ha' the siller? Do they nae think I've friends and relatives o' my ain that ha' the first call upon me? Wad they, had they the chance, help every stranger that came tae them and asked? Hoo comes it folk can lose their self-respect sae?

There's folk, I've seen them a' ma life, who put sae muckle effort into trying to get something for nowt that they ha' no time or leisure to work. They're aye sae busy writin' begging letters or working it aroond sae as to get to see a man or a woman they ken has mair siller than he or she needs that they ha' nae the time to mak' any effort by their ain selves. Wad they but put half the cleverness into honest toil that they do into writin' me a letter or speerin' a tale o' was to wring my heart, they could earn a' the siller they micht need for themselves.

In ma time I've helped many a yin. And whiles I've been sorry, I've been impressed by an honest tale o' sorrow and distress. I've gi'en its teller what he asked, or what I thocht he needed. And I've seen the effect upon him. I've seen hoo he's thocht, after that, that there was aye the sure way to fill his needs, wi'oot effort or labor.

'T'is a curious thing hoo such things hang aboot the stage. They're aye an open handed lot, the folks o' the stage. They help one another freely. They're always the first to gie their services for a benefit when there's a disaster or a visitation upon a community. They'll earn their money and gie it awa' to them that's in distress. Yet there's few to help them, save themselves, when trouble comes to them.

There's another curious thing I've foond. And that's the way that many a man wull go tae ony lengths to get a free pass for the show. He'll come tae me. He'll be wanting tae tak' me to dinner, he'll ask me and the wife to ride in a motor, he'll do ought that comes into his head-- and a' that he may be able to look to me for a free ticket for the playhoose! He'll be seekin' to spend ten times what the tickets wad cost him that he may get them for nothing. I canna understand that in a man wi' sense enough to mak' a success in business, yet every actor kens weel that it's sae.

What many a man calls meanness I call prudence. I think if we talked more o' that virtue, prudence, and less o' that vice, meanness--for I'm as sure as you can be that meanness is a vice--we'd come nearer to the truth o' this matter, mayhap.

Tak' a savage, noo. He'll no be mean or savin': He'll no be prudent, either. He lives frae hand tae mooth. When mankind became a bit more prudent, when man wanted to know, any day, where the next day's living was to come frae, then civilization began, and wi' it what many miscall meanness. Man wad be laying aside some o' the food frae a day o' plenty against the time o' famine. Why, all literature is fu' o' tales o' such things. We all heard the yarn o' the grasshopper and the ant at our mither's knee. Some o' us ha' ta'en profit from the same; some ha' nicht. That's the differ between the prudent man and the reckless yin. And the prudent man can afford to laugh when the ither calls him mean. Or sae I'll gae on thinkin' till I'm proved wrong, at any rate.

I've in mind a man I know weel. He's a sociable body. He likes fine to gang aboot wi' his friends. But he's no rich, and he maun be carefu' wi' his siller, else the wife and the bairns wull be gae'in wi'oot things he wants them to have. Sae, when he'll foregather, of an evening, wi' his friends, in a pub., maybe, he'll be at the bar. He's no teetotaller, and when some one starts standing a roond o' drinks he'll tak' his wi' the rest. And he'll wait till it comes his turn to stand aroond, and he'll do it, too.

But after he's paid for the drinks, he'll aye turn toward the door, and nod to all o' them, and say:

"Weel, lads, gude nicht. I'll be gae'n hame the noo."

They'll be thinking he's mean, most like. I've heard them, after he's oot the door, turn to ane anither, and say:

"Did ye ever see a man sae mean as Wully?"

And he kens fine the way they're talking, but never a bean does he care. He

kens, d'ye see, hoo he maun be using his money. And the siller a second round o'
drinks wad ha' cost him went to his family-- and, sometimes, if the truth be known,
one o' them that was no sae "mean" wad come aroond to see Wully at his shop.

"Man, Wull," he'd say. "I'm awfu' short. Can ye no lend me the loan o' five bob
till Setterday?"

And he'd get the siller--and not always be paying it back come Setterday, neither. But Wull wad no be caring, if he knew the man needed it. Wull, thanks to his
"meanness," was always able to find the siller for sicca loan. And I mind they did
no think he was so close then. And he's just one o' many I've known; one o' many
who's heaped coals o' fire on the heads of them that's thocht to mak' him a laughing
stock.

I'm a grand hand for saving. I believe in it. I'll preach thrift, and I'm no ashamed
to say I've practiced it. I like to see it, for I ken, ye'll mind, what it means to be puir
and no to ken where the next day's needs are to be met. And there's things worth
saving beside siller. Ha' ye ne'er seen a lad who spent a' his time a coortin' the wee
lassies? He'd gang wi' this yin and that. Nicht after nicht ye'd see him oot--wi' a
different lassie each week, belike. They'd a' like him fine; they'd be glad tae see him
comin' to their door. He'd ha' a reputation in the toon for being a great one wi' the
lassies, and ither men, maybe, wad envy him.

Oftimes there'll be a chiel o' anither stamp to compare wi' such a one as that.
They'll ca' him a woman hater, when the puir laddie's nae sicca thing. But he's no
the trick o' making himsel' liked by the bit lassies. He'd no the arts and graces o'
the other. But all the time, mind ye, he's saving something the other laddie's spending.

I mind twa such laddies I knew once, when I was younger. Andy could ha' his
way wi' any lassie, a'most, i' the toon. Just so far he'd gang. Ye'd see him, in the
gloamin', roamin' wi' this yin and that one. They'd talk aboot him, and admire him.
Jamie--he was reserved and bashfu', and the lassies were wont to laugh at him. They
thocht he was afraid of them; whiles they thocht he had nae use for them, whatever, and was a woman hater. It was nae so; it was just that Jamie was waiting. He
knew that, soon or late, he'd find the yin who meant mair to him than a' the ither
lassies i' the world put together.

And it was sae. She came to toon, a stranger. She was a wee, bonnie creature, wi' bricht een and bright cheeks; she had a laugh that was like music in your ears. Half the young men in the toon went coortin' her frae the moment they first clapped een upon her. Andy and Jamie was among them--aye, Jamie the woman hater, the bashfu' yin! And, wad ye believe it, it was Jamie hung on and on when all the ithers had gie'n up the chase and left the field to Andy? She liked them both richt weel; that much we could all see. But noo it was that Andy found oot that he'd been spending what he had wi' tae free a hand. Noo that he loved a lassie as he'd never dreamed he could love anyone, he found he could say nowt to her he had no said to a dozen or a score before her. The protestations that he made rang wi' a familiar sound in his ain ears--hoo could he mak' them convincing to her?

And it was sae different wi' Jamie; he'd ne'er wasted his treasure o' love, and thrown a wee bit here and a wee bit there. He had it a' to lay at the feet o' his true love, and there was little doot in ma mind, when I saw hoo things were gae'in, o' what the end on't wad be. And, sure enow, it was no Andy, the graceful, the popular one, who married her--it was the puir, salt Jamie, who'd saved the siller o' his love--and, by the way, he'd saved the ither sort o' siller, tae, sae that he had a grand little hoose to tak' his bride into, and a hoose well furnished, and a' paid for, too.

Aye, I'll no be denyin' the Scot is a close fisted man. But he's close fisted in more ways than one. Ye'll ca' a man close fisted and mean by that just that he's slow to open his fist to let his siller through it. But doesna the closed fist mean more than that when you come to think on't? Gie'n a man strike a blow wi' the open hand--it'll cause anger, maybe a wee bit pain. But it's the man who strikes wi' his fist closed firm who knocks his opponent doon. Ask the Germans what they think o' the close fisted Scots they've met frae ane end o' France to the other!

And the Scot wull aye be slow to part wi' his siller. He'll be wanting to know why and hoo comes it he should be spending his bawbees. But he'll be slow to part wi' other things, too. He'll keep his convictions and his loyalty as he keeps his cash. His love will no be lyin' in his open palm for the first comer to snatch awa'. Sae wull it be, tae, wi' his convictions. He had them yesterday; he keeps them to- day; they'll still be his to-morrow. Aye, the Scott'll be a close fisted, hard man--a strang man, tae, an' one for ye to fear if you're his enemy, but to respect withal, and to trust. Ye ken whaur the man stands who deals wi' his love and his friends and his siller as does the Scot. And ne'er think ye can fash him by callin' him mean.

Wull it sound as if I were boastin' if I talk o' what Scots did i' the war? What British city was it led the way, in proportion to its population, in subscribing to the war loans? Glasga, I'm tellin' ye, should ye no ken for yersel'. And ye'll no be needing me to tell ye hoo Scotland poured out her richest treasure, the blood of her sons, when the call came. The land that will spend lives, when the need arises, as though they were water, is the land that men ha' called mean and close! God pity the man who canna tell the difference between closeness and common sense!

There's nae merit in saving, I'll admit, unless there's a reason for't. The man who willna spend his siller when the time comes I despise as much as can anyone. But I despise, too, or I pity, the poor spendthrift who canna say "No!" when it wad be folly for him to spend his siller. Sicca one can ne'er meet the real call when it comes; he's bankrupt in the emergency. And that's as true of a nation as of a man by himsel'.

In the wartime men everywhere came to learn the value o' saving--o' being close fisted. Men o' means went proodly aboot, and showed their patched clothes, where the wife had put a new seat in their troosers-- 't'was a badge of honor, then, to show worn shoes, old claes.

Weel, was it only then, and for the first time, that it was patriotic for a man to be cautious and saving? Had we all practiced thrift before the war, wad we no hae been in a better state tae meet the crisis when it came upon us? Ha' we no learned in all these twa thousand years the meaning o' the parable o' the wise virgin and her lamp?

It's never richt for a man or a country tae live frae hand to mooth, save it be necessary. And if a man breaks the habit o' sae doin' it's seldom necessary. The amusement that comes frae spendin' siller recklessly dinna last; what does endure is the comfort o' kennin' weel that, come what may, weel or woe, ye'll be ready. Siller in the bank is just a symbol o' a man's ain character; it's ane o' many ways ither man have o' judging him and learnin' what sort he is.

So I'm standing up still for Scotland and my fellow countrymen. Because they'd been close and near in time of plenty they were able to spend as freely as was needfu' when the time o' famine and sair trouble came. So let's be havin' less chattering o' the meanness o' the Scot, and more thocht o' his prudence and what that last has meant to the Empire in the years o' war.

CHAPTER XIII

Folk ask me, whiles, hoo it comes that I dwell still sae far frae the centre o' the world--as they've a way o' dubbin London! I like London, fine, ye'll ken. It's a grand toon. I'd be an ungrateful chiel did I no keep a warm spot for the place that turned me frae a provincial comic into what I'm lucky enow to be the day. But I'm no wishfu' to pass my days and nichts always in the great city. When I've an engagement there, in the halls or in a revue, 'tis weel enow, and I'm happy. But always and again there'll be somethin' tae mak' me mindfu' o' the Clyde and ma wee hoose at Dunoon, and ma thochts wull gae fleein' back to Scotland.

It's ma hame--that's ane thing. There's a magic i' that word, for a' it's sae auld. But there's mair than that in the love I ha' for Dunoon and all Scotland. The city's streets--aye, they're braw, whiles, and they've brocht me happiness and fun, and will again, I'm no dootin'. Still--oh, listen tae me whiles I speak o' the city and the glen! I'm a loon on that subject, ye'll be thinkin', maybe, but can I no mak' ye see, if ye're a city yin, hoo it is I feel?

London's the most wonderfu' city i' the world, I do believe. I ken ithers will be challenging her. New York, Chicago--braw cities, both. San Francisco is mair picturesque than any, in some ways. In Australia, Sydney, Melbourne, Adelaide--I like them a'. But old London, wi' her traditions, her auld history, her wondrous palaces-- and, aye, her slums!

I'm no a city man. I'm frae the glen, and the glen's i' the blood o' me to stay. I've lived in London. Whiles, after I first began to sing often in London and the English provinces, I had a villa at Tooting--a modest place, hamely and comfortable. But the air there was no the Scottish air; the heather wasna there for ma een to see when they opened in the morn; the smell o' the peat was no in ma nostrils.

I gae a walkin' in the city, and the walls o' the hooses press in upon me as if they would be squeezing the breath frae ma body. The stones stick to the soles o' ma shoon and drag them doon, sae that it's an effort to lift them at every step. And at hame, I walk five miles o'er the bonny purple heather and am no sae tired as after I've trudged the single one o'er London brick and stone.

Ye ken ma song, "I love a lassie"? Aweel, it's sae that I think of my Scottish countryside. London's a grand lady, in her silks and her satins, her paint and her patches. But the country's a bonnie, bonnie lassie, as pure as the heather in the dell. And it's the wee lassie that I love.

There's a sicht ye can see as oft in the city as in the country. It's that o' a lover and his lass a walkin' in the gloamin'. And it's a sicht that always tears at my heart in the city, and fills me wi' sorrow and wi' sympathy for the puir young creatures, that's missin' sae much o' the best and bonniest time o' their lives, and ne'er knowin' it, puir things!

Lang agane I'd an engagement at the Paragon Music Hall--it must be many and many a year agane. One evening I was going through the City in my motor car-- the old City, that echoes to the tread of the business man by day, and at nicht is sae lane and quiet, wi' all the folk awa'. The country is quiet at nicht, tae, but it's quiet in a different way. For there the hum o' insects fills the air, and there's the music o' a brook, and the wind rustling in the tops o' the trees, wi' maybe a hare starting in the heather. It's the quiet o' life that's i' the glen at nicht, but i' the auld, auld City the quiet is the quiet o' death.

Weel, that nicht I was passing through Threadneedle street, hard by the Bank of England, that great, grey building o' stane. And suddenly, on the pavement, I saw them--twa young things, glad o' the stillness, his arm aboot her waist, their een turned upon one another, thinking o' nothing else and no one else i' a' the world.

I was sae sorry for them, puir weans! They had'na e'er ta'en a bit walk by their twa selves in the purple gloaming. They knew nothing o' the magic of a shady lane, wi' the branches o' old trees meeting over their heads. When they wad be togither they had to flee tae some such dead spot as this, or flaunt their love for one another in a busy street, where all who would micht laugh at them, as folk ha' a way o' doing, thoughtlessly, when they see the miracle o' young love, that is sae old that it is always young.

And yet, I saw the lassie's een. I saw the way he looked at her. It was for but a moment, as I passed. But I wasna sorry for them mair. For the miracle was upon them. And in their een, dinna doot it, the old, grey fronts o' the hooses were green trees. The pavement beneath their feet was the saft dirt o' a country road, or the bonny grass.

City folk do long, I'm sure o' it, for the glen and the beauty o' the countryside. Why else do they look as they do, and act as they do, when I sing to them o' the same? And I've the memory of what many a one has said to me, wi' tears in his een.

"Oh, Harry--ye brocht the auld hame to ma mind when ye sang o' roaming in the gloaming! And--the wee hoose amang the heather!"

'Tis the hamely songs I gie 'em o' the country they aye love best, I find. But why will they be content wi' what I bring them o' the glen and the dell? Why will they no go back or oot, if they're city born, and see for themselves? It's business holds some; others ha' other reasons. But, dear, dear, 'tis no but a hint o' the glamour and the freshness and the beauty o' the country that ma songs can carry to them. No but a hint! Ye canna bottle the light o' the moon on Afton Water; ye canna bring the air o' a Hieland moor to London in a box.

Will ye no seek to be oot sae much o' the year as ye can? It may be true that your affairs maun keep you living in the city. But whiles ye can get oot in the free air. Ye can lee doon upon yer back on the turf and look up at the blue sky and the bricht sun, and hear the skylark singing high above ye, or the call o' the auld hoot owl at nicht.

I think it's the evenings, when I'm held a prisoner in the city, mak' me lang maist for the country. There's a joy to a country evening. Whiles it's winter. But within it's snug. There's the wind howling doon the chimney, but there's the fire blazing upon the hearth, and the kettle singing it's bit sang on the hob. And all the family will be in frae work, tired but happy. Some one wull start a sang to rival the kettle; we've a poet in Scotland. 'Twas the way ma mither wad sing the sangs o' Bobby Burns made me sure, when I was a bit laddie, that I must, if God was gude tae me, do what I could to carry on the work o' that great poet.

There's plenty o' folk who like the country for rest and recreation. But they canna understand hoo it comes that folk are willing to stay there all their days and do the "dull country work." Aye, but it's no sae dull, that work in the country. There's less monotony in it, in ma een, than in the life o' the clerk or the shop-keeper, doing the same thing, day after day, year after year. I' the country they're producing--they're making food and ither things yon city dweller maun ha'.

It's the land, when a's said a's done, that feeds us and sustains us; clothes us and keeps us. It's the countryman, wi' his plough, to whom the city liver owes his food. We in Britain had a sair lesson in the war. Were the Germans no near bein' able to starve us oot and win the war wi' their submarines, And shouldna Britain ha' been able, as she was once, to feed hersel' frae her ain soil?

I'm thinking often, in these days, of hoo the soldiers must be feeling who are back frae France and the years i' the trenches. They've lived great lives, those o' them that ha' lived through it. Do ye think they'll be ready tae gang back to what they were before they dropped their pens or their tape measures and went to war to save the country?

I hae ma doots o' that. There's some wull go back, and gladly--them that had gude posts before the fichtin' came. But I'm wondering about the clerks that sat, stooped on their high stools, and balanced books. Wull a man be content to write doon, o'er and o'er again, "To one pair shoes, eighteen and sixpence, to five yards cotton print----" Oh, ye ken the sort o' thing I mean. Wull he do that, who's been out there, facin' death, clear eyed, hearing the whistle o' shell o'er his head, seeing his friends dee before his een?

I hault nothing against the man who's a clerk or a man in a linen draper's shop. It's usefu', honest work they do. But it's no the sort of work I'm thinking laddies like those who've fought the Hun and won the war for Britain and humanity wull be keen tae be doing in the future.

The toon, as it is, lives frae hand to mooth on the work the country does. Man canna live, after a', on ledgers and accounts. Much o' the work that's done i' the city's just the outgrowth o' what the country produces. And the trouble wi' Britain is that sae many o' her sons ha' flocked tae the cities and the toons that the country's deserted. Villages stand empty. Farms are abandoned--or bought by rich men who make park lands and lawns o' the fields where the potato and the mangel wurzel, the corn and the barley, grew yesteryear.

America and Australia feed us the day. Aye--for the U-boats are driven frae the depths o' the sea. But who's kennin' they'll no come back anither day? Shouldna we be ready, truly ready, in Britain, against the coming of anither day o' wrath? Had we been able to support ourselves, had we nae had to divert sae much o' our energy to beating the U-boats, to keep the food supply frae ower the seas coming freely, we'd ha' saved the lives o' thousands upon thousands o' our braw lads.

Ah, me, I may be wrang! But in ma een the toon's a parasite. I'm no sayin' it's no it's uses. A toon may be a braw and bonnie place enow-- for them that like it. But gie me the country.

Do ye ken a man that'll e'er be able tae love his hame sae well if it were a city he was born in, and reared in? In a city folk move sae oft! The hame of a man's faithers may be unknown tae him; belike it's been torn doon, lang before his own bairns are weaned.

In the country hame has a different meaning. Country folk make a real hame o' a hoose. And they grow to know all the country round aboot. It's an event when an auld tree is struck by lightning and withered. When a hoose burns doon it's a sair calamity, and all the neighbors turn to to help. Ah, and there's anither thing! There's neighborliness in the country that's lacking in the city.

And 'tis not because country folk are a better, or a different breed. We're all alike enow at bottom. It's just that there's more room, more time, more o' maist o' the good things that make life hamely and comfortable, i' the country than i' the city. Air, and sunshine, and space to run and lepp and play for the children. Broad fields--not hot, paved streets, full o' rushin' motor cars wi' death under their wheels for the wee bairns.

But I come back, always, in ma thochts, to the way we should be looking to being able to support oorselves in the future. I tak' shame to it that my country should always be dependent upon colonies and foreign lands for food. It is no needfu', and it is no richt. Meat! I'll no sing o' the roast beef o' old England when it comes frae Chicago and the Argentine. And ha' we no fields enow for our cattle to graze in, and canna we raise corn to feed them witha'?

I've a bit farm o' my ain. I didna buy it for masel'. It was to hae been for ma son, John. But John lies sleepin' wi' many another braw laddie, oot there in France. And I've ma farm, wi' its thousands o' acres o' fertile fields. I've no the time to be doing so much work upon it masel' as I'd like. But the wife and I ne'er let it wander far frae our thochts. It's a bonnie place. And I'm proving there that farmin' can be made to pay its way in Britain--aye, even in Scotland, the day.

I can wear homespun clothes, made frae wool ta'en frae sheep that ha' grazed and been reared on ma ain land. All the food I ha' need to eat frae ane end o' the year to the other is raised on my farm. The leather for ma shoon can be tanned frae the skins o' the beasties that furnish us wi' beef. The wife and I could shut ourselves up together in our wee hoose and live, so long as micht be needfu', frae our farm --aye, and we could support many a family, beside ourselves.

Others are doing so, tae. I'm not the only farmer who's showing the way back to the land.

I'm telling ye there's anither thing we must aye be thinkin' of. It's in the country, it's on the farms, that men are bred. It's no in the city that braw, healthy lads and lassies grow up wi' rosy cheeks and sturdy arms and legs. They go tae the city frae the land, but their sons and their sons' sons are no sae strong and hearty--when there are bairns. And ye ken, and I ken, that 'tis in the cities that ye'll see man and wife wi' e'er a bairn to bless many and many sicca couple, childless, lonely. Is it the hand o' God? Is it because o' Providence that they're left sae?

Ye know it is not--not often. Ye know they're traitors to the land that raised them, nourished them. They've taken life as a loan, and treated it as a gift they had the richt to throw awa' when they were done wi' the use of it. And it is no sae! The life God gives us he gibe's us to hand on to ithers--to our children, and through them to generations still to come. Oh, aye, I've heard folk like those I'm thinkin' of shout loudly o' their patriotism. But they're traitors to their country--they're traitors as surely as if they'd helped the Hun in the war we've won. If there's another war, as God forbid, they're helping now to lose it who do not do their part in giving Britain new sons and new dochters to carry on the race.

CHAPTER XIV

Tis strange thing enow to become used to it no to hea to count every bawbee before ye spend it. I ken it weel. It was after I made my hit in London that things changed sae greatly for me. I was richt glad. It was something to know, at last, for sure, that I'd been richt in thinking I had a way wi' me enow to expect folk to pay their siller in a theatre or a hall to hear me sing. And then, I began to be fair sure that the wife and the bairn I'd a son to be thinkin' for by then--wad ne'er be wanting.

It's time, I'm thinkin', for all the folk that's got a wife and a bairn or twa, and the means to care for them and a', to be looking wi' open een and open minds at all the talk there is. Shall we be changing everything in this world? Shall a man no ha' the richt tae leave his siller to his bairn? Is it no to be o' use any mair to be lookin' to the future?

I wonder if the folk that feel so ha' taken count enow o' human nature. It's a grand thing, human nature, for a' the dreadfu' things it leads men tae do at times. And it's an awfu' persistent thing, too. There was things Adam did that you'll be doing the day, and me, tae, and thousands like us. It's human tae want to be sure o' whaur the next meal's coming frae. And it's human to be wanting to mak' siccar that the wife and the bairns will be all richt if a man dees before his time.

And then, we're a' used to certain things. We tak' them for granted. We're sae used to them, they're sae muckle a part o' oor lives, that we canna think o' them as lacking. And yet--wadna many o' them be lost if things were changed so greatly and sae suddenly as those who talk like the Bolsheviki wad be havin' them?

I'm a' for the plain man. It's him I can talk wi'; it's him I understand, and who understands me. It's him I see in the audience, wi' his wife, and his bairns, maybe. And it's him I saw when I was in France--Briton, Anzac, Frenchman, American,

Canadian, South African, Belgian. Aye, and it was plain men the Hun commanders sent tae dee. We've seen what comes to a land whaur the plain man has nae voice in the affairs o' the community, and no say as to hoo things shall be done.

In Russia--though God knows what it'll be like before ye read what I am writing the noo!--the plain man has nae mair to say than he had in Germany before the ending o' the war. The plain man wants nowt better than tae do his bit o' work, and earn his wages or his salary plainly --or, maybe, to follow his profession, and earn his income. It's no the money a man has in the bank that tells me whether he's a plain man or no. It's the way he talks and thinks and feels.

I've aye felt mysel' a plain man. Oh, I've made siller--I've done that for years. But havin' siller's no made me less a plain man. Nor have any honors that ha' come to me. They may call me Sir Harry Lauder the noo, but I'm aye Harry to my friends, and sae I'll be tae the end o' the chapter. It wad hurt me sair tae think a bit title wad mak' a difference to ma friends.

Aye, it was a strange thing in yon days to be knowing that the dreams the wife and I had had for the bairn could be coming true. It was the first thing we thocht, always, when some new stroke o' fortune came-- there'd be that much mair we could do for the bairn. It surprised me to find hoo much they were offering me tae sing. And then there was the time when they first talked tae me o' singin' for the phonograph! I laughed fit to kill masel' that time. But it's no a laughin' matter, as they soon made me see.

It's no just the siller there's to be earned frae the wee discs, though there's a muckle o' that. It's the thocht that folk that never see ye, and never can, can hear your voice. It's a rare thing, and an awesome one, tae me, to be thinkin' that in China and India, and everywhere where men can carry a bit box, my songs may be heard.

I never work harder than when I'm makin' a record for the phonograph. It's a queer feelin'. I mind weel indeed the first time ever I made a record. I was no takin' the gramophone sae seriously as I micht ha' done, perhaps--I'd no thocht, as I ha' since. Then, d'ye ken, I'd not heard phonographs singin' in ma ain voice in America, and Australia, and Honolulu, and dear knows where beside. It was a new idea tae me, and I'd no notion 'twad be a gude thing for both the company and me tae ha' me makin' records. Sae it was wi' a laugh on ma lips that I went into the recording room o' one o' the big companies for the first time.

They had a' ready for me. There was a bit orchestra, waitin', wi' awfu' funny looking instruments--sawed off fiddles, I mind, syne a' the sound must be concentrated to gae through the horn. They put me on a stool, syne I'm such a wee body, and that raised my head up high enow sae that ma voice wad carry straight through the horn to the machine that makes the master record's first impression.

"Ready?" asked the man who was superintending the record.

"Aye," I cried. "When ye please!"

Sae I began, and it wasna sae bad. I sang the first verse o' ma song. And then, as usual, while the orchestra played a sort o' vampin' accompaniment, I sprang a gag, the way I do on the stage. I should ha' gone straight on, then. But I didn't. D'ye ken what? Man, I waited for the applause! Aye, I did so--there in front o' that great yawnin' horn, that was ma only listener, and that cared nae mair for hoo I sang than a cat micht ha' done!

It was a meenit before I realized what a thing I was doing. And then I laughed; I couldna help it. And I laughed sae hard I fell clean off the stool they'd set me on! The record was spoiled, for the players o' the orchestra laughed wi' me, and the operator came runnin' oot tae see what was wrang, and he fell to laughin', too.

"Here's a daft thing I'm doing for ye!" I said to the manager, who stud there, still laughin' at me. "Hoo much am I tae be paid for this, I'll no mak' a fool o' masel', singing into that great tin tube, unless ye mak' the reason worth my while."

He spoke up then--it had been nae mair than an experiment we'd planned, ye'll ken. And I'll tell ye straight that what he tauld me surprised me--I'd had nae idea that there was sae muckle siller to be made frae such foolishness, as I thocht it a' was then. I'll admit that the figures he named fair tuk my breath awa'. I'll no be tellin' ye what they were, but, after he'd tauld them tae me, I'd ha' made a good record for my first one had I had to stay there trying all nicht.

"All richt," I said. "Ca' awa'--I'm the man for ye if it's sae muckle ye're willin' tae pay me."

"Oh, aye--but we'll get it all back, and more beside," said the manager. "Ye're a rare find for us, Harry, my lad. Ye'll mak' more money frae these records we'll mak' together than ye ha' ever done upon the stage. You're going to be the most popular comic the London halls have ever known, but still, before we're done with you, we'll pay you more in a year than you'll make from all your theatrical engagements."

"Talk sense, man," I tauld him, wi' a laugh. "That can never be."

Weel, ye'll not be asking me whether what he said has come true or nicht. But I don't mind tellin' ye the man was no sica fool as I thocht him!

Eh, noo--here's what I'm thinking. Here am I, Harry Lauder. For ane reason or anither, I can do something that others do not do, whether or no they can--as to that I ken nothing. All I know is that I do something others ha' nae done, and that folk enow ha' been willin' and eager to pay me their gude siller, that they've worked for. Am I a criminal because o' that? Has any man the richt to use me despitefully because I've hit upon a thing tae do that ithers do no do, whether or no they can? Should ithers be fashed wi' me because I've made ma bit siller? I canna see why!

The things that ha' aye moved me ha' moved thousands, aye millions o' other men. There's joy in makin' ithers happy. There's hard work in it, tae, and the laborer is worthy o' his hire.

Then here's anither point. Wad I work as I ha' worked were I allowed but such a salary as some committee of folk that knew nothing o' my work, and what it cost me, and meant tae me in time ta'en frae ma wife and ma bairn at hame? I'll be tellin' ye the answer tae that question, gi'en ye canna answer it for yersel'. It's NO! And it's sae, I'm thinkin', wi' most of you who read the words I've written. Ye'll mind yer own affairs, and sae muckle o' yer neighbors as he's not able to keep ye from findin' oot when ye tak' the time for a bit gossip!

It'll be all verra weel to talk of socialism and one thing and another. We've much tae do tae mak' the world a better place to live in. But what I canna see, for the life o' me, is why it should be richt to throw awa' all our fathers have done. Is there no good in the institutions that have served the world up to now? Are we to mak' everything ower new? I'm no thinking that, and I believe no man is thinking that, truly. The man who preaches the destruction of everything that is and has been has some reasons of his own not creditable to either his brain or his honesty, if you'll ask me what I think.

Let us think o' what these folk wad be destroying. The hame, for one thing. The hame, and the family. They'll talk to us o' the state. The state's a grand thing--a great thing. D'ye ken what the state is these new fangled folk are aye talkin' of?

It's no new thing. It's just the bit country Britons ha' been dying for, a' these weary years in the trenches. It's just Britain, the land we've a' loved and wanted to see happy and safe--safe frae the Hun and frae the famine he tried to bring upon it. Do these radicals, as they call themselves--they'd tak' every name they please to themselves!--think they love their state better than the boys who focht and deed and won loved their country?

Eh, and let's think back a bit, just a wee bit, into history. There's a reason for maist of the things there are in the world. Sometimes it's a good reason; whiles it's a bad one. But there's a reason, and you maun e'en be reasonable when you come to talk o' making changes.

In the beginning there was just man, wasna there, wi' his woman, when he could find her, and catch her, and tak' her wi' him tae his cave, and their bairns. And a man, by his lane, was in trouble always wi' the great beasties they had in yon days. Sae it came that he found it better and safer tae live close by wi' other men, and what more natural than that they should be those of his ane bluid kin? Sae the family first, and then the clan, came into being. And frae them grew the tribe, and finally the nation.

Ye ken weel that Britain was no always the ane country. There were many kings in Britain lang agane. But whiles it was so armies could come from over the sea and land, and ravage the country. And sae, in the end, it was found better tae ha' the ane strong country and the ane strong rule. Syne then no foreign invader has e'er set foot in Britain. Not till they droppit frae the skies frae Zeppelins and German Gothas ha' armed men stood on British soil in centuries--and they, the baby killers frae the skies, were no alarming when they came doon to earth.

Now, wull we be changing all the things all our centuries ha' taught us to be good and useful? Maybe we wull. Change is life, and all living things maun change, just as a man's whole body is changed in every seven years, they tell us. But change that is healthy is gradual, too.

Here's a thing I've had tae tak' note of. I went aboot a great deal during the war, in Britain and in America. I was in Australia and New Zealand, too, but it was in Britain and America that I saw most. There were, in both lands, pro-Germans. Some were honest; they were wrang, and I thocht them wicked, but I could respect them, in a fashion, so lang as they came oot and said what was in their minds, and took the consequences. They'd be interned, or put safely oot o' the way. But there were others that skulked and hid, and tried to stab the laddies who were doing the fichtin' in the back. They'd talk o' pacifism, and they'd be conscientious objectors, who had never been sair troubled by their conscience before.

Noo, it's those same folk, those who helped the Hun during the war by talking of the need of peace at any price, who said that any peace was better than any war, who are maist anxious noo that we should let the Bolsheviks frae Russia show us how to govern ourselves. I'm a suspicious man, it may be. But I cannot help thinking that those who were enemies of their countries during the war should not be taken very seriously now when they proclaim themselves as the only true patriots.

They talk of internationalism, and of the common interests of the proletariat against capitalism. But of what use is internationalism unless all the nations of the world are of the same mind? How shall it be safe for some nations to guide themselves by these fine sounding principles when others are but lying in wait to attack them when they are unready? I believe in peace. I believe the laddies who fought in France and in the other battlegrounds of this war won peace for humanity. But they began the work; it is for us who are left to finish it.

And we canna finish it by talk. There must be deeds as weel as words. And what I'm thinking more and more is that those who did not do their part in these last years ha' small call to ask to be heard now. There'd be no state for them to talk o' sae glibly noo had it no been for those who put on uniforms and found the siller for a' the war loans that had to be raised, and to pay the taxes.

Aye, and when you speak o' taxes, there's another thing comes to mind. These folk who ha' sae a muckle to say aboot the injustice of conditions pay few taxes. They ha' no property, as a rule, and no great stake in the land. But they're aye ready to mak' rules and regulations for those who've worked till they've a place in the world. If they were busier themselves, maybe they'd not have so much time to see how much is wrong. Have you not thought, whiles, it was strange you'd not noticed all these terrible things they talk to you aboot? And has it not been just that you've had too many affairs of your ain to handle?

There are things for us all to think about, dear knows. We've come, of late years, we were doing it too much before the war, to give too great weight to things that were not of the spirit. Men have grown used to more luxury than it is good for man to have. Look at our clubs. Palaces, no less, some of them. What need has a man of a temple or a palace for a club. What should a club be? A comfortable place, is it no, whaur a man can go to meet his friends, and smoke a pipe, maybe--find a bit and a sup if the wife is not at hame, and he maun be eating dinner by his lane. Is there need of marble columns and rare woods?

And a man's own hoose. We've been thinking lately, it seems to me, too much of luxury, and too little of use and solid comfort. We wasted much strength and siller before the war. Aweel, we've to pay, and to go on paying, noo, for a lang time. We've paid the price in blood, and for a lang time the price in siller will be kept in our minds. We'll ha' nae choice aboot luxury, maist of us. And that'll be a rare gude thing.

Things! Things! It's sae easy for them to rule us. We live up to them. We act as if they owned us, and a' the time it's we who own them, and that we maun not forget. And we grow to think that a'thing we've become used to is something we can no do wi'oot. Oh, I'm as great a sinner that way as any. I was forgetting, before the war came to remind me, the days when I'd been puir and had had tae think longer over the spending of a saxpence than I had need to in 1914, in you days before the Kaiser turned his Huns loose, over using a hundred poonds.

I'm not blaming a puir body for being bitter when things gae wrong. All I'm saying is he'll be happier, and his troubles will be sooner mended if he'll only be thinking that maybe he's got a part in them himsel'. It's hard to get things richt when you're thinking they're a' the fault o' some one else, some one you can't control. Ca' the guilty one what you will--a prime minister, a capitalist, a king. Is it no hard to mak' a wrong thing richt when it's a' his fault?

But suppose you stop and think, and you come tae see that some of your troubles lie at your ain door? What's easier then than to mak' them come straight? There are things that are wrong wi' the world that we maun all pitch in together to mak' richt--I'm kenning that as well as anyone. But there's muckle that's only for our own selves to correct, and until that's done let's leave the others lie.

It's as if a man waur sair distressed because his toon was a dirty toon. He'd be thinking of hoo it must look when strangers came riding through it in their motor cars. And he'd aye be talking of what a bad toon it was he dwelt in; how shiftless, how untidy. And a' the time, mind you, his ain front yard would be full o' weeds, and the grass no cut, and papers and litter o' a' sorts aboot.

Weel, is it no better for that man to clean his ain front yard first? Then there'll be aye ane gude spot for strangers to see. And there'll be the example for his neighbors, too. They'll be wanting their places to look as well as his, once they've seen his sae neat and tidy. And then, when they've begun tae go to work in sic a fashion, soon the whole toon will begin to want to look weel, and the streets will look as fine as the front yards.

When I hear an agitator, a man who's preaching against all things as they are, I'm always afu' curious aboot that man. Has he a wife? Has he bairns o' his ain? And, if he has, hoo does he treat them?

There's men, you know, who'll gang up and doon the land talkin' o' humanity. But they'll no be kind to the wife, and their weans will run and hide awa' when they come home. There's many a man has keen een for the mote in his neighbor's eye who canna see the beam in his own-- that's as true to-day as when it was said first twa thousand years agane.

I ken fine there's folk do no like me. I've stood up and talked to them, from the stage, and I've heard say that Harry Lauder should stick to being a comic, and not try to preach. Aye, I'm no preacher, and fine I ken it. And it's no preaching I try to do; I wish you'd a' understand that. I'm only saying, whiles I'm talking so, what I've seen and what I think. I'm but one plain man who talks to others like him.

"Harry," I've had them say to me, in wee toons in America, "ca' canny here. There's a muckle o' folk of German blood. Ye'll be hurtin' their feelings if you do not gang easy----"

It was a lee! I ne'er hurt the feelings o' a man o' German blood that was a decent body--and there were many and many o' them. There in America the many had to suffer for the sins of the few. I've had Germans come tae me wi' tears in their een and thank me for the way I talked and the way I was helping to win the war. They were the true Germans, the ones who'd left their native land because they cauldna endure the Hun any more than could the rest of the world when it came to know him.

But I couldna ha gone easy, had I known that I maun lose the support of thousands of folk for what I said. The truth as I'd seen it and knew it I had to tell. I've a muckle to say on that score.

CHAPTER XV

It was as great a surprise tae me as it could ha' been to anyone else when I discovered that I could move men and women by speakin' tae them. In the beginning, in Britain, I made speeches to help the recruiting. My boy John had gone frae the first, and through him I knew much about the army life, and the way of it in those days. Sae I began to mak' a bit speech, sometimes, after the show.

And then I organized my recruiting band--Hieland laddies, wha went up and doon the land, skirling the pipes and beating the drum. The laddies wad flock to hear them, and when they were brocht together so there was easy work for the sergeants who were wi' the band. There's something about the skirling of the pipes that fires a man's blood and sets his feet and his fingers and a' his body to tingling.

Whiles I'd be wi' the band masel'; whiles I'd be off elsewhere. But it got sae that it seemed I was being of use to the country, e'en though they'd no let me tak' a gun and ficht masel'. When I was in America first, after the war began, America was still neutral. I was ne'er one o' those who blamed America and President Wilson for that. It was no ma business to do sae. He was set in authority in that country, and the responsibility and the authority were his. They were foolish Britons, and they risked much, who talked against the President of the United States in yon days.

I keened a' the time that America wad tak' her stand on the side o' the richt when the time came. And when it came at last I was glad o' the chance to help, as I was allowed tae do. I didna speak sae muckle in favor of recruiting; it was no sae needfu' in America as it had been in Britain, for in America there was conscription frae the first. In America they were wise in Washington at the verra beginning. They knew the history of the war in Britain, and they were resolved to profit by oor mistakes.

But what was needed, and sair needed, in America, was to mak' people who were sae far awa' frae the spectacle o' war as the Hun waged it understand what it meant. I'd been in France when I came back to America in the autumn o' 1917. My boy was in France still; I'd knelt beside his grave, hard by the Bapaume road. I'd seen the wilderness of that country in Picardy and Flanders. We'd pushed the Hun back frae a' that country I'd visited--I'd seen Vimy Ridge, and Peronne, and a' the other places.

I told what I'd seen. I told the way the Hun worked. And I spoke for the Liberty Loans and the other drives they were making to raise money in America--the Red Cross, the Y. M. C. A., the Salvation Army, the Knights of Columbus, and a score of others. I knew what it was like, over yonder in France, and I could tell American faithers and mithers what their boys maun see and do when the great transports took them oversea.

It was for me, to whom folk would listen, tae tell the truth as I'd seen it. It was no propaganda I was engaged in--there was nae need o' propaganda. The truth was enow. Whiles, I'll be telling you, I found trouble. There were places where folk of German blood forgot they'd come to America to be free of kaisers and junkers. They stood by their old country, foul as her deeds were. They threatened me, more than once; they were angry enow at me to ha' done me a mischief had they dared. But they dared not, and never a voice was raised against me publicly--in a theatre or a hall where I spoke, I mean.

I went clear across America and back in that long tour. When I came back it was just as the Germans began their last drive. Ye'll be minding hoo black things looked for a while, when they broke our British line, or bent it back, rather, where the Fifth Army kept the watch? Mind you, I'd been over all that country our armies had reclaimed frae the Hun in the long Battle o' the Somme. My boy John, the wean I'd seen grow frae a nursling in his mither's arms, had focht in that battle.

He'd been wounded, and come hame tae his mither to be nursed back to health. She'd done that, and she'd blessed him, and kissed him gude bye, and he'd gone oot there again. And--that time, he stayed. There's a few words I can see, written on a bit o' yellow paper, each time I close ma een.

"Captain John Lauder, killed, December 28. Official."

Aye, I'd gone all ower that land in which he'd focht. I'd seen the spot where he was killed. I'd lain doon beside his grave. And then, in the spring of 1918, as I travelled back toward New York, across America, the Hun swept doon again through Peronne and Bapaume. He took back a' that land British blood had been spilled like watter to regain frae him.

The pity of it! Sae I was thinking each day as I read the bulletins! Had America come in tae late? I'd read the words of Sir Douglas Haig, that braw and canny Scot wha held the British line in France, when he said Britain was fichtin' wi' her back tae the wall. Was Ypres to be lost, after four years? Was the Channel to be laid open to the Hun? It lookit sae, for a time.

I was like a man possessed by a de'il, I'm thinking, in you days. I couldna think of ought but the way the laddies were suffering in France. And it filled me wi' rage tae see those who couldna or wouldna understand. They'd sit there when I begged them to buy Liberty Bonds, and they'd be sae slow to see what I was driving at. I lost ma temper, sometimes. Whiles I'd say things to an audience that were no so, that were unfair. If I was unjust to any in those days, I'm sorry. But they maun understand that ma heart was in France, wi' them that was deein' and suffering new tortures every day. I'd seen what I was talking of.

Whiles, in America, I was near to bein' ashamed, for the way I was always seekin' to gain the siller o' them that came to hear me sing. I was raising money for ma fund for the Scotch wounded. I'd a bit poem I'd written that was printed on a card to be sold, and there were some wee stamps. Mrs. Lauder helped me. Each day, as an audience went oot, she'd be in the lobby, and we raised a grand sum before we were done. And whiles, too, when I spoke on the stage, money would come raining doon, so that it looked like a green snowstorm.

I maun no be held to account too strictly, I'm thinking, for the hard things I sometimes said on that tour. I tak' back nothing that was deserved; there were toons, and fine they'll ken themselves wi'oot ma naming them, that ought to be ashamed of themselves. There was the book I wrote. Every nicht I'd auction off a copy to the highest bidder--the money tae gae tae the puir wounded laddies in Scotland. A copy went for five thousand dollars ane nicht in New York!

That was a grand occasion, I'm tellin' ye. It was in the Metropolitan Opera Hoose, that great theatre where Caruso and Melba and a' the stars of the opera ha' sung sae often. Aye, Harry Lauder had sung there tae--sung there that nicht! The hoose was fu', and I made my talk.

And then I held up my book, "A Minstrel in France." I asked that they should buy a copy. The bidding started low. But up and up it ran. And when I knocked it doon at last it was for twenty-five hundred dollars --five hundred poonds! But that wasna a'. I was weel content. But the gentleman that bocht it lookit at it, and then sent it back, and tauld me to auction it all ower again. I did, and this time, again, it went for twenty-five hundred dollars. So there was five thousand dollars--a thousand poonds--for ma wounded laddies at hame in Scotland.

Noo, think o' the contrast. There's a toon--I'll no be writing doon its name--where they wadna bid but twelve dollars--aboot twa poond ten shillings--for the book! Could ye blame me for being vexed? Maybe I said more than I should, but I dinna think so. I'm thinking still those folk were mean. But I was interested enough to look to see what that toon had done, later, and I found oot that its patriotism must ha' been awakened soon after, for it bocht its share and more o' bonds, and it gave its siller freely to all the bodies that needed money for war work. They were sair angry at old Harry Lauder that nicht he tauld them what he thocht of their generosity, but it maybe he did them gude, for a' that!

I'd be a dead man the noo, e'en had I as many lives as a dozen nine lived cats, had a' the threats that were made against me in America been carried oot. They'd tell me, in one toon after anither, that it wadna be safe tae mak' ma talk against the Hun. But I was never frightened. You know the old saying that threatened men live longest, and I'm a believer in that. And, as it was, the towns where there were most people of German blood were most cordial to me.

I ken fine how it was that that was so. All Germans are not Huns. And in America the decent Germans, the ones who were as filled with horror when the Lusitania was sunk as were any other decent bodies, were anxious to do all they could to show that they stood with the land of their adoption.

I visited many an American army camp. I've sung for the American soldiers, as well as the British, in America, and in France as well. And I've never seen an American regiment yet that did not have on its muster rolls many and many a German name. They did well, those American laddies wi' the German names. They were heroes like the rest.

It's a strange thing, the way it fell to ma lot tae speak sae much as I did during the war. I canna quite believe yet that I was as usefu' as my friends ha' told me I was. Yet they've come near to making me believe it. They've clapped a Sir before my name to prove they think so, and I've had the thanks of generals and ministers and state. It's a comfort to me to think it's so. It was a sair grief tae me that when my boy was dead I couldna tak' his place. But they a' told me I'd be wasted i' the trenches.

A man must do his duty as he's made to see it. And that's what I tried to do in the war. If I stepped on any man's toes that didna deserve it, I'm sorry. I'd no be unfair to any man. But I think that when I said hard things to the folk of a toon they were well served, as a rule, and I know that it's so that often and often folk turned to doing the things I'd blamed them for not doing even while they were most bitter against me, and most eager to see me ridden oot o' toon upon a rail, wi' a coat o' tar and feathers to cover me! Sae I'm not minding much what they said, as long as what they did was a' richt.

All's well that ends well, as Wull Shakespeare said. And the war's well ended. It's time to forget our ain quarrels the noo as to the way o' winning; we need dispute nae mair as to that. But there's ane thing we maun not forget, I'm thinking. The war taught us many and many a thing, but none that was worth mair to us than this. It taught us that we were invincible sae lang as we stood together, we folk who speak the common English tongue.

Noo, there's something we knew before, did we no? Yet we didna act upon our knowledge. Shall we ha' to have anither lesson like the one that's past and done wi', sometime in the future? Not in your lifetime or mine, I mean, but any time at a'? Would it no be a sair pity if that were so? Would it no mak' God feel that we were a stupid lot, not worth the saving?

None can hurt us if we but stand together, Britons and Americans. We've a common blood and a common speech. We've our differences, true enough. We do not do a' things i' the same way. But what matter's that, between friends? We've learned we can be the best o' friends. Our laddies learned that i' France, when Englishman and Scot, Yankee and Anzac, Canadian and Irishman and Welshman, broke the Hindenburg line together.

We've the future o' the world, that those laddies saved, to think o' the noo. And we maun think of it together, and come to the problems that are still left together, if we would solve them in the richt way, and wi'oot havin' to spill more blood to do so.

When men ha' fought together and deed together against a common foe they should be able to talk together aboot anything that comes up between them, and mak' common cause against any foe that threatens either of them. And I'm thinking that no foe will ever threaten any of the nations that fought against the Hun that does no threaten them a'!

CHAPTER XVI

I t's a turning point in the life of any artist like myself to mak' a London success. Up tae that time in his career neithing is quite certain. The provinces may turn on him; it's no likely, but they may. It's true there's many a fine artist has ne'er been able to mak' a London audience care for him, and he's likely to stay in the provinces a' his life long, and be sure, always, o' his greetin' frae those who've known him a lang time. But wi' London having stamped success upon ye ye can be sure o' many things. After that there's still other worlds to conquer, but they're no sae hard tae reach.

For me that first nicht at Gatti's old hall in the Westminster Bridge road seems like a magic memory, even the noo. I'm sorry the wife was no wi' me; had I been able to be sure o' getting the show Tom Tinsley gied me I'd ha' had her doon. As it was it wad ha' seemed like tempting Providence, and I've never been any hand tae do that. I'm no superstitious, exactly--certainly I'm no sae for a Scot. But I dinna believe it's a wise thing tae gave oot o' the way and look for trouble. I'll no walk under a ladder if I can help it, I'll tell ye, if ye ask me why, that I avoid a ladder because I've heard o' painters dropping paint and costin' them that was beneath the price o' the cleaning of their claes, and ye can believe that or no, as ye've a mind!

Ye've heard o' men who went to bed themselves at nicht and woke up famous. Weel, it was no like that, precisely, wi' me after the nicht at Gatti's. I was no famous i' the morn. The papers had nowt to say o' me; they'd not known Mr. Harry Lauder was to mak' his first appearance in the metropolis. And, e'en had they known, I'm no thinking they'd ha' sent anyone to write me up. That was tae come to me later on. Aye, I've had my share of write-ups in the press; I'd had them then, in the provincial papers. But London was anither matter.

Still, there were those who knew that a new Scotch comic had made an audience like him. It's a strange thing how word o' a new turn flies aboot amang those regulars of a hall's audiences. The second nicht they were waiting for my turn, and I got a rare hand when I stepped oot upon the stage--the nicht before there'd been dead silence i' the hoose. Aye, the second nicht was worse than the first. The first nicht success micht ha' been an accident; the second aye tells the tale. It's so wi' a play. I've friends who write plays, and they say the same thing--they aye wait till the second nicht before they cheer, no matter how grand a success they think they ha' the first nicht, and hoo many times they ha' to step oot before the curtain and bow, and how many times they're called upon for a speech.

So when the second nicht they made me gie e'en more encores than the first I began to be fair sure. And the word had spread, I learned, to the managers o' other halls; twa-three of them were aboot to hear me. My agent had seen to that; he was glad enough to promise me all the London engagements I wanted noo that I'd broken the ice for masel'! I didna blame him for havin' been dootfu'. He knew his business, and it would ha' been strange had he ta'en me at my word when I told him I could succeed where others had failed that had come wi' reputations better than my own.

I think I'd never quite believed, before, the tales I'd heard of the great sums the famous London artists got. It took the figures I saw on the contracts I was soon being asked to sign for appearances at the Pavilion and the Tivoli and all the other famous music halls to make me realize that all I'd heard was true. They promised me more for second appearances, and my agent advised me against making any long term engagements then.

"The future's yours, now, Harry, my boy," he said. "Wait--and you can get what you please from them. And then--there's America to think about."

I laughed at him when he said that. My mind had not carried me sae far as America yet. It seemed a strange thing, and a ridiculous one, that he who'd been a miner digging coal for fifteen shillings a week not so lang syne, should be talking about making a journey of three thousand miles to sing a few wee songs to folk who had never heard of him. And, indeed, it was a far cry frae those early times in London to my American tours. I had much to do before it was time for me to be thinking seriously of that.

For a time, soon after my appearance at Gatti's, I lived in London. A man can be busy for six months in the London halls, and singing every nicht at more than one. There is a great ring of them, all about the city. London is different frae New York or any great American city in that. There is a central district in which maist of the first class theatres are to be found, just like what is called Broadway in New York. But the music halls--they're vaudeville theatres in New York, o' coorse--are all aboot London.

Folk there like to gae to a show o' a nicht wi'oot travelling sae far frae hame after dinner. And in London the distances are verra great, for the city's spread oot much further than New York, for example. In London there are mair wee hooses; folk don't live in apartments and flats as much as they do in New York. So it's a pleasant thing for your Londoner that he can step aroond the corner any nicht and find a music hall. There are half a dozen in the East End; there are more in Kensington, and out Brixton way. There's one in Notting Hill, and Bayswater, and Fulham--aye, there a' ower the shop.

And it's an interesting thing, the way ye come to learn the sort o' thing each audience likes. I never grow tired of London music-hall audiences. A song that makes a great hit in one will get just the tamest sort of a hand in another. You get to know the folk in each hoose when you've played one or twa engagements in it; they're your friends. It's like having a new hame everywhere you go.

In one hoose you'll find the Jews. And in another there'll be a lot o' navvies in the gallery. Sometimes they'll be rough customers in the gallery of a London music hall. They're no respecters of reputations. If they like you you can do nae wrong; if they don't, God help you! I've seen artists who'd won a great name on the legitimate stage booed in the halls; I've been sorry for mair than one o' the puir bodies.

You maun never be stuck up if you'd mak' friends and a success in the London halls. You maun remember always that it's the audience you're facing can make you or break you. And, another thing. It's a fatal mistake to think that because you've made a success once you're made for life. You are--if you keep on giving the audience what you've made it like once. But you maun do your best, nicht after nicht, or they'll soon ken the difference--and they'll let you know they ken it, too.

I'm often asked if I'm no sorry I'm just a music hall singer. It's a bonnie thing to be a great actor, appearing in fine plays. No one admires a great actor in a great play more than I do, and one of the few things that ever makes me sorry my work is what it is is that I can sae seldom sit me doon in a stall in a theatre and watch a play through. But, after a', why should I envy any other man his work? I do my best. I study life, and the folk that live it, and in my small way I try to represent life in my songs. It's my way, after a', and it's been a gude way for me. No, I'm no sorry I'm just a music hall singer.

I've done a bit o' acting. My friend Graham Moffatt wrote a play I was in, once, that was no sicca poor success--"A Scrape o' the Pen" it was called. I won't count the revues I've been in; they're more like a variety show than a regular theatrical performance, any nicht in the week.

I suppose every man that's ever stepped before the footlichts has thought o' some day appearing in a character from Wull Shakespeare's plays, and I'm no exception tae the rule. I'll gae further; I'll say that every man that's ever been any sort of actor at a' has thought o' playing Hamlet, Prince of Denmark. But I made up ma mind, lang ago, that Hamlet was nae for me. Syne then, though, I've thought of another o' Shakespeare's characters I'd no mind playing. It's a Scottish part --Macbeth.

They've a' taken Macbeth too seriously that ha' played him. I'm thinking Shakespeare's ghost maun laugh when it sees hoo all the great folk ha' missed the satire o' the character. Macbeth was a Scottish comedian like masel'--that's why I'd like to play him. And then, I'm awfu' pleased wi' the idea o' his make-up. He wears great whiskers, and I'm thinkin' they'd be a great improvement to me, wi' the style o' beauty I have. I notice that when a character in one o' ma songs wears whiskers I get an extra round o' applause when I come on the stage.

And then, while Macbeth had his faults, he was a verra accomplished pairson, and I respect and like him for that. He did a bit o' murdering, but that was largely because of his wife. I sympathize wi' any man that takes his wife's advice, and is guided by it. I've done that, ever since I was married. Tae be sure, I made a wiser choice than did Macbeth, but it was no his fault the advice his lady gied him was bad, and he should no be blamed as sair as he is for the way he followed it. He was punished, tae, before ever Macduff killed him-- wasna he a victim of insomnia, and is there anything worse for a man tae suffer frae than that?

Aye, if ever the time comes when I've a chance to play in one of Wull Shakespeare's dramas, it's Macbeth I shall choose instead of Hamlet. So I gie you fair warning. But it's only richt to say that the wife tells me I'm no to think of doing any such daft thing, and that my managers agree wi' her. So I think maybe I'll have to be content just to be a music hall singer a' my days--till I succeed in retiring, that is, and I think that'll be soon, for I've a muckle tae do, what wi twa-three mair books I've promised myself to write.

Weel, I was saying, a while back, before I digressed again, that soon after that nicht at Gatti's I moved to London for a bit. It was wiser, it seemed tae me. Scotland was a lang way frae London, and it was needfu' for me to be in the city so much that I grew tired of being awa' sae much frae the wife and my son John. Sae, for quite a spell, I lived at Tooting. It was comfortable there. It wasna great hoose in size, but it was well arranged. There was some ground aboot it, and mair air than one can find, as a rule, in London. I wasna quite sae cramped for room and space to breathe as if I'd lived in the West End --in a flat, maybe, like so many of my friends of the stage. But I always missed the glen, and I was always dreaming of going back to Scotland, when the time came.

It was then I first began to play the gowf. Ye mind what I told ye o' my first game, wi' Mackenzie Murdoch? I never got tae be much more o' a hand than I was then, nae matter hoo much I played the game. I'm a gude Scot, but I'm thinkin' I didna tak' up gowf early enough in life. But I liked to play the game while I was living in London. For ane thing it reminded me of hame; for another, it gie'd me a chance to get mair exercise than I would ha done otherwise.

In London ye canna walk aboot much. You ha' to gae tae far at a time. Thanks to the custom of the halls, I was soon obliged to ha' a motor brougham o' my ain. It was no an extravagance. There's no other way of reaching four or maybe five halls in a nicht. You've just time to dash from one hall, when your last encore's given, and reach the next for your turn. If you depended upon the tube or even on taxi-cabs, you could never do it.

It was then that my brother-in-law, Tom Vallance, began to go aboot every-where wi' me. I dinna ken what I'd be doing wi'oot Tom. He's been all ower the shop wi' me--America, Australia, every where I gae. He knows everything I need in ma songs, and he helps me tae dress, and looks after all sorts of things for me. He packs all ma claes and ma wigs; he keeps ma sticks in order. You've seen ma sticks? Weel, it's Tom always hands me the richt one just as I'm aboot to step on the stage.

If he gied me the stick I use in "She's Ma Daisy" when I was aboot to sing "I Love a Lassie" I believe I'd have tae ha' the curtain rung doon upon me. But he never has. I can trust old Tom. Aye, I ca' trust him in great things as well as sma'.

It took me a lang time to get used to knowing I had arrived, as the saying is. Whiles I'd still be worried, sometimes, aboot the future. But soon it got so's I could scarce imagine a time when getting an engagement had seemed a great thing. In the old days I used to look in the wee book I kept, and I'd see a week's engagement marked, a long time ahead, and be thankfu' that that week, at least, there'd be siller coming in.

And noo--well, the noo it's when I look in the book and see, maybe a year ahead, a blank week, when I've no singing the do, that I'm pleased.

"Eh, Tom," I'll say. "Here's a bit o' luck! Here's the week frae September fifteenth on next year when I've no dates!"

"Aye, Harry," he'll answer me. "D'ye no remember? We'll be on the ocean then, bound for America. That's why there's no dates that week."

But the time will be coming soon when I can stop and rest and tak' life easy. 'Twill no be as happy a time as I'd dreamed it micht be. His mither and I had looked forward to settling doon when ma work was done, wi' my boy John living nearby. I bought my farm at Dunoon that he micht ha' a place o' his ain to tak' his wife tae when he married her, and where his bairns could be brought up as bairns should be, wi' glen and hill to play wi'. Aweel, God has not willed that it should be sae. Mrs. Lauder and I canna have the grandchildren we'd dreamed aboot to play at our knees.

But we've one another still, and there's muckle tae be thankfu' for.

One thing I liked fine aboot living in London as I did. I got to know my boy better than I could ha' done had we stayed at hame ayant the Tweed. I could sleep hame almost every nicht, and I'd get up early enough i' the morning to spend some time wi' him. He was at school a great deal, but he was always glad tae see his dad. He was a rare hand wi' the piano, was John--a far better musician than ever I was or shall be. He'd play accompaniments for me often, and I've never had an accompanist I liked sae well. It's no because he was my boy I say that he had a touch, and a way of understanding just what I was trying tae do when I sang a song, that made his accompaniment a part of the song and no just something that supported ma voice.

But John had no liking for the stage or the concert platform. It was the law that interested him. That aye seemed a little strange tae me. But I was glad that he should do as it pleased him. It was a grand thing, his mother and I thought, that we could see him gae to Cambridge, as we'd dreamed, once, many years before it ever seemed possible, that he micht do. And before the country called him to war he took his degree, and was ready to begin to read law.

We played many a game o' billiards together, John and I, i' the wee hoose at Tooting. We were both fond o' the game, though I think neither one of us was a great player. John was better than I, but I was the stronger in yon days, and I'd tak' a great swipe sometimes and pocket a' the balls. John was never quite sure whether I meant to mak' some o' the shots, but he was a polite laddie, and he'd no like to be accusing his faither o' just being lucky.

"Did ye mean that shot, pal" he'd ask me, sometimes. I'd aye say yes, and, in a manner o' speaking, I had.

Aweel, yon days canna come again! But it's gude to think upon them. And it's better to ha' had them than no, no matter what Tennyson sang once. "A sorrow's crown of sorrow--to remember happier things." Was it no sae it went? I'm no thinking sae! I'm glad o' every memory I have of the boy that lies in France.

CHAPTER XVII

There was talk that I micht gae to America lang before the time came. I'd offers--oh, aye! But I was uncertain. It was a tricky business, tae go sae far frae hame. A body would be a fool to do sae unless he waur sure and siccar against loss. All the time I was doing better and better in Britain. And it seems that American visitors to Britain, tourists and the like, came to hear me often, and carried hame reports--to say nothing of the scouts the American managers always have abroad.

Still, I was verra reluctant tae mak' the journey. I was no kennin' what sort of a hand I'd be for an ocean voyage. And then, I was liking my ain hame fine, and the idea of going awa' frae it for many months was trying tae me. It was William Morris persuaded me in the end, of course. There's a man would persuade a'body at a' tae do his will. He'll be richt sae, often, you see, that you canna hault oot against the laddie at all. I'm awfu' fond o' Wullie Morris. He should ha' been a Scot.

He made me great promises. I didna believe them a', for it seemed impossible that they could be true. But I liked the man, and I decided that if the half of what he said was true it would be verra interesting--verra interesting indeed. Whiles, when you deal w' a man and he tells you more than you think he can do, you come to distrust him altogether. It was not so that I felt aboot Wull Morris.

It was a great time when I went off to America at last. My friends made a great to-do aboot my going. There were pipers to play me off--I mind the way they skirled. Verra soft they were playing at the end, ane of my favorite tunes--"Will ye no come back again?" And so I went.

I was a better sailor than I micht ha' thought. I enjoyed the voyage. And I'll ne'er forget my first sicht o' New York. It's e'en more wonderfu' the noo; there's skyscrapers they'd not dared dream of, so high they are, when I was first there.

Maybe they've reached the leemit now, but I hae ma doots--I'm never thinking a Yankee has reached a leemit, for I've ma doots that he has ane!

I kenned fine that they'd heard o' me in America. Wull Morris and others had told me that. I knew that there'd be Scots there tae bid me welcome, for the sake of the old country. Scots are clansmen, first and last; they make much of any chance to keep the memory and the spirit of Scotland fresh in a strange land, when they are far frae hame. And so I thought, when I saw land, that I'd be having soon a bit reception frae some fellow Scots, and it was a bonny thing to think upon, sae far frae all I'd known all my life lang.

I was no prepared at a' for what really happened. The Scots were oot-- oh, aye, and they had pipers to greet me, and there were auld friends that had settled doon in New York or other parts o' the United States, and had come to meet me. Scots ha' a way o' makin' siller when they get awa' frae Scotland, I'm findin' oot. At hame the competition is fierce, sae there are some puir Scots. But when they gang away they've had such training that no ithers can stand against them, and sae the Scot in a foreign place is like to be amang the leaders.

But it wasna only the Scots turned oot to meet me. There were any number of Americans. And the American reporters! Unless you've come into New York and been met by them you've no idea of what they're like, yon. They made rare sport of me, and I knew they were doing it, though I think they thought, the braw laddies, they were pulling the wool over my een!

There was much that was new for me, and you'll remember I'm a Scot. When I'm travelling a new path, I walk cannily, and see where each foot is going to rest before I set it doon. Sae it was when I came to America. I was anxious to mak' friends in a new land, and I wadna be saying anything to a reporter laddie that could be misunderstood. Sae I asked them a' to let me off, and not mak' me talk till I was able to give a wee bit o' thought to what I had tae say.

They just laughed at one another and at me. And the questions they asked me! They wanted to know what did I think of America? And o' this and o' that that I'd no had the chance tae see. It was a while later before I came to understand that they were joking wi' themselves as well as wi' me. I've learned, since then, that American reporters, and especially those that meet the ships that come in to New York, have had cause to form impressions of their ain of a gude many famous folk that would no be sae flattering to those same folk as what they usually see written aboot themselves.

Some of my best friends in America are those same reporters. They've been good tae me, and I've tried to be fair wi' them. The American press is an institution that seems strange to a Briton, but to an artist it's a blessing. It's thanks to the papers that the people learn sae much aboot an artist in America; it's thanks tae them that they're sae interested in him.

I'm no saying the papers didn't rub my fur the wrang way once or twice; they made mair than they should, I'm thinking, o' the jokes aboot me and the way I'd be carfu' wi' ma siller. But they were aye good natured aboot it. It's a strange thing, that way that folk think I'm sae close wi' my money. I'm canny; I like to think that when I spend my money I get its value in return. But I'm no the only man i' the world feels sae aboot it; that I'm sure of. And I'll no hand oot siller to whoever comes asking. Aye, I'll never do that, and I'd think shame to masel' if I did. The only siller that's gude for a man to have, the only siller that helps him, i' the end, is that which he's worked hard to earn and get.

Oh, gi'e'n a body's sick, or in trouble o' some sair sort, that's different; he deserves help then, and it's nae the same thing. But what should I or any other man gie money to an able bodied laddie that can e'en work for what he needs, the same as you and me? It fashes me to ha' such an one come cadging siller frae me; I'd think wrong to encourage him by gi'e'n it the him.

You maun work i' this world. If your siller comes tae you too easily, you'll gain nae pleasure nor profit frae the spending on't. The things we enjoy the maist are not those that are gi'e'n to us; they're those that, when we look at, mean weeks or months or maybe years of work. When you've to work for what you get you have the double pleasure. You look forward for a lang time, while you're working, to what your work will bring you. And then, in the end, you get it--and you know you're beholden tae no man but yourself for what you have. Is that no a grand feeling?

Aweel, it's no matter. I'm glad for the laddies to hae their fun wi' me. They mean no harm, and they do no harm. But I've been wishfu', sometimes, that the American reporters had a wee bit less imagination. 'Tis a grand thing, imagination; I've got it masel, tae some extent. But those New York reporters--and especially the first ones I met! Man, they put me in the shade altogether!

I'd little to say to them the day I landed; I needed time tae think and assort my impressions. I didna ken my own self just what I was thinking aboot New York and America. And then, I'd made arrangements wi' the editor of one of the great New York papers to write a wee piece for his journal that should be telling his readers hoo I felt. He was to pay me weel for that, and it seemed no more than fair that he should ha' the valuable words of Harry Lauder to himself, since he was willing to pay for them.

But did it mak' a wee bit of difference tae those laddies that I had nought to say to them? That it did--not! I bade them all farewell at my hotel. But the next morning, when the papers were brought to me, they'd all long interviews wi' me. I learned that I thought America was the grandest country I'd ever seen. One said I was thinking of settling doon here, and not going hame to Scotland at a' any more! And another said I'd declared I was sorry I'd not been born in the United States, since, noo, e'en though I was naturalized--as that paper said I meant tae be!--I could no become president of the United States!

Some folk took that seriously--folk at hame, in the main. They've an idea, in America, that English folk and Scots ha' no got a great sense of humor. It's not that we've no got one; it's just that Americans ha' a humor of a different sort. They've a verra keen sense o' the ridiculous, and they're as fond of a joke that's turned against themselves as of one they play upon another pairson. That's a fine trait, and it makes it easy to amuse them in the theatre.

I think I was mair nervous aboot my first appearance in New York than I'd ever been in ma life before. In some ways it was worse than that nicht in the old Gatti's in London. I'd come tae New York wi' a reputation o' sorts, ye ken; I'd brought naethin' o' the sort tae New York.

When an artist comes tae a new country wi' sae much talk aboot him as there was in America concerning me, there's always folk that tak' it as a challenge.

"Eh!" they'll say. "So there's Harry Lauder coming, is there? And he's the funniest wee man in the halls, is he? He'd make a graven image laugh, would he? Well, I'll be seeing! Maybe he can make me laugh-- maybe no. We'll just be seeing."

That's human nature. It's natural for people to want to form their own judgments aboot everything. And it's natural, tae, for them tae be almost prejudiced against anyone aboot whom sae much has been said. I realized a' that; I'd ha' felt the same way myself. It meant a great deal, too, the way I went in New York. If I succeeded there I was sure to do well i' the rest of America. But to fail in New York, to lose the stamp of a Broadway approval--that wad be laying too great a handicap altogether upon the rest of my tour.

In London I'd had nothing to lose. Gi'e'n I hadna made my hit that first nicht in the Westminster Bridge Road, no one would have known the difference. But in New York there'd be everyone waiting. The critics would all be there--not just men who write up the music halls, but the regular critics, that attend first nichts at the theatre. It was a different and a mair serious business than anything I'd known in London.

It was a great theatre in which I appeared--one o' the biggest in New York, and the greatest I'd ever playcd in, I think, up tae that time. And when the nicht came for my first show the hoose was crowded; there was not a seat to be had, e'en frae the speculators.

Weel, there's ane thing I've learned in my time on the stage. You canna treat an audience in any verra special way, just because you're anxious that it shall like you. You maun just do your best, as you've been used to doing it. I had this much in my favor--I was singing auld songs, that I knew weel the way of. And then, tae, many of that audience knew me. There were a gude few Scots amang it; there were American friends I'd made on the other side, when they'd been visiting. And there was another thing I'd no gi'en a thocht, and that was the way sae many o' them knew ma songs frae havin' heard them on the gramaphone.

It wasna till after I'd been in America that I made sae many records, but I'd made enough at lime for some of my songs tae become popular, and so it wasna quite sicca novelty as I'd thought it micht be for them to hear me. Oh, aye, what wi' one thing and another it would have been my ain fault had that audience no liked hearing me sing that nicht.

But I was fairly overwhelmed by what happened when I'd finished my first song. The house rose and roared at me. I'd never seen sic a demonstration. I'd had applause in my time, but nothing like that. They laughed frae the moment I first waggled my kilt at them, before I did more than laugh as I came oot to walk aroond. But there were cheers when I'd done; it was nae just clapping of the hands they gie'd me. It brought the tears to my een to hear them. And I knew then that I'd made a whole new countryful of friends that nicht--for after that I couldna hae doots aboot the way they'd be receiving me elsewhere.

Even sae, the papers surprised me the next morning. They did sae much more than just praise me! They took me seriously--and that was something the writers at hame had never done. They saw what I was aiming at wi' my songs. They understood that I was not just a comedian, not just a "Scotch comic." I maun amuse an audience wi' my songs, but unless I mak' them think, and, whiles, greet a bit, too, I'm no succeeding. There's plenty can sing a comic song as weel as I can. But that's no just the way I think of all my songs. I try to interpret character in them. I study queer folk o' all the sorts I see and know. And, whiles, I think that in ane of my songs I'm doing, on a wee scale, what a gifted author does in a novel of character.

Aweel, it went straight to my heart, the way those critics wrote about me. They were not afraid of lowering themselves by writing seriously about a "mere music hall comedian." Aye, I've had wise gentlemen of the London press speak so of me. They canna understand, yon gentry, why all the fuss is made about Harry Lauder. They're a' for the Art Theatre, and this movement and that. But they're no looking for what's natural and unforced i' the theatre, or they'd be closer to-day to having a national theatre than they'll ever be the gait they're using the noo!

They're verra much afraid of hurting their dignity, or they were, in Britain, before I went to America. I think perhaps it woke them up to read the New York reviews of my appearance. It's a sure thing they've been more respectful tae me ever since. And I dinna just mean that it's to me they're respectful. It's to what I'm trying tae do. I dinna care a bit what a'body says or thinks of me. But I tak' my work seriously. I couldna keep on doing it did I not, and that's what sae many canna understand. They think a man at whom the public maun laugh if he's to rate himsel' a success must always be comical; that he can never do a serious thing. It is a mistaken idea altogether, yon.

I'm thinking Wull Morris must ha' breathed easier, just as did I, the morning after that first nicht show o' mine. He'd been verra sure-- but, man, he stood to lose a lot o' siller if he'd found he'd backed the wrang horse! I was glad for his sake as well as my own that he had not.

After the start my first engagement in New York was one long triumph. I could ha' stayed much longer than I did, but there were twa reasons against making any change in the plans that had been arranged. One is that a long tour is easy to throw oot o' gear. Time is allotted long in advance, and for a great many attractions. If one o' them loses it's week, or it's three nichts, or whatever it may be, it's hard to fit it in again. And when a tour's been planned so as to eliminate so much as possible of doubling back in railway travel, everything may be spoiled by being a week or so late in starting it.

Then, there was another thing. I was sure to be coming back to New York again, and it was as weel to leave the city when it was still hard to be buying tickets for my show. That's business; I could see it as readily as could Wull Morris, who was a revelation tae me then as a manager. He's my friend, as well as my manager, the noo, you'll ken; I tak' his advice aboot many and many a thing, and we've never had anything that sounded like even the beginnings of a quarrel.

Sae on I went frae New York. I was amazed at the other cities--Boston, Philadelphia, Washington, Baltimore, Chicago, Pittsburgh--in a' o' them the greeting New York had gi'en me was but just duplicated. They couldna mak' enough of me. And everywhere I made new friends, and found new reason to rejoice over having braved the hazardous adventure of an American tour.

Did I tell you how I was warned against crossing the ocean? It was the same as when I'd thought of trying ma luck in London. The same sort of friends flocked about me.

"Why will you be risking all you've won, Harry?" they asked me. "Here in Britain you're safe--your reputation's made, and you're sure of a comfortable living, and more, as long as you care to stay on the stage. There they might not understand you, and you would suffer a great blow to your prestige if you went there and failed."

I didna think that, e'en were I to fail in America, it would prevent me frae coming back to Britain and doing just as well as ever I had. But, then, too, I didna think much o' that idea. Because, you see, I was so sure I was going to succeed, as I had succeeded before against odds and in the face of all the croakers and prophets of misfortune had to say.

CHAPTER XVIII

It was a hard thing for me to get used to thinking o' the great distances of travel in America. In Britain aboot the longest trip one wad be like to make wad be frae London tae Glasga or the other way around. And that's but a matter of a day or a nicht. Wull Morris showed me a route for my tour that meant travelling, often and often, five hundred miles frae ane toon tae the next. I was afraid at first, for it seemed that I'd ha' tae be travelling for months at a time. I'd heard of the hotels in the sma' places, and I knew they couldna be tae good.

It's harder than one wha hasna done it can realize the travel and gie twa shows a day for any length of time. If it was staying always a week or mair in the ane city, it would be better. But in America, for the first time, I had to combine long travelling wi' constant singing. Folks come in frae long distances to a toon when a show they want to see is booked to appear, and it's necessary that there should be a matinee as well as a nicht performance whenever it's at a' possible.

They all told me not to fret; that I didna ken, until I'd seen for myself, how comfortable travel in America could be made. I had my private car--that was a rare thing for me to be thinking of. And, indeed, it was as comfortable as anyone made me think it could be. There was a real bedroom--I never slept in a berth, but in a brass bed, just as saft and comfortable as ever I could ha' known in ma own wee hoose at hame. Then there was a sitting room, as nice and hamely as you please, where I could rest and crack, whiles we were waiting in a station, wi' friends wha came callin'.

I wasna dependent on hotels at all, after the way I'd been led to fear them. It was only in the great cities, where we stayed a week or mair, that I left the car and stopped in a hotel. And even then it was mair because the yards, where the car would wait, would be noisy, and would be far awa' frae the theatre, than because the hotel was mair comfortable, that we abandoned the car.

Our own cook travelled wi' us. I'm a great hand for Scottish cooking. Mrs. Lauder will bake me a scone, noo and then, no matter whaur we are. And the parritch and a' the other Scottish dishes tickle my palate something grand. Still it was a revelation to me, the way that negro cooked for us! Things I'd never heard of he'd be sending to the table each day, and when I'd see him and tell him that I liked something special he'd made, it was a treat to see his white teeth shining oot o' his black face.

I love to sit behind the train, on the observation platform, while I'm travelling through America. It's grand scenery--and there's sae much of it. It's a wondrous sicht to see the sun rise in the desert. It puts me in mind o' the moors at home, wi' the rosy sheen of the dawn on the purple heather, but it's different.

There's no folk i' the world more hospitable than Americans. And there's no folk prouder of their hames, and more devoted to them. That's a thing to warm the cockles of a Scots heart. I like folk who aren't ashamed to let others know the way they feel. An Englishman's likely to think it's indelicate to betray his feelings. We Scots dinna wear our hearts upon our sleeves, precisely, but we do love our hame, and we're aye fond o' talking about it when we're far awa'.

In Canada, especially, I always found Scots everywhere I went. They'd come to the theatre, whiles I was there; nearly every nicht I'd hear the gude Scots talk in my dressing room after my turn. There'd be dinners they'd gie me--luncheons, as a rule, rather, syne my time was ta'en up sae that I couldna be wi' em at the time for the evening meal. Whiles I'd sing a bit sang for them; whiles they'd ask me tae speak to them.

Often there'd be some laddie I'd known when we were boys together; once or twice I'd shake the hand o' one had worked wi' me in the pit. Man, is there anything like coming upon an old friend far frae hame I didna think sae. It's a feeling that you always have, no matter how oft it comes to you. For me, I know weel, it means a lump rising in my throat, and a bit o' moisture that's verra suspicious near my een, so that I maun wink fast, sometimes, that no one else may understand.

I'm a great one for wearing kilts. I like the Scottish dress. It's the warmest, the maist sensible, way of dressing that I ken. I used to have mair colds before I took to wearing kilts than ever I've had since I made a practice of gie'in up my troosers.

And there's a freedom aboot a kilt that troosers canna gie ye.

I've made many friends in America, but I'm afraid I've made some enemies, too. For there's a curious trait I've found some Americans have. They've an audacity, when they're the wrang sort, I've never seen equalled in any other land. And they're clever, tae--oh, aye-- they're as clever as can be!

More folk tried tae sell me things I didna want on that first tour o' mine. They'd come tae me wi' mining stocks, and tell me how I could become rich overnicht. You'd no be dreaming the ways they'd find of getting a word in my ear. I mind times when men wha wanted to reach me, but couldna get to me when I was off the stage, hired themselves as stage hands that they micht catch me where I could not get away.

Aye, they've reached me in every way. Selling things, books, insurance, pictures; plain begging, as often as not. I've had men drive cabs so they could speak to me; I mind a time when one, who was to drive me frae the car, in the yards, tae the theatre, took me far oot of ma way, and then turned.

"Now then, Harry Lauder!" he said. "Give me the thousand dollars!"

"And what thousand dollars wi' that be, my mannie?" I asked him.

"The thousand I wrote and told you I must have!" he said, as brash as you please.

"Noo, laddie, there's something wrang," I said. "I've had nae letter from you aboot that thousand dollars!"

"It's the mails!" he said, and cursed. "I'm a fule to trust to them. They're always missending letters and delaying them. Still, there's no harm done. I'm telling you now I need a thousand dollars. Have you that much with you?"

"I dinna carrie sae muckle siller wi' me, laddie," I said. I could see he was but a salt yin, and none to be fearing. "I'll gie you a dollar on account."

And, d'ye ken, he was pleased as Punch? It was a siller dollar I gie'd him, for it was awa' oot west this happened, where they dinna have the paper money so much as in the east.

That's a grand country, that western country in America, whichever side of the line you're on, in Canada or in the States. There's land, and there's where real men work upon it. The cities cannot lure them awa'--not yet, at any rate. It's an adventure to work upon one of those great farms. You'll see the wheat stretching awa' further than the een can reach. Whiles there'll be a range, and you can see maybe five thousand head o' cattle that bear a single brand grazing, wi' the cowboys riding aboot here and there.

I've been on a round up in the cattle country in Texas, and that's rare sport. Round up's when they brand the beasties. It seems a cruel thing, maybe, to brand the bit calves the way they do, but it's necessary, and it dosna hurt them sae much as you'd think. But ot's the life that tempts me! It's wonderfu' to lie oot under the stars on the range at nicht, after the day's work is done. Whiles I'd sing a bit sang for the laddies who were my hosts, but oft they'd sing for me instead, and that was a pleasant thing. It made a grand change.

I've aye taken it as a great compliment, and as the finest thing I could think aboot my work, that it's true men like those cowboys, and like the soldiers for whom I sang sae much when I was in France, o' all the armies, who maist like to hear me sing. I've never had audiences that counted for sae much wi' me. Maybe it's because I'm singing, when I sing for them, for the sheer joy of doing it, and not for siller. But I think it's mair than that. I think it's just the sort of men they are I know are listening tae me. And man, when you hear a hundred voices--or five thousand!--rising in a still nicht to join in the chorus of a song of yours its something you canna forget, if you live to any age at a'.

I've had strange accompaniments for my stings, mair than once. Oot west the coyote has played an obligato for me; in France I've had the whustling o' bullets over my head and the cooming of the big guns, like the lowest notes of some great organ. I can always sing, ye ken, wi'oot any accompaniments frae piano or band. 'Deed, and there's one song o' mine I always sing alone. It's "The Wee Hoose Amang the Heather." And every time I appear, I think, there's some one asks for that.

Whiles I think I've sung a song sae often everyone must be tired of it. I'm fond o' that wee song masel', and it was aye John's favorite, among all those in my repertory. But it seems I canna sing it often enough, for more than once, when I've not sung it, the audience hasna let me get awa' without it. I'll ha' gie'n as many encores as I usually do; I'll ha' come back, maybe a score of times, and bowed. But a' over the hoose I'll hear voices rising--Scots voices, as a rule.

"Gie's the wee hoose, Harry," they'll roar. And: "The wee hoose 'mang the heather, Harry," I'll hear frae another part o' the hoose. It's many years since I've no had to sing that song at every performance.

Sometimes I've been surprised at the way my audiences ha' received me. There's toons in America where maist o' the folk will be foreigners-- places where great lots o' people from the old countries in Europe ha' settled doon, and kept their ain language and their ain customs. In Minnesota and Wisconsin there'll be whole colonies of Swedes, for example. They're a fine, God fearing folk, and, nae doot, they've a rare sense of humor o' their ain. But the older ones, sometimes, dinna understand English tae well, and I feel, in such a place, as if it was asking a great deal to expect them to turn oot to hear me.

And yet they'll come. I've had some of my biggest audiences in such places, and some of my friendliest. I'll be sure, whiles I'm singing, that they canna understand. The English they micht manage, but when I talk a wee bit o' Scots talk, it's ayant them altogether. But they'll laugh--they'll laugh at the way I walk, I suppose, and at the waggle o' ma kilts. And they'll applaud and ask for mair. I think there's usually a leaven o' Scots in sic a audience; just Scots enough so I'll ha' a friend or twa before I start. And after that a's weel.

It's a great sicht to see the great crowds gather in a wee place that's happened to be chosen for a performance or twa because there's a theatre or a hall that's big enough. They'll come in their motor cars; they'll come driving in behind a team o' horses; aye, and there's some wull come on shanks' mare. And it's a sobering thing tae think they're a' coming, a' those gude folk, tae hear me sing. You canna do ought but tak' yourself seriously when they that work sae hard to earn it spend their siller to hear you.

I think it was in America, oot west, where the stock of the pioneers survives to this day, that I began to realize hoo much humanity counted for i' this world. Yon's the land of the plain man and woman, you'll see. Folk live well there, but they live simply, and I think they're closer, there, to living as God meant man tae do, than they are in the cities. It's easier to live richtly in the country. There's fewer ways to hand to waste time and siller and good intentions.

It was in America I first came sae close to an audience as to hae it up on the stage wi' me. When a hoose is sair crowded there they'll put chairs aroond upon the stage--mair sae as not to disappoint them as may ha' made a lang journey tae get in than for the siller that wad be lost were they turned awa'. And it's a rare thing for an artist to be able tae see sae close the impression that he's making. I'll pick some old fellow, sometimes, that looks as if nothing could mak' him laugh. And I'll mak' him the test. If I canna make him crack a smile before I'm done my heart will be heavy within me, and I'll think the performance has been a failure. But it's seldom indeed that I fail.

There's a thing happened tae me once in America touched me mair than a'most anything I can ca' to mind. It was just two years after my boy John had been killed in France. It had been a hard thing for me to gae back upon the stage. I'd been minded to retire then and rest and nurse my grief. But they'd persuaded me to gae back and finish my engagement wi' a revue in London. And then they'd come tae me and talked o' the value I'd be to the cause o' the allies in America.

When I began my tour it was in the early winter of 1917. America had not come into the war yet, wi' her full strength, but in London they had reason to think she'd be in before long--and gude reason, tae, as it turned oot. There was little that we didna ken, I've been told, aboot the German plans; we'd an intelligence system that was better by far than the sneaking work o' the German spies that helped to mak' the Hun sae hated. And, whiles I canna say this for certain, I'm thinking they were able to send word to Washington frae Downing street that kept President Wilson and his cabinet frae being sair surprised when the Germans instituted the great drive in the spring of 1918 that came sae near to bringing disaster to the Allies.

Weel, this was the way o' it. I'll name no names, but there were those who knew what they were talking of came tae me.

"It's hard, Harry," they said. "But you'll be doing your country a good service if you'll be in America the noo. There's nae telling when we may need all her strength. And when we do it'll be for her government to rouse the country and mak' it realize what it means to be at war wi' the Hun. We think you can do that better than any man we could be sending there--and you can do it best because you'll no be there just for propaganda. Crowds will come to hear you sing, and they'll listen to you if you talk to them after your performance, as they'd no be listening to any other man we might send."

In Washington, when I was there before Christmas, I saw President Wilson, and he was maist cordial and gracious tae me. Yon' a great man, for a' that's said against him, and there was some wise men he had aboot him to help him i' the conduct of the war. Few ken, even the noo, how great a thing America did, and what a part she played in ending the war when it was ended. I'm thinking the way she was making ready saved us many a thousand lives in Britain and in France, for she made the Hun quit sooner than he had a mind to do.

At any rate, they made me see in Washington that they agreed wi' those who'd persuaded me to make that tour of America. They, too, thought that I could be usefu', wi' my speaking, after what I'd seen in France. Maybe, if ye'll ha' heard me then, ye'll ha' thought I just said whatever came into my mind at the moment. But it was no so. The things I said were thought oot in advance; their effect was calculated carefully. It was necessary not to divulge information that micht ha' been of value to the enemy, and there were always new bits of German propoganda that had tae be met and discounted without referring to them directly. So I was always making wee changes, frae day to day. Sometimes, in a special place, there'd be local conditions that needed attention; whiles I could drop a seemingly careless or unstudied suggestion that would gain much more notice than an official bulletin or speech could ha' done.

There's an art that conceals art, I'm told. Maybe it was that I used in my speaking in America during the war. It may be I gave offence sometimes, by the vehemence of my words, but I'm hoping that all true Americans understood that none was meant. I'd have to be a bit harsh, whiles, in a toon that hadna roused itself to the true state of affairs. But what's a wee thing like that between friends and allies?

It's the New Year's day I'm thinking of, though. New Year's is aye a sacred day for a' us Scots. When we're frae hame we dinna lik it; it's a day we'd fain celebrate under our ain rooftree. But for me it was mair so than for maist, because it was on New Year's day I heard o' my boy's death.

Weel, it seemed a hard thing tae ha' the New Year come in whiles I was journeying in a railroad car through the United States. But here's the thing that touched me sae greatly. The time came, and I was alane wi' the wife. Tom Vallance had disappeared. And then I heard the skirl o' the pipes, and into the car the pipers who travelled wi' me came marching. A' the company that was travelling wi' me followed them, and they brocht wee presents for me and for the wife. There were tears in our een, I'm telling you; it was a kindly thought, whoever amang them had it, and ane I'll ne'er forget. And there, in that speeding car, we had a New Year's day celebration that couldna ha' been matched ootside o' Scotland.

But, there, I've aye found folk kindly and thoughtfu' tae me when I've had tae be awa' frae hame on sic a day, And it happens often, for it's just when folk are making holiday that they'll want maist to see and hear me in their theatres, and sae it's richt seldom that I can mak' my way hame for the great days o' the year. But I wull, before sae lang--I'm near ready to keep the promise I've made sae often, and retire. You're no believing I mean that? You've heard the like of that tale before? Aye, I ken that fine. But I mean it!

CHAPTER XIX

I've had much leisure to be thinking of late. A man has time to wonder and to speculate concerning life and what he's seen o' it when he's taking a long ocean voyage. And I've been meditating on some curious contrasts. I was in Australia when I heard of the coming of the war. My boy John was with me, then; he'd come there tae meet his mither and me. He went hame, straight hame; I went to San Francisco.

Noo I'm on ma way hame frae Australia again, and again I've made the lang journey by way of San Francisco and the States. And there's a muckle to think upon in what I've seen. Sad sichts they were, a many of them. In yon time when I was there before the world was a' at peace. Men went aboot their business, you in Australia, underneath the world, wi' no thought of trouble brewing. But other men, in Europe, thousands of miles way, were laying plans that meant death and the loss of hands and een for those braw laddies o' Australia and New Zealand that I saw-- those we came to ken sae weel as the gallant Anzacs.

It makes you realize, seeing countries so far awa' frae a' the war, and yet suffering so there from, how dependent we all are upon one another. Distance makes no matter; differences make none. We cannot escape the consequences of what others do. And so, can we no be thinking sometimes, before we act, doing something that we think concerns only ourselves, of all those who micht suffer for what we did?

I maun think of labor when I think of the Anzacs. Yon is a country different frae any I have known. There's no landed aristocracy in the land of the Anzac. Yon's a country where all set out on even terms. That's truer there, by far, than in America, even. It's a young country and a new country, still, but it's grown up fast. It has the strength and the cities of an old country, but it has a freshness of its own.

And there labor rules the roost. It's one of the few places in the world where a government of labor has been instituted. And yet, I'm wondering the noo if those labor leaders in Australia have reckoned on one or twa things I think of? They're a' for the richts of labor--and so am I. I'd be a fine one, with the memory I have of unfairness and exploitation of the miners in the coal pits at Hamilton, did I not agree that the laboring man must be bound together with his fellows to gain justice and fair treatment from his employers.

But there's a richt way and a wrong way to do all things. And there was a wrong way that labor used, sometimes, during the war, to gain its ends. There was sympathy for all that British labor did among laboring men everywhere, I'm told--in Australia, too. But let's bide a wee and see if labor didn't maybe, mak' some mistakes that it may be threatening to mak' again noo that peace has come.

Here's what I'm afraid of. Labor used threats in the war. If the government did not do thus and so there'd be a strike. That was meanin' that guns would be lacking, or shell, or rifles, or hand grenades, or what not in the way of munitions, on the Western front. But the threat was sae vital that it won, tae often I'm no saying it was used every time. Nor am I saying labor did not have a richt to what it asked. It's just this--canna we get alang without making threats, one to the other?

And there were some strikes that had serious consequences. There were strikes that delayed the building of ships, and the making of cannon and shell. And as a result of them men died, in France, and in Gallipoli, and in other places, who need no have died. They were laddies who'd dropped all, who'd gi'en up all that was dear to them, all comfort and safety, when the country called.

They had nae voice in the matters that were in dispute. None thought, when sic a strike was called, of hoo those laddies in the trenches wad be affected. That's what I canna forgie. That's what makes me wonder why the Anzacs, when they reach home, don't have a word to say themselves aboot the troubles that the union leaders would seem to be gaein' to bring aboot.

We're in a ficht still, even though peace has come. We're in a ficht wi' poverty, and disease, and all the other menaces that still threaten our civilization. We'll beat them, as we ha' beaten the other enemies. But we'll no beat them by quarrelling amang oorselves, any more than we'd ever have beaten the Hun if France and Britain had stopped the war, every sae often, to hae oot an argument o' their own. We had differences with our gude friends the French, fraw time to time. Sae did the Americans, and whiles we British and our American cousins got upon ane anither's nerves. But there was never real trouble or difficulty, as the result and the winning of the war have shown.

Do you ken what it is we've a' got to think of the noo? It's production. We must produce more than we ha' ever done before. It's no a steady raise in wages that will help. Every time wages gang up a shilling or twa, everything else is raised in proportion. The workingman maun mak' more money; everyone understands that. But the only way he can safely get more siller is to earn more--to increase production as fast as he knows how.

It's the only way oot--and it's true o' both Britain and America. The more we mak' the more we'll sell. There's a market the noo for all we English speaking folk can produce. Germany is barred, for a while at least; France, using her best efforts and brains to get back upon her puir, bruised feet, canna gae in avily for manufactures for a while yet. We, in Britain, have only just begun to realize that the war is over. It took us a long time to understand what we were up against at the beginning, and what sort of an effort we maun mak' if we were to win the war.

And then, before we'd done, we were doing things we'd never ha dreamed it was possible for us tae do before the need was upon us. We in Britain had to do without things we'd regarded as necessities and we throve without them. For the sake of the wee bairns we went without milk for our tea and coffee, and scarce minded it. Aye, in a thousand little ways that had not seemed to us to matter at all we were deprived and harried and hounded.

Noo, what I'm thinking sae often is just this. We had a great problem to meet in the winning of the war. We solved it, though it was greater than any of those we were wont to call insoluble. Are there no problems left? There's the slum. There's the sort of poverty that afflicts a man who's willing tae work and can nicht find work enough tae do tae keep himself and his family alive and clad. There's all sorts of preventible disease. We used to shrug our shoulders and speak of such things as the act of God. But I'll no believe they're acts of God. He doesna do things in such a fashion. They're acts of man, and it's for man to mak' them richt and end what's wrong wi' the world he dwells in.

They used to shrug their shoulders in Russia, did those who had enough to eat and a warm, decent hoose tae live in. They'd hear of the sufferings of the puir, and they'd talk of the act of God, and how he'd ordered it that i' this world there maun always be some suffering.

And see what's come o' that there! The wrong sort of man has set to work to mak' a wrong thing richt, and he's made it worse than it ever was. But how was it he had the chance to sway the puir ignorant bodies in Russia? How was it that those who kenned a better way were not at work long agane? Ha' they anyone but themselves to blame that Trotzky and the others had the chance to persuade the Russian people tae let them ha' power for a little while'?

Oh, we'll no come to anything like that in Britain and America. I've sma' patience wi' those that talk as if the Bolsheviki would be ruling us come the morrow. We're no that sort o' folk, we Britons and Americans. We've settled our troubles our ain way these twa thousand years, and we'll e'en do sae again. But we maun recognize that there are things we maun do tae mak' the lot of the man that's underneath a happier and a better one.

He maun help, tae. He maun realize that there's a chance for him. I'm haulding mysel' as one proof of that--it's why I've told you sae muckle in this book of myself and the way that I've come frae the pit tae the success and the comfort that I ken the noo.

I had to learn, lang agane, that my business was not only mine. Maybe you'll think that I'm less concerned with others and their affairs than maist folk, and maybe that's true, tae. But I. canna forget others, gi'en I would. When I'm singing I maun have a theatre i' which to appear. And I canna fill that always by mysel'. I maun gae frae place to place, and in the weeks of the year when I'm no appearing there maun be others, else the theatre will no mak' siller enough for its owners to keep it open.

And then, let's gie a thought to just the matter of my performance. There must be an orchestra. It maun play wi' me; it maun be able to accompany me. An orchestra, if it is no richt, can mak' my best song sound foolish and like the singing o' some one who dinna ken ane note of music frae the next. So I'm dependent on the musicians--and they on me. And then there maun be stage hands, to set the scenes. Folk wouldna like it if I sang in a theatre wi'oot scenery. There maun be those that sell tickets, and tak' them at the doors, and ushers to show the folk their seats.

And e'en before a'body comes tae the hoose to pay his siller for a ticket there's others I'm dependent upon. How do they ken I'm in the toon at a'? They've read it in the papers, maybe--and there's reporters and printers I've tae thank. Or they've seen my name and my picture on a hoarding, and I've to think o' the men who made the lithograph sheets, and the billposters who put them up. Sae here's Harry Lauder and a' the folk he maun have tae help him mak' a living and earn his bit siller! More than you'd thought' Aye, and more than I'd thought, sometimes.

There's a michty few folk i' this world who can say they're no dependant upon others in some measure. I ken o' none, myself. It's a fine thing to mind one's ain business, but if one gies the matter thought one will find, I think, that a man's business spreads oot more than maist folk reckon it does.

Here, again. In the States there's been trouble about the men that work on the railways. Can I say it's no my business? Is it no? Suppose they gae oot on strike? How am I to mak' my trips frae one toon the the next? And should I no be finding oot, if there's like that threatening to my business, where the richt lies? You will be finding it's sae, too, in your affairs; there's little can come that willna affect you, soon or late.

We maun all stand together, especially we plain men and women. It was sae that we won the war--and it is sae that we can win the peace noo that it's come again, and mak' it a peace sae gude for a' the world that it can never be broken again by war. There'd be no wars i' the world if peace were sae gude that all men were content. It's discontented men who stir up trouble in the world, and sae mak' wars possible.

We talk much, in these days, of classes. There's a phrase it sickens me tae hear-- class consciousness. It's ane way of setting the man who works wi' his hands against him who works wi' his brain. It's no the way a man works that ought to count--it's that he works at all. Both sorts of work are needful; we canna get along without either sort.

Is no humanity a greater thing than any class? We are all human. We maun all be born, and we maun all die in the end. That much we ken, and there's nae sae much more we can be siccar of. And I've often thought that the trouble with most of our hatreds an' our envy and malice is that folk do not know one another well enough. There's fewer quarrels among folk that speak the same tongue. Britain and

America dwelt at peace for mair than a hundred years before they took the field together against a common enemy. America and Canada stand side by side--a great strong nation and a small one. There's no fort between them; there are no fichting ships on the great lakes, ready to loose death and destruction.

It's easier to have a good understanding when different peoples speak the same language. But there's a hint o' the way things must be done, I'm thinking, in the future. Britain and France used tae have their quarrels. They spoke different tongues. But gradually they built up a gude understanding of one another, and where's the man in either country the noo that wadna laugh at you if you said there was danger they micht gae tae war?

It's harder, it may be, to promote a gude understanding when there's a different language for a barrier. But walls can be climbed, and there's more than the ane way of passing them. We've had a great lesson in that respect in the war. It's the first time that ever a coalition of nations held together. Germany and Austria spoke one language. But we others, with a dozen tongues or mair to separate us, were forged into one mighty confederation by our peril and our consciousness of richt, and we beat doon that barrier of various languages, sae that it had nae existence.

And it's not only foreign peoples that speak a different tongue at times. Whiles you'll find folk of the same family, the same race, the same country, who gie the same words different meanings, and grow confused and angry for that reason. There's a way they can overcome that, and reach an understanding. It's by getting together and talking oot all that confuses and angers them. Speech is a great solvent if a man's disposed any way at all to be reasonable, and I've found, as I've gone about the world, that most men want to be reasonable.

They'll call me an optimist, maybe. I'll no be ashamed of that title. There was a saying I've heard in America that taught me a lot. They've a wee cake there they call a doughnut--awfu' gude eating, though no quite sae gude as Mrs. Lauder's scones. There's round hole in the middle of a doughnut, always. And the Americans have a way of saying: "The optimist sees the doughnut; the pessimist sees the hole." It's a wise crack, you, and it tells you a good deal, if you'll apply it.

There's another way we maun be thinking. We've spent a deal of blood and siller in these last years. We maun e'en have something to show for all we've spent. For a muckle o' the siller we've spent we've just borrowed and left for our bairns and their bairns to pay when the time comes. And we maun leave the world better for those that are coming, or they'll be saying it's but a puir bargain we've made for them, and what we bought wasna worth the price.

CHAPTER XX

There's no sadder sicht my een have ever seen than that of the maimed and wounded laddies that ha' come hame frae this war that is just over. I ken that there's been a deal of talk aboot what we maun do for them that ha' done sae much for us. But I'm thinking we can never think too often of those laddies, nor mak' too many plans to mak' life easier for them. They didna think before they went and suffered. They couldna calculate. Jock could not stand, before the zero hour came in the trenches, and talk' wi' his mate.

He'd not be saying: "Sandy, man, we're going to attack in twa-three meenits. Maybe I'll lose a hand, Sandy, or a leg. Maybe it'll be you'll be hit. What'll we be doing then? Let's mak' our plans the noo. How'll we be getting on without our legs or our arms or if we should be blind?"

No, it was not in such fashion that the laddies who did the fichting thought or talked wi' one another. They'd no time, for the one thing. And for another, I think they trusted us.

Weel, each government has worked out its own way of taking care of the men who suffered. They're gude plans, the maist of them. Governments have shown more intelligence, more sympathy, more good judgment, than ever before in handling such matters. That's true in America as well as in Britain. It's so devised that a helpless man will be taken care of a' his life lang, and not feel that he's receiving any charity. It's nae more than richt that it should be so; it would be a black shame, indeed, if it were otherwise. But still there's more tae be done, and it's for you and me and all the rest of us that didna suffer sae to do it.

There's many things a laddie that's been sair wounded needs and wants when he comes hame. Until he's sure of his food and his roof, and of the care of those dependent on him, if such there be, he canna think of anything else. And those things, as is richt and proper, his country will take in its charge.

But after that what he wants maist is tae know that he's no going to be helpless all his days. He wants to feel that he's some use in the world. Unless he can feel sae, he'd raither ha' stayed in a grave in France, alongside the thousands of others who have stayed there. It's an awfu' thing to be a laddie, wi' maist of the years of your life still before you to be lived, and to be thinking you micht better be dead.

I know what I'm talking aboot when I speak of this. Mind ye, I've passed much time of late years in hospitals. I've talked to these laddies when they'd be lying there, thinking--thinking. They'd a' the time in the world to think after they began to get better. And they'd be knowing, then, that they would live--that the bullet or the shell or whatever it micht be that had dropped them had not finished them. And they'd know, too, by then, that the limb was lost for aye, or the een or whatever it micht be.

Noo, think of a laddie coming hame. He's discharged frae the hospital and frae the army. He's a civilian again. Say he's blind. He's got his pension, his allowance, whatever it may be. There's his living. But is he to be just a hulk, needing some one always to care for him? That's a' very fine at first. Everyone's glad tae do it. He's a hero, and a romantic figure. But let's look a wee bit ahead.

Let's get beyond Jock just at first, when all the folks are eager to see him and have him talk to them. They're glad to sit wi' him, or tae tak' him for a bit walk. He'll no bore them. But let's be thinking of Jock as he'll be ten years frae noo. Who'll be remembering then hoo they felt when he first came home? They'll be thinking of the nuisance it is tae be caring for him a' the time, and of the way he's always aboot the hoose, needing care and attention.

What I'm afraid of is that tae many of the laddies wull be tae tired to fit themselves tae be other than helpless creatures, despite their wounds or their blindness. They can do wonders, if we'll help them. We maun not encourage those laddies tae tak' it tae easy the noo. It's a cruel hard thing to tell a boy like yon that he should be fitting himself for life. It seems that he ought to rest a bit, and tak' things easy, and that it's a sma' thing, after all he's done, to promise him good and loving care all his days.

Aye, and that's a sma' thing enough--if we're sure we can keep our promise. But after every war--and any old timer can tell ye I'm tellin' ye the truth the noo-

-there have been crippled and blinded men who have relied upon such promises--and seen them forgotten, seen themselves become a burden. No man likes to think he's a burden. It irks him sair. And it will be irksome specially tae laddies like those who have focht in France.

It's no necessary that any man should do that. The miracles of to-day are all at the service of the wounded laddies. And I've seen things I'd no ha' believed were possible, had I had to depend on the testimony o' other eyes than my own. I've seen men sae hurt that it didna seem possible they could ever do a'thing for themselves again. And I've seen those same men fend for themselves in a way that was as astonishing as it was heart rending.

The great thing we maun all do wi' the laddies that are sae maimed and crippled is never tae let them ken we're thinking of their misfortunes. That's a hard thing, but we maun do it. I've seen sic a laddie get into a 'bus or a railway carriage. And I've seen him wince when een were turned upon him. Dinna mistake me. They were kind een that gazed on him. The folk were gude folk; they were fu' of sympathy. They'd ha' done anything in the world for the laddie. But--they were doing the one thing they shouldna ha' done.

Gi'en you're an employer, and a laddie wi' a missing leg comes tae ye seeking a job. You've sent for him, it may be; ye ken work ye can gie him that he'll be able tae do. A' richt--that's splendid, and it's what maun be done. But never let him know you're thinking at a' that his leg's gone. Mak' him feel like ithers. We maun no' be reminding the laddies a' the time that they're different noo frae ither folk. That's the hard thing.

Gi'en a man's had sic a misfortune. We know--it's been proved a thousand times ower--that a man can rise above sic trouble. But he canno do it if he's thinking of it a' the time. The men that have overcome the handicaps of blindness and deformity are those who gie no thought at all to what ails them--who go aboot as if they were as well and as strong as ever they've been.

It's a hard thing not to be heeding such things.

But it's easier than what these laddies have had to do, and what they must go on doing a' the rest of their lives. They'll not be able to forget their troubles very long; there'll be plenty to remind them. But let's not gae aboot the streets wi' our een like a pair of looking glasses in which every puir laddie sees himsel' reflected.

It's like the case of the lad that's been sair wounded aboot the head; that's had his face sae mangled and torn that he'd be a repulsive sicht were it not for the way that he became sae. If he'd been courting a lassie before he was hurt wadna the thought of how she'd be feeling aboot him be amang his wairst troubles while he lay in hospital? I've talked wi' such, and I know.

Noo, it's a hard thing to see the face one loves changed and altered and made hideous. But it's no sae hard as to have tha face! Who wull say it is? And we maun be carefu' wi' such boys as that, tae. They're verra sensitive; all those that have been hurt are sensitive. It's easy to wound their feelings. And it should be easy for all of us to enter into a conspiracy amang ourselves to hide the shock of surprise we canna help feeling, whiles, and do nothing that can make a lad-die wha's fresh frae the hospital grow bitter over the thocht that he's nae like ither men the noo.

Yon's a bit o' a sermon I've been preaching, I'm afraid. But, oh, could ye ha' seen the laddies as I ha' seen them, in the hospitals, and afterward, when they were waiting tae gae hame! They wad ask me sae often did I think their ain folk could stand seeing them sae changed.

"Wull it be sae hard for them, Harry?" they've said the me, over and over again. "Whiles I've thocht it would ha' been better had I stayed oot there----"

Weel, I ken that that's nae sae. I'd gie a' the world tae ha' my ain laddie back, no matter hoo sair he'd been hurt. And there's never a faither nor a mither but wad feel the same way--aye, I'm sure o' that. Sae let us a' get together and make sure that there's never a look in our een or a shrinking that can gie' any o' these laddies, whether they're our kin or no, whether we saw them before, the feeling that there's any difference in our eyes between them and ourselves.

The greatest suffering any man's done that's been hurt is in his spirit, in his mind--not in his body. Bodily pain passes and is forgotten. But the wounds of the human spirit lie deep, and it takes them a lang time tae heal. They're easily reopened, tae; a careless word, a glance, and a' a man has gone through is brought back to his memory, when, maybe, he'd been forgetting. I've seen it happen too oft.

CHAPTER XXI

I've said sae muckle aboot myself in this book that I'm a wee bit reluctant tae say mair. But still, there's a thing I've thought about a good deal of late, what wi' all this talk of hoo easy some folk have it, and how hard others must work. I think there's no one makes a success of any sort wi'oot hard work--and wi'oot keeping up hard work, what's mair. I ken that's so of all the successful men I've ever known, all over the world. They work harder than maist folk will ever realize, and it's just why they're where they are.

Noawadays it's almost fashionable to think that any man that's got mair than others has something wrong about him. I know folks are always saying to me that I'm sae lucky; that all I have tae do is to sing twa-three songs in an evening and gae my ain gait the rest of my time. If they but knew the way I'm working!

Noo, I'd no be having anyone think I'm complaining. I love my work. It's what I'd rather do, till I retire and tak' the rest I feel I've earned, than any work i' a' the world. It's brought me happiness, my work has, and friends, and my share o' siller. But--it's *work*.

It's always been work. It's work to-day. It'll be work till I'm ready to stop doing it altogether. And, because, after all, a man knows more of his own work than of any other man's, I think I'll tell you just hoo I do work, and hoo much of my time it takes beside the hour or two I'll be in the theatre during a performance.

Weel, to begin with, there's the travelling. I travel in great comfort. But I dinna care how comfortable ye are, travel o' the sort I do is bound tae be a tiring thing. It's no sae hard in England or in Scotland. Distances are short. There's seldom need of spending a nicht on a train. So there it's easy. But when it comes to the United States and Canada it's a different matter.

There it's almost always a case of starting during the nicht, after a performance.

That means switching the car, coupling it to a train. I'm a gude sleeper, but I'll defy any man tae sleep while his car is being hitched to a train, or whiles it's being shunted around in a railroad yard. And then, as like as not, ye'll come tae the next place in the middle of the nicht, or early in the morning, whiles you're taking your beauty sleep. The beauty sleeps I've had interrupted in America by having a switching engine come and push and haul me aboot! 'Is it any wonder I've sae little o' my manly beauty left?

There's a great strain aboot constant travelling, too. There will aye be accidents. No serious ones, maist of them, but trying tae the nerves and disturbing tae the rest. And there's aye some worry aboot being late. Unless you've done such work as mine, you canna know how I dread missing a performance. I've the thought of all the folk turning oot, and having them disappointed. There's a sense of responsibility one feels toward those who come oot sae to hear one sing. One owes them every care and thought.

Sae it's the nervous strain as much as the actual weariness of travel that I'm thinking of. It's a relief, on a long tour, tae come to a city where one's booked for a week. I'm no ower fond of hotels, but there's comfort in them at such times. But still, that's another thing. I miss my hame as every man should when he's awa frae it. It's hard work to keep comfortable and happy when I'm on tour so much.

Oh, aye, I can hear what you're saying to yourself! You're saying I've talked sae much about hoo fond I am of travelling. You'll be thinking, maybe, you'd be glad of the chance to gae all around the world, travelling in comfort and luxury. Aye, and so am I. It's just that I want you to understand that it's all wear and tear. It all takes it out of me.

But that's no what I'm meaning when I talk of the work I do. I'm thinking of the wee songs themselves, and the singing of them. Hoo do you think I get the songs I sing? Do you think they're just written richt off? Weel, it's not so.

A song, for me, you'll ken, is muckle mair than just a few words and a melody. It must ha' business. The way I'll dress, the things I do, the way I'll talk between verses--it's all one. A song, if folks are going to like it, has to be thought out wi' the greatest care.

I keep a great scrapbook, and it gaes wi' me everywhere I go. In it I put doon everything that occurs tae me that may help to make a new song, or that will make an old one go better. I'll see a queer yin in the street, maybe. He'll do something wi' his hands, or he'll stand in a peculiar fashion that makes me laugh. Or it'll be something funny aboot his claes.

It'll be in Scotland, maist often, of course, that I'll come upon something of the sort, but it's no always there. I've picked up business for my songs everywhere I've ever been. My scrap book is almost full now--my second one, I mean. And I suppose that there must be ideas buried in it that are better by far than any I've used, for I must confess that I can't always read the notes I've jotted down. I dash down a line or two, often, and they must seem to me to be important at the time, or I'd no be doing it. But later, when I'm browsing wi' the old scrapbook, blessed if I can make head or tail of them! And when I can't no one else can; Mrs. Lauder has tried, often enough, and laughed at me for a salt yin while she did it.

But often and often I've found a treasure that I'd forgotten a' aboot in the old book. I mind once I saw this entry----

"Think about a song called the 'Last of the Sandies'."

I had to stop and think a minute, and then I remembered that I'd seen the bill of a play, while I was walking aboot in London, that was called "The Last of the Dandies." That suggested the title for a song, and while I sat and remembered I began to think of a few words that would fit the idea.

When I came to put them together to mak' a song I had the help of my old Glasga friend, Rob Beaton, who's helped me wi' several o' my songs. I often write a whole song myself; sometimes, though, I can't seem to mak' it come richt, and then I'm glad of help frae Beaton or some other clever body like him. I find I'm an uncertain quantity when it comes to such work; whiles I'll be able to dash off the verses of a song as fast as I can slip the words doon upon the paper. Whiles, again, I'll seem able never to think of a rhyme at a', and I just have to wait till the muse will visit me again.

There's no telling how the idea for a song will come. But I ken fine how a song's made when once you have the idea! It's by hard work, and in no other way. There's nae sic a thing as writing a song easily--not a song folk will like. Don't let anyone tell you any different--or else you may be joining those who are sae sure I've refused the best song ever written--theirs!

The ideas come easily--aye! Do you mind a song I used to sing called "I Love a

Lassie?" I'm asked ower and again to sing it the noo, so I'm thinking perhaps ye'll ken the yin I mean. It's aye been one of the songs folk in my audiences have liked best. Weel, ane day I was just leaving a theatre when the man at the stage door handed me a letter--a letter frae Mrs. Lauder, I'll be saying.

"A lady's handwriting, Harry," he said, jesting. "I suppose you love the lassies,"

"Oh, aye--ye micht say so," I answered. "At least--I'm fond o' all the lassies, but I only love yin."

And I went off thinking of the bonnie lassie I'd loved sae well sae lang.

"I love ma lassie," I hummed to myself. And then I stopped in my tracks. If anyone was watching me they'd ha' thought I was daft, no doot!!

"I love a lassie!" I hummed. And then I thocht: "Noo--there's a bonny idea for a bit sang!"

That time the melody came to me frae the first. It was wi' the words I had the trouble. I couldna do anything wi' them at a' at first. So I put the bit I'd written awa'. But whiles later I remembered it again, and I took the idea to my gude friend Gerald Grafton. We worked a long time before we hit upon just the verses that seemed richt. But when we'd done we had a song that I sang for many years, and that my audiences still demand from me.

That's aye been one great test of a song for me. Whiles I'll be a wee bit dootful aboot a song-in my repertory for a season. Then I'll stop singing it for a few nichts. If the audiences ask for it after that I know that I should restore it to its place, and I do.

I do not write all my own songs, but I have a great deal to do with the making of all of them. It's not once in a blue moon that I get a song that I can sing exactly as it was first written. That doesna mean it's no a good song it may mean that I'm no just the man tae sing it the way the author intended. I've my ain ways of acting and singing, and unless I feel richt and hamely wi' a song I canna do it justice. Sae it's no reflection on an author if I want to change his song about.

I keep in touch with several song writers--Grafton, J. D. Harper and several others. So well do they understand the way I like to do that they usually send me their first rough sketch of a song--the song the way it's born in their minds, before they put it into shape at all. They just give an outline of the words, and that gives me a notion of the story I'll have to be acting out to sing the song.

If I just sang songs, you see, it would be easy enough. But the song's only a part of it. There must aye be a story to be told, and a character to be portrayed, and studied, and interpreted. I always accept a song that appeals to me, even though I may not think I can use it for a long time to come. Good ideas for songs are the scarcest things in the world, I've found, and I never let one that may possibly suit me get away from me.

Often and often there'll be nae mair than just the bare idea left after we get through rebuilding and writing a new song. It may be just a title-a title counts for a great deal in a song with me.

I get a tremendous lot of songs frae ane year's end tae the other. All sorts of folk that ha' heard me send me their compositions, and though not one in fifty could possibly suit me I go through them a'. It doesna tak' much time; I can tell by a single glance at the verses, as a rule, if it's worth my while tae go on and finish reading. At the same time it has happened just often enough that a good song has come to me so, frae an author that's never been heard of before, that I wullna tak' the chance of missing one.

It may be, you'll understand, that some of the songs I canna use are very good. Other singers have taken a song I have rejected and made a great success wi' it. But that means just nothing at a' tae me. I'm glad the song found it's place--that's all. I canna put a song on unless it suits me--unless I feel, when I'm reading it, that here's something I can do so my audience will like to hear me do it. I flatter myself that I ken weel enough what the folk like that come to hear me--and, in any case, I maun be the judge.

But, every sae oft, there'll be a batch of songs I've put aside to think aboot a wee bit more before I decide. And then I'll tell my wife, of a morning, that I'd like tae have her listen tae a few songs that seemed to me micht do.

"All richt," she'll say. "But hurry up I'm making scones the day."

She's a great yin aboot the hoose, is Mrs. Lauder. We've to be awa' travelling sae much that she says it rests her to work harder than a scullery maid whiles she's at hame. And it's certain I'd rather eat scones of her baking than any I've ever tasted.

I always sit sae that I can watch her whiles I'm reading. She never lets me get very far wi'oot some comment.

"No bad," she'll murmur, whiles, and I'll gae on, for that means a muckle frae her. Then, maybe, instead o' that, she'll just listen, and I'll see she's no sure. If she mutters a little I'll gae on, too, for that still means she's making up her mind. But when she says, "Stop yer ticklin'!" I always stop. For that means the same thing they meant in Rome when they turned their thumbs doon toward a gladiator. And her judgments aye been gude enow for me.

Sometimes I'll get long letters frae authors wha send me their songs-- but nearly always they're frae those that wad be flattered tae be called authors, puir bodies who've no proper notion of how to write or how to go aboot getting what they've written accepted when they've done it. I mind a man in Lancashire who sent me songs for years. The first was an awfu' thing--it had nae meaning at a' that I could see. But his letter was a delight.

"Dear Harry," he wrote. "I've been sorry for a long time that so clever a man as you had such bad songs to sing. And so, though I'm busy most of the time, I've written one for you. I like you, so I'll only charge you a guinea for every time you sing it, and let you set your own music to it, too!"

It was a generous offer, surely, but I did not see my way clear to accept it, and the song went back immediately. A little later I got another. He wrote a very dignified letter this time; he'd evidently made up his mind to forgie me for the way I'd insulted him and his song before, but he wanted me to understand he'd have nae nonsense frae me. But this time he wanted only fifteen shilling a performance.

Weel, he kept on sending me songs, and each one was worse than the one before, though you'd never have thought it possible for anything to be worse than any one of them if you'd seen them! And each time his price went doon! The last one was what he called a "grand new song."

"I'm hard up just now, Harry," he said, "and you know how fond I've always been of you. So you can have this one outright for five shillings, *cash down*."

D'ye ken, I thought his persistence deserved a reward of some sort, sae I sent him the five shillings, and put his song in the fire. I rather thought I was a fool tae do sae, because I expected he'd be bombarding me wi' songs after that bit of encouragement. But it was not so; I'm thankfu' to say I've never heard of him or his songs frae that day tae this.

I've had many a kind word said tae me aboot my songs and the way I sing them.

But the kindest words have aye been for the music. And it's true that it's the lilt of a melody that makes folk remember a song. That's what catches the ear and stays wi' those who have heard a song sung.

It would be wrong for me to say I'm no proud of the melodies that I have introduced with the songs I've sung. I have never had a music lesson in my life. I can sit doon, the noo, at a piano, and pick out a harmony, but that's the very limit of my powers wi' any instrument. But ever since I can remember anything I have aye been humming at some lilt or another, and it's been, for the maist part, airs o' my ain that I've hummed. So I think I've a richt to be proud of having invented melodies that have been sung all over the world, considering how I had no musical education at a'.

Certainly it's the melody that has muckle tae do wi' the success of any song. Words that just aren't quite richt will be soon overlooked if the melody is one o' the sort the boys in the gallery pick up and whustle as they gae oot.

I'm never happy, when a gude verse comes tae me, till I've wedded a melody tae the words. When the idea's come tae me I'll sit doon at the piano and strum it ower and ower again, till I maun mak' everyone else i' the hoose tired. 'Deed, and I've been asked, mair than once, tae gie the hoose a little peace.

I dinna arrange my songs, I needn't say, having no knowledge of the principles. But always, after a song's accompaniment has been arranged for the orchestra, I'll listen carefully at a rehearsal, and often I can pick out weak spots and mak' suggestions that seem to work an improvement. I've a lot of trouble, sometimes, wi' the players, till they get sae that they ken the way I like my accompaniment tae be. But after that we aye get alang fine together, the orchestra and me.

CHAPTER XXII

I've talked a muckle i' this book aboot what I think. Do you know why? It's because I'm a plain man, and I think the way plain men think all ower this world. It was the war taught me that I could talk to folk as well as sing tae them. If I've talked tae much in this book you maun forgie me--and you maun think that it's e'en yor ain fault, in a way.

During the war, whiles I'd speak aboot this or that after my show, people paid an attention tae me that wad have been flattering if I hadn't known sae well that it was no to me they were listening. It wasna old Harry Lauder who interested them-- it was what he had to tell them. It was a great thing to think that folk would tak' me seriously. I've been amusing people for these many years. It seemed presumptuous, at first, when I set out to talk to them of other and more serious things.

"Hoots!" I said, at first, when they wanted me tae speak for the war and the recruiting or a loan. "They'll no be wanting to listen tae me. I'm just a comedian."

"You'll be a relief to them, Harry," I was told. "There's been too much serious speaking already."

Weel, I ken what they meant. It's serious speaking I've done, and serious think-ing. But there's nae harm if I crack a bit joke noo and again; it makes the medicine gae doon the easier. And noo the medicine's swallowed. There's nae mair fichting tae be done, thank God! We've saved the hoose our ancestors built.

But its walls are crackit here and there. The roof's leaking. There's paint need-ed on all sides. There's muckle for us tae do before the' hoose we've saved is set in order. It's like a hoose that's been afire. The firemen come and play their hose upon it. They'll put oot the fire, a' richt. But is it no a sair sicht, the hoose they leave be-hind them when they gae awa'?

Ye'll see a wee bit o' smoke, an hour later, maybe, coming frae some place where they thocht it was a' oot. And ye'll have tae be taking a bucket of water and putting oot the bit o' fire that they left smouldering there, lest the whole thing break oot again. And here and there the water will ha' done a deal of damage. Things are better than if the fire had just burnt itself oot, but you've no got the hoose you had before the fire! 'Deed, and ye have not!

Nor have we. We had our fire--the fire the Kaiser lighted. It was arson caused our fire--it was a firebug started it, no spontaneous combustion, as some wad ha' us think. And we called the firemen--the braw laddies frae all the world, who set to work and never stopped till the fire was oot. Noo they've gaed hame aboot their other business. We'll no be wanting to call them oot again. It was a cruel, hard task they had; it was a terrible ficht they had tae make.

It's sma' wonder, after such a conflagration, that there's spots i' the world where there's a bit of flame still smouldering. It's for us tae see that they're a' stamped oot, those bits of fire that are still burning. We can do that ourselves--no need to ca' the tired firemen oot again. And then there's the hoose itself!

Puir hoose! But how should it have remained the same? Man, you'd no expect to sleep in your ain hoose the same nicht there'd been a fire to put out? You'd be waiting for the insurance folks. And you'd know that the furniture was a' spoiled wi' water, and smoke. And there'll be places where the firemen had to chop wi' their axes. They couldna be carfu' wi' what was i' the hoose--had they been sae there'd be no a hoose left at a' the noo.

Sae are they no foolish folk that were thinking that sae soon as peace came a' would be as it was before yon days in August, 1914? Is it but five years agane? It is--but it'll tak' us a lang time tae bring the world back to where it was then. And it can't be the same again. It can't. Things change.

Here's what there is for us tae do. It's tae see that the change is in the richt direction. We canna stand still the noo. We'll move. We'll move one way or the other--forward or back.

And I say we dare not move back. We dare not, because of the graves that have been filled in France and Gallipoli and dear knows where beside in these last five years. We maun move forward. They've left sons behind them, many of the laddies that died to save us. Aye, there's weans in Britain and America, and in many another land, that will ne'er know a faither.

We owe something to those weans whose faithers deed for this world's salvation. We owe it to them and to their faithers tae see that they have a better world to grow up in than we and their faithers knew. It can be a better world. It can be a bonnier world than any of us have ever dreamed of. Dare I say that, ye'll be asking me, wi' the tears of the widow and the orphan still flowing fresh, wi' the groans of those that ha' suffered still i' our ears?

Aye, I dare say it. And I'll be proving it, tae, if ye'll ha' patience wi' me. For it's in your heart and mine that we'll find the makings of the bonnier world I can see, for a' the pain.

Let's stop together and think a bit. We were happy, many of us, in yon days before the war. Our loved yins were wi' us. There was peace i' a' the world. We had no thought that any wind could come blowing frae ootside ourselves that would cast down the hoose of our happiness. Wasna that sae? Weel, what was the result?

I think we were selfish folk, many, too many, of us. We had no thought, or too little, for others. We were so used to a' we had and were in the habit of enjoying that we forgot that we owed much of what we had to others. We were becoming a very fierce sort of individualists. Our life was to ourselves. We were self-sufficient. One of the prime articles of our creed was Cain's auld question:

"Am I my brother's keeper?"

We answered that question wi' a ringing "No!" The day was enow for the day. We'd but to gae aboot our business, and eat and drink, and maybe be merry. Oh, aye--I ken fine it was sae wi' me. Did I have charity, Weel, it may be that the wife and I did our wee bit tae be helping some that was less fortunate than ourselves. But here I'll be admitting why I did that. It was for my ain selfish satisfaction and pleasure. It was for the sake of the glow of gude feeling, the warmth o' heart, that came wi' the deed.

And in a' the affairs of life, it seems to me, we human folk were the same. We took too little thought of God. Religion was a failing force in the world. Hame ties were loosening; we'd no the appreciation of what hame meant that our faithers had had. Not all of us, maybe, but too many. And a' the time, God help us, we were like those folk that dwell in their wee hooses on the slopes of Vesuvius--puir folk and wee hooses that may be swept awa' any day by an eruption of the volcano.

All wasna sae richt and weel wi' the world as we thought it in you days. We'd closed our een to much of bitterness and hatred and malice that was loose and seeking victims in the hearts of men. Aye, it was the Hun loosed the war upon us. It was he who was responsible for the calamity that overtook the world--and that will mak' him suffer maist of all in the end, as is but just and richt. But we'd ha' had trouble, e'en gi'en there'd been no war.

It wouldna ha' been sae great, perhaps. There'd not be sae much grief and sae much unhappiness i' the world today, save for him. But there was something wrang wi' the world, and there had tae be a visitation of some sort before the world could be made better.

There's few things that come to a man or a nation in the way of grief and sorrow and trouble that are no punishments for some wickedness and sin o' his ain. We dinna always ken what it is we ha' done. And whiles the innocent maun suffer wi' the guilty--aye, that's a part of the punishment of the guilty, when they come to realize hoo it is they've carried others, maybe others they love, doon wi' them into the valley of despair.

I love Britain. I think you'll all be knowing that I love my native land better than anything i' the world. I'd ha' deed for her gladly-- aye, gladly. It was a sair grief tae me that they wadna tak' me. I tried, ye ken? I tried even before the Huns killed my boy, John. And I tried again after he'd been ta'en. Sae I had tae live for my country, and tae do what I could to help her.

But that doesna mean that I think my country's always richt. Far frae it. I ken only tae well that she's done wrang things. I'm minded of one of them the noo.

I've talked before of history. There was 1870, when Prussia crushed France. We micht ha' seen the Hun then, rearing himself up in Europe, showing what was in his heart. But we raised no hand. We let France fall and suffer. We saw her humbled. We saw her cast down. We'd fought against France--aye. But we'd fought a nation that was generous and fair; a nation that made an honorable foe, and that played its part honorably and well afterward when we sent our soldiers to fight beside hers in the Crimea.

France had clear een even then. She saw, when the Hun was in Paris, wi' his hand at her throat and his heel pressed doon upon her, that he meant to dominate all Europe, and, if he could, all the world. She begged for help--not for her sake alone, but for humanity. Humanity refused. And humanity paid for its refusal.

And there were other things that were wrang wi' Britain. Our cause was holy, once we began to ficht. Oh, aye--never did a nation take up the sword wi' a holier reason. We fought for humanity, for democracy, for the triumph of the plain man, frae the first. There are those will tell ye that Britain made war for selfish reasons. But it's no worth my while tae answer them. The facts speak for themselves.

But here's what I'm meaning. We saw Belgium attacked. We saw France threatened wi' a new disaster that would finish the murder her ain courage and splendor had foiled in 1871. We sprang to the rescue this time--oh, aye! The nation's leaders knew the path of honor--knew, too, that it was Britain's only path of safety, as it chanced. They declared war sae soon as it was plain how Germany meant to treat the world.

Sae Britain was at war, and she called oot her young men. Auld Britain--wi' sons and daughters roond a' the Seven Seas. I saw them answering the call, mind you. I saw them in Australia and New Zealand. I kissed my ain laddie gude bye doon there in Australia when he went back--to dee.

Never was there a grander outpouring of heroic youth. We'd no conscription in those first days. That didna come until much later. Sae, at the very start, a' our best went forth to ficht and dee. Thousands--hundreds of thousands--millions of them. And sae I come to those wha were left.

It's sair I am to say it. But it was in the hearts of sae many of those who stayed behind that we began tae be able tae see what had been wrang wi' Britain--and what was, and remains, wrang wi' a' the world to-day.

There were our boys, in France. We'd no been ready. We'd no spent forty years preparing ourselves for murder. Sae our boys lacked guns and shells, and aircraft, and a' the countless other things they maun have in modern war. And at hame the men in the shops and factories haggled and bargained, and thought, and talked. Not all o' them--oh, understand that in a' this I say that is harsh and bears doon hard upon this man and that, I'm only meaning a few each time! Maist of the plain folk i' the world are honest and straight and upright in their dealings.

But do you ken hoo, in a basket of apples, ane rotten one wi' corrupt the rest? Weel, it's sae wi' men. Put ane who's disaffected, and discontented, and nitter, in a shop and he'll mak' trouble wi' all the rest that are but seeking the do their best.

"Ca' Canny!" Ha' ye no heard that phrase?

It's gude Scots. It's a gude Scots motto. It means to go slow--to be sure before you leap. It sums up a' the caution and the findness for feeling his way that's made the Scot what he is in the wide world over. But it's a saying that's spread to England, and that's come to have a special meaning of its own. As a certain sort of working-man uses it it means this:

"I maun be carfu' lest I do too much. If I do as much as I can I'll always have to do it, and I'll get no mair pay for doing better--the maister'll mak' all the profit. I maun always do less than I could easily manage--sae I'll no be asked to do mair than is easy and comfortable in a day's work."

Restriction of output! Aye, you've heard those words. But do you ken what they were meaning early i' the war in Britain? They were meaning that we made fewer shells than we could ha' made. Men deed in France and Flanders for lack of the shells that would ha' put our artillery on even terms with that of the Germans.

It didna last, you'll be saying. Aye, I ken that. All the rules union labor had made were lifted i' the end. Labor in Britain took its place on the firing line, like the laddies that went oot there to ficht. Mind you, I'm saying no word against a man because he stayed at hame and didna ficht. There were reasons to mak' it richt for many a man tae do that. I've no sympathy wi' those who went aboot giving a white feather to every young man they saw who was no in uniform. There was much cruel unfairness in a' that.

But I'm saying it was a dreadfu' thing that men didna see for themselves, frae the very first, where their duty lay. I'm saying it was a dreadfu' thing for a man to be thinking just of the profit he could be making for himself oot of the war. And we had too many of that ilk in Britain--in labor and in capital as well. Mind you there were men i' London and elsewhere, rich men, who grew richer because of their work as profiteers.

And do you see what I mean now? The war was a great calamity. It cost us a great toll of grief and agony and suffering. But it showed us, a' too plainly, where the bad, rotten spots had been. It showed us that things hadna been sae richt as we'd supposed before. And are we no going to mak' use of the lesson it has taught us?

CHAPTER XXIII

I've had a muckle to say in this book aboot hoo other folk should be acting. That's what my wife tells me, noo that she's read sae far. "Eh, man Harry," she says, "they'll be calling you a preacher next. Dinna forget you're no but a wee comic, after a'!"

Aye, and she's richt! It's a good thing for me to remember that. I'm but old Harry Lauder, after a'. I've sung my songs, and I've told my stories, all over the world to please folk. And if I've done a bit more talking, lately, than some think I should, it's no been all my ain fault. Folk have seemed to want to listen to me. They've asked me questions. And there's this much more to be said aboot it a'.

When you've given maist of the best years of your life to the public you come to ken it well. And--you respect it. I've known of actors and other artists on the stage who thought they were better than their public--aye. And what's come tae them? We serve a great master, we folk of the stage. He has many minds and many tongues, and he tells us quickly when we please him--and when we do not. And always, since the nicht when I first sang in public, so many yearst agane that it hurts a little to count the tale o' them, I've been like a doctor who keeps his finger on the pulse of his patient.

I've tried to ken, always, day in, day oot, how I was pleasing you-- the public. You make up my audiences. And--it is you who send the other audiences, that hae no heard me yet, to come to the theatre. To- morrow nicht's audience is in the making to-nicht. If you folk who are out in front the noo, beyond the glare of the footlights, dinna care for me, dinna like the way I'm trying to please you, and amuse you, there'll be empty seats in the hoose to-morrow and the next day.

Sae that's my answer, I'm thinking, to my wife when she tells me to beware of turning into a preacher. I mind, do you ken, the way I've talked to audiences at hame, and in America and Australia, these last twa or three years. It was the war led me to do it first. I was surprised, in the beginning. I had just the idea of saying a few words. But you who were listening to me would not let me stop. You asked for more and more--you made me think you wanted to know what old Harry Lauder was thinking.

There was a day in Kansas City that I remember well. Kansas City is a great place. And it has a wonderful hall--a place where national conventions are held. I was there in 1918 just before the Germans delivered their great assault in March, when they came so near to breaking our line and reaching the Channel ports we'd held them from through all the long years of the war. I was nervous, I'll no be denying that. What Briton was not, that had a way of knowing how terrible a time was upon us? And I knew--aye, it was known, in London and in Washington, that the Hun was making ready for his last effort.

Those were dark and troubled days. The great American army that General Pershing has led hame victorious the noo was still in the making. The Americans were there in France, but they had not finished their training. And it was in the time when they were just aboot ready to begin to stream into France in really great numbers. But at hame, in America, and especially out West, it was hard to realize how great an effort was still needed.

America had raised her great armies. She had done wonders--and it was natural for those folk, safe at hame, and far, far away frae all the turmoil and the stress of the fighting, to think that they had done enough.

The Americans knew, you'll ken, that they were resistless. They knew that the gigantic power of America could crush half a dozen Germanys-- in time. But what we were all fearing, we who knew how grave the situation was, how tremendous the Hun's last effort would be, was that the line in France would be broken. The French had fought almost to the last gasp. Their young men were gone. And if the Hun broke through and swept his way to Paris, it was hard to believe that we could have gathered our forces and begun all over again, as we would have had to do.

In Kansas City there was a great chance for me, I was told. The people wanted to hear me talk. They wanted to hear me--not just at the theatre, but in the great hall where the conventions met. There was only the one time when I could speak, and I said so--that was at noon. It was the worst time of all the day to gather an audience of great size. I knew that, and I was sorry. But I had been booked for two performances a day while I was in Kansas City, and there was no choice.

Well, I agreed to appear. Some of my friends were afraid it would be what they called a frost. But when the time came for me to make my way to the platform the hall was filled. Aye--that mighty hall! I dinna ken how many thousand were there, but there were more than any theatre in the world could hold--more than any two theatres, I'm thinking. And they didna come to hear me sing or crack a joke. They came to hear me talk--to hear me preach, if you'll be using that same word that my wife is sae fond of teasing me with.

I'm thinking I did preach to them, maybe. I told them things aboot the war they'd no heard before, nor thought of, maybe, as seriously as they micht. I made them see the part they, each one of them, man, and woman, and child, had to play. I talked of their president, and of the way he needed them to be upholding him, as their fathers and mothers had upheld President Lincoln.

And they rose to me--aye, they cheered me until the tears stood in my een, and my voice was so choked that I could no go on for a space. So that's what I'm meaning when I say it's no all my fault if I preach, sometimes, on the stage, or when I'm writing in a book. It's true, too, I'm thinking, that I'm no a real author. For when I sit me doon to write a book I just feel that I maun talk wi' some who canna be wi' me to hear my voice, and I write as I talk. They'll be telling me, perhaps, that that's no the way to write a book, but it's the only way I ken.

Oh, I've had arguments aboot a' this! Arguments, and to spare! They'll come tae me, good friends, good advisers. They'll be worried when I'm in some place where there's strong feeling aboot some topic I'm thinking of discussing wi' my friends in the audience.

"Now, Harry, go easy here," I mind a Scots friend told me, once during the war. I was in a town I'll no be naming. "This is a queer place. There are a lot of good Germans here. They're unhappy about the war, but they're loyal enough. They don't want to take any great part in fighting their fatherland, but they won't help against their new country, either. They just want to go about their business and forget that there's a war."

Do you ken what I did in that town I talked harder and straighter about the war than I had in any place I'd talked in up to then! And I talked specially to the

Germans, and told them what their duty was, and how they could no be neutral.

I've small use for them that would be using the soft pedal always, and seeking to offend no one. If you're in the richt the man who takes offence at what you say need not concern you. Gi'en you hold a different opinion frae mine. Suppose I say what's in my mind, and that I think that I am richt and you are wrong. Wull ye be angry wi' me because of that? Not if you know you're richt! It's only the man who is'na sure of his cause who loses his temper and flies into a rage when he heard any one disagree wi' him.

There's a word they use in America aboot the man who tries to be all things to a' men--who tries to please both sides when he maun talk aboot some question that's in dispute. They call him a "pussyfooter." Can you no see sicca man? He'll no put doon his feet firmly--he'll walk on the balls of them. His een will no look straight ahead, and meet those of other men squarely. He'll be darting his glances aboot frae side to side, looking always for disapproval, seeking to avoid it. But wall he? Can he? No--and weel ye ken that--as weel as I! Show me sicca man and I'll show you one who ends by having no friends at all--one who gets all sides down upon him, because he was so afraid of making enemies that he did nothing to make himself freinds.

Think straight--talk straight. Don't be afraid of what others will say or think aboot ye. Examine your own heart and your own mind. If what you say and what you do suits your ain conscience you need ha' no concern for the opinions of others. If you're wrong--weel, it's as weel for you to ken that. And if you're richt you'll find supporters enough to back you.

I said, whiles back, that I'd in my mind cases of artists who thocht themselves sae great they need no think o' their public. Weel, I'll be naming no names--'twould but mak' hard feeling, you'll ken, and to no good end. But it's sae, richt enough. And it's especially sae in Britain, I think, when some great favorite of the stage goes into the halls to do a turn.

They're grand places to teach a sense of real value, the halls! In the theatre so muckle counts--the play, the rest of the actors, reputation, aye, a score of things. But in a music hall it's between you and the audience. And each audience must be won just as if you'd never faced one before. And you canna be familiar wi' your audience. Friendly--oh, aye! I've been friendly wi' my audiences ever since I've had them. But never familiar.

And there's a vast difference between friendliness and what I mean when I say familiarity. When you are familiar I think you act as though you were superior--that's what I mean by the word, at least, whether I'm richt or no. And it's astonishing how quickly an audience detects that--and, of course, resents it. Your audience will have no swank frae ye--no side. Ye maun treat it wi' respect and wi' consideration.

Often, of late, I've thocht that times were changing. Folk, too many of them, seem to have a feeling that ye can get something for nothing. Man, it's no so--it never will be so. We maun work, one way or another, for all we get. It's those lads and lassies who come tae the halls, whiles, frae the legitimate stage, that put me in mind o' that.

Be sure, if they've any real reputation upon the stage, they have earned it. Oh, I ken fine that there'll be times when a lassie 'll mak' her way tae a sort of success if she's a pretty face, or if she's gained a sort of fame, I'm sorry to say, frae being mixed up in some scandal or another. But--unless she works hard, unless she has talent, she'll no keep her success. After the first excitement aboot her is worn off, she's judged by what she can do--not by what the papers once said aboot her. Can ye no think of a hundred cases like that? I can, without half trying.

Weel, then, what I'm meaning is that those great actors and actresses, before they come to the halls to show us old timers what's what, and how to get applause, have a solid record of hard work behind them. And still some of them think the halls are different, and that there they'll be clapped and cheered just because of their reputations. They'd be astonished tae hear the sort of talk goes on in the gallery of the Pav., in London--just for a sample. I've heard!

"Gaw bli'me, Alf--'oo's this toff? Comes on next. 'Mr. Arthur Andrews, the Celebrated Shakespearian Actor.'"

"Never heard on him," says Alf, indifferently.

And so it goes. Mr. Andrews appears, smiling, self-possessed, waiting gracefully for the accustomed thunders of applause to subside. Sometimes he gets a round or two--from the stalls. More often he doesn't. Music hall audiences give their applause after the turn, not before, as a rule, save when some special favorite like Miss Vesta Tilley or Mr. Albert Chevalier or--oh, I micht as weel say it like old Harry

Lauder!--comes on!

And then Mr. Andrews, too often, goes stiffly through a scene from a play, or gives a dramatic recitation. In its place what he does would be splendid, and would be splendidly received. The trouble, too often, is that he does not realize that he must work to please this new audience. If he does, his regard will be rich in the event of success. I dinna mean just the siller he will earn, either.

It's true, I think, that there's a better living, for the really successful artist, in varieties than there is on the stage. There's more certainty--less of a speculative, dubious element, such as ye canna escape when there's a play involved. The best and most famous actors in the world canna keep a play frae being a failure if the public does not tak' to it. But in the halls a good turn's a good turn, and it can be used longer than even the most successful plays can run.

But still, it's no just the siller I was thinking of when I spoke of the rich rewards of a real success in the halls. An artist makes real friends there--warm-hearted, personal friends, who become interested in him and his career; who think of him, and as like as not, call him by his first name. Oh--aye, I've known artists who were offended by that! I mind a famous actor who was with me once when I was taking a walk in London, and a dozen costers, recognizing me, wished me good luck--it was just before I was tae mak' my first visit to America.

It was "Good luck, Harry," and "God bless you, Harry!" frae them. 'Deed, and it warmed the cockles of my heart to hear them! But my friend was quite shocked.

"I say, Harry--do you know those persons?" he said.

"Never saw them before," I told him, cheerfully.

"But they addressed you in the most familiar fashion," he persisted.

"And why not?" I asked. "I never saw them before--but they've seen me, thanks be! And as for familiarity--they helped to buy the shoon and the claes I'm wearing! They paid for the parritch I had for breakfast, and the bit o' beef I'll be eating for my dinner. If it wasna for them and the likes of them I'd still be digging coal i' the pit in Scotland! It'll be the sair day for me when they call me Mr. Lauder!"

I meant that then, and I mean it now. And if ever I hear a coster call out, "There goes Sir Harry Lauder," I'll ken it's time for me to be really doing what I'm really going tae do before sae long--retire frae the stage and gae hame to my wee hoose amang the heather at Dunoon tae live!

I'd no be having you think I'm meaning to criticize all the actors and actresses of the legitimate stage who have done a turn in the halls. Many of them are among our prime favorites, and our most successful artists. Some have given up appearing in plays to stick to the halls; some gae tae the halls only when they can find no fitting play to occupy their time and their talent. Some of the finest and most talented folk in the world are, actors and artists; whiles I think all the most generous and kindly folk are! And I can count my friends, warm, dear, intimate friends amang them by the score--I micht almost say by the hundred.

No, it's just the flighty ones that gie the rest a bad name I'm addressing my criticisms to. There'll be those that accept an opportunity to appear in the halls scornfully. They'll be lacking an engagement, maybe. And so they'll turn to the halls tae earn some siller easily, with their lips curling the while and their noses turned up. They see no need tae give of their best.

"Why should I really *act* for these people?" I heard one famous actor say once. "The subtleties of my art would be wasted upon them. I shall try to bring myself down to their level!"

Now, heard you ever sae hopeless a saying as that? It puts me in mind of a friend of mine--a novelist. He's a grand writer, and his readers, by the million, are his friends. It's hard for his publishers to print enough of his books to supply the demand. And he's a kindly, simple wee man; he ust does his best, all the time, and never worries aboot the results. But there are those that are envious of him. I mind the only time I ever knew him to be angry was when one of these, a man who could just get his books published, and no mair, was talking.

"Oh, I suppose I'll have to do it!" he said. "Jimmy"--Jimmy was the famous novelist my friend--"tell me how you write one of your best sellers? I think I'll turn out one or two under a pen name. I need some money."

Man, you can no even mak' money in that fashion! I ken fine there's men succeed, on the stage, and in literature, and in every other walk of life, who do not do the very best of work. But, mind you, they've this in common--they do the best they can! You may not have to be the best to win the public--but you maun be sincere, or it will punish you.

CHAPTER XXIV

When every one's talking sae much of Bolsheviki and Soviets it's hard to follow what it's just all about. It's a serious subject--aye, I'd be the last to say it wasna that! But, man--there's sae little in this world that's no got its lighter side, if we'll but see it!

I'm a great yin for consistency. Men are consistent--mair than women, I think. My wife will no agree with that, but it shall stand in spite of her. I'll be maister in my ain book, even if I canna be such in my ain hoose! And when it comes to all this talk of Bolshevism, I'm wondering how the ones that are for it would like it if their principles were really applied consistently to everything?

Tak' the theatre, just for an example. I mind a time when there was nearly a strike. It was in America, once, and I was on tour in the far West. Wall Morris, he that takes care of all such affairs for me, had given me a grand company. On those tours, ye ken, I travel with my ain company. That time there were my pipers, of coorse--it wouldna be my performance without those braw laddies. And there was a bonnie lassie to sing Scots songs in her lovely voice--a wee bit of a lassie she was, that surprised you with the strength of her voice when she sang.

There was a dancer, and some Japanese acrobats, and a couple more turns-- another singer, a man, and two who whistled like birds. And then there was just me, tae come on last.

Weel, there'd be trouble, once in sae often, aboot how they should gae on. None of them liked tae open the show; they thocht they were too good for that. And so they were, all of them, bless their hearts. There was no a bad act amang the lot. But still--some one had to appear first! And some one had to give orders. I forget, the noo, just how it was settled, but settled it was, at any rate, and all was peaceful and happy.

And then, whoever it was that did open got ill one nicht, and there was a terrible disturbance. No one was willing to take the first turn. And for a while it looked as if we could no get it settled any way at all. So I said that I would open the show, and they could follow, afterward, any way they pleased--or else that so and so must open, and no more argument. They did as I said.

But now, suppose there'd been a Bolshevik organization of the company? Suppose each act had had a vote in a council. Each one would have voted for a different one to open, and the fight could never have been settled. It took some one to decide it--and a way of enforcing the decision--to mak' that simple matter richt.

I'm afraid of these Bolsheviki because I don't think they know just what they are doing. I can deal with a man, whether I agree with him or no, if he just knows what it is he wants to do, and how. I'll find some common ground that we can both stand on while we have out our differences. But these folk aren't like that. They say what they don't mean. And they tell you, if you complain of that, they are interested only in the end they want to attain, and that the means they use don't matter.

Folk like that make an agreement never meaning to stick to it, ust to get the better of you for a little while. They mak' any promise you demand of them to get you quieted and willing to leave them alone, and then when the time comes and it suits them they'll break it, and laugh in your face. I'm not guessing or joking. And it's not the Bolshevists in Russia I'm thinking of--it's the followers of them in Britain and America, no matter what they choose to call themselves.

I've nothing to say about an out-and-out union labor fight. I've been oot on strike maself and I ken there's times when men have to strike to get their rights. They've reason for it then, and it's another matter. But some of the new sort of leaders of the men think anything is fair when they're dealing with an employer. They'll mak' agreements they've no sort of thought of keeping. I'll admit it's to their credit that they're frank.

They say, practically: "We'll make promises, but we won't keep them. We'll make a truce, but no peace. And we'll choose the time when the truce is to be broken."

And what I'm wanting to know is how are we going to do business that way, and live together, and keep cities and countries going? And suppose, just suppose, noo, doctrine like that was consistently applied?

Here's Mr. Radical. He's courtin' a lassie--supposing he's no one of those that believe in free love--and maybe if he is! I've found that the way to cure those that have such notions as that is to let the right lassie lay her een upon them. She'll like him fine as a suitor, maybe. She'll like the way he'll be taking her to dances, and spending his siller on presents for her, and on taking her oot to dinner, and the theatre. But, ye'll ken, she's no thocht of marrying him.

Still, just to keep him dangling, she promises she wull, and she'll let him slip his arm aboot her, and kiss her noo and again. But whiles she finds the lad she really loves, and she's off wi' him. Mr. Radical comes and reminds her of her promise.

"Oh, aye," she'll say, wi' a flirt of her head. "But that was like the promise you made at the works that you'd keep the men at work for a year on the new scale--when you called them oot on strike again within a month! Good day to you!"

Wull Mr. Radical say that's all richt, and that what's all sound and proper when he does it is the same when it's she does it tae him? Wull he? Not he! He'll call her false, and tell the tale of her perfidy tae all that wull listen to him!

But there's a thing we folk that want to keep things straight must aye remember. And that's that if everything was as it should be, Mr. Radical and his kind could get no following. It's because there's oppression and injustice in this bonny world of ours that an opening is made for those who think as do Trotzky and Lenine and the other Russians whose names are too hard for a simple plain man to remember.

We maun e'en get ahead of the agitators and the trouble makers by mending what's wrong. It's the way they use truth that makes them dangerous. Their lies wull never hurt the world except for a little while. It's because there's some truth in what they say that they make so great an impression as they do. Folk do starve that ask nothing better than a chance to earn money for themselves and their families by hard work. There is poverty and misfortune in the world that micht be prevented--that wull be prevented, if only we work as hard for humanity now that we have peace as we did when we were at war.

Noo, here's an example of what I'm thinking of. I said, a while back, that the folk that don't have bairns and raise them to make good citizens were traitors. Well, so they are. But, after a', it's no always their fault. When landlords wull not let their property to the families that have weans, it's a hard thing to think about. And it's that sort of thing makes folk turn into hating the way the world is organized and conducted. No man ought to have the richt to deny a hame to a man and his wife because they've a bairn to care for.

And then, too, there's many an employer bears doon upon those who work for him, because he's strong and they're weak. He'll say his business is his ain, to conduct as he sees fit. So it is--up to a certain point. But he canna conduct it by his lane, can he? He maun have help, or he would not hire men and women and pay them wages. And when he maun have their help he makes them his partners, in a way.

Jock'll be working for such an employer. He'll be needing more money, because the rent's been raised, and the wife's ailing. And his employer wull say he's sorry, maybe, but he canna afford to pay Jock more wages, because the cost of, diamonds such as his wife would be wearing has gone up, and gasolene for his motor car is more expensive, and silk shirts cost more. Oh, aye--I ken he'll no be telling Jock that, but those wull be his real reasons, for a' that!

Noo, what's Jock to do? He can quit--oh, aye! But Jock hasna the time, whiles he's at work, to hunt him anither job. He maun just tak' his chances, if he quits, and be out of work for a week or twa, maybe. And Jock canna afford that; he makes sae little that he hasna any siller worth speaking of saved up. So when his employer says, short like: "I cannot pay you more, Jock--tak' it or leave it!" there's nothing for Jock to do. And he grows bitter and discontented, and when some Bolshevik agitator comes along and tells Jock he's being ill used and that the way to make himself better off is to follow the revolutionary way, Jock's likely to believe him.

There's a bit o' truth, d'you see, in what the agitator tells Jock. Jock is ill used. He knows his employer has all and more than he needs or can use--he knows he has to pinch and worry and do without, and see his wife and his bairns miserable, so that the employer can live on the fat of the land. And he's likely, is he no, to listen to the first man who comes along and tells him he has a way to cure a' that? Can ye blame a man for that?

The plain truth is that richt noo, when there's more prosperity than we've ever seen before, there are decent, hard workingmen who canna afford to have as many bairns as they would wish, for lack of the siller to care for them properly after they come. There are men who mak' no more in wages than they did five years ago, when everything cost half what it does the noo. And they're listening to those who preach of general strikes, and overthrowing the state, and all the other wild remedies the agitators recommend.

Now, we know, you and I, that these remedies wouldn't cure the faults that we can see. We know that in Russia they're worse off for the way they've heeded Lenine and Trotzky and their crew. We know that you can't alter human nature that way, and that when customs and institutions have grown up for thousands of years it's because most people have found them good and useful. But here's puir Jock! What interests him is how he's to buy shoes for Jean and Andy, and a new dress for the wife, and milk for the wean that's been ailing ever since she was born. He hears the bairns crying, after they're put to bed, because they're hungry. And he counts his siller wi' the gude wife, every pay day, and they try to see what can they do without themselves that the bairns may be better off.

"Eh, man Jock, listen to me," says the sleek, well fed agitator. "Join us, and you'll be able to live as well as the King himself. Your employer's robbing you. He's buying diamonds for his wife with the siller should be feeding your bairns."

Foolishness? Oh, aye--but it's easier for you and me to see than for Jock, is it no?

And just suppose, noo, that a union comes and Jock gets a chance to join it--a real, old fashioned union, not one of the new sort that's for upsetting everything. It brings Jock and Sandy and Tom and all the rest of the men in the works together. And there's one man, speaking for a' of them, to talk to the employer.

"The men maun have more money, sir," he'll say, respectfully.

"I cannot pay it," says the employer.

"Then they'll go out on strike," says the union leader.

And the employer will whine and complain! But, do you mind, the shoe's on the other foot the noo! For now, if they all quit, it hurts him. He wouldna mind Jock quitting, sae lang as the rest stayed. But when they all go out together it shuts doon his works, and he begins to lose siller. And so he's likely to find that he can squeeze out a few shillings extra for each man's pay envelope, though that had seemed so impossible before. Jock, by himself, is weak, and at his employer's mercy. But Jock, leagued with all the other men in the works, has power.

Now, I hear a lot of talk from employers that sounds fine but is no better, when you come to pick it to pieces, than the talk of the agitators. Oh, I'll believe you if you tell me they're sincere, and believe what they say! But that does not mak' it richt for me to believe them, too!

Here's your employer who won't deal with a union.

"Every man in my shop can come to my office at any time and talk to me," he'll say. "He needs no union delegate to speak for him. I'll talk to the men any time, and do everything I can to adjust any legitimate grievance they may have. But I won't deal with men who presume to speak for them--with union delegates and leaders."

But can he no see, or wull he no see, that it's only when all the men in his shop bind themselves together that they can talk to him as man to man, as equal to equal? He's stronger than any one or twa of them, but when the lot of them are leagued together they are his match. That's what's meant by collective bargaining, and the employer who won't recognize that right is behind the times, and is just inviting trouble for himself and all the rest of us.

Let me tell you a story I heard in America on my last tour. I was away oot on the Pacific coast. It was when America was beginning her great effort in the war, and she was trying to build airplanes fast enough to win the mastery of the air frae the Hun. She needed spruce for them--and to supply us and France and Italy, as well. That spruce grew in great, damp forests in the States of Oregon and Washington--one great tree, that was suitable for making aircraft, to an acre, maybe. It was a great task to select those trees and hew them doon, and split and cut them up.

And in those forests lumbermen had been working for years. It was hard, punishing work; work for strong, rough men. And those who owned the forests and employed the men were strong, hard men themselves, as they had need to be. But they could not see that the men they employed had any richt to organize themselves. So always they fought, when a union appeared in the forests, and they had beaten them all.

The men were weak, dealing, each by himself, with his employer. The employers were strong. But presently a new sort of union came--the I. W. W. It did as it pleased. It cheated and lied. It made promises and didn't keep them. It didn't fight fair, the way the old unions did. And the men flocked to it--not because they liked to fight that way, but because that was the first time they had had a chance to deal with their employers on even terms.

So, very quickly, the I. W. W. had organized most of the men who worked in the forests. There had been a strike, the summer before I was there, and, after the men went back to work, they still soldiered on their jobs and did as little as they could--that was the way the I. W. W. taught them to do.

"Don't stay out on strike and lose your pay," the I. W. W. leaders said. "That's foolish. Go back--but do as little as you can and still not be dismissed. Poll a log whenever you can without being caught. Make all the trouble and expense you can for the bosses."

And here was the world, all humanity, needing the spruce, and these men acting so! The American army was ordered to step in. And a wise American officer, seeing what was wrong, soon mended matters. He was stronger than employers and men put together. He put all that was wrong richt. He saw to it that the men got good hours, good pay, good working conditions. He organized a new union among them that had nothing to do with the I. W. W. but that was strong enough to make the employers deal fairly with it.

And sae it was that the I. W. W. began to lose its members. For it turned out that the men wanted to be fair and honorable, if the employers would but meet them half way, and so, in no time at all, work was going on better than ever, and the I. W. W. leaders could make no headway at all among the workers. It is only men who are discontented because they are unfairly treated who listen to such folk as those agitators. And is there no a lesson for all of us in that?

CHAPTER XXV

I've heard much talk, and I've done much talking myself, of charity. It's a beautiful word, yon. You mind St. Paul--when be spoke of Faith, Hope, Charity, and said that the greatest of these was Charity? Aye-- as he meant the word! Not as we've too often come to think of it.

What's charity, after a'? It's no the act of handing a saxpence to a beggar in the street. It's a state of mind. We should all be charitable--surely all men are agreed on that! We should think weel of others, and believe, sae lang as they wull let us, that they mean to do what's right and kind. We should not be bitter and suspicious and cynical. God hates a cynic.

But charity is a word that's as little understood as virtue. You'll hear folk speak of a woman as virtuous when she may be as evil and as wretched a creature as walks this earth. They mean that she's never sinned the one sin men mean when they say a lassie's not virtuous! As if just abstaining frae that ane sin could mak' her virtuous!

Sae it's come to be the belief of too many folk that a man can be called charitable if he just gives awa' sae muckle siller in a year. That's not enough to mak' him charitable. He maun give thought and help as well as siller. It's the easiest thing in the world to gie siller; easier far than to refuse it, at times, when the refusal is the more charitable thing for one to be doing.

I ken fine that folk think I'm close fisted and canny wi' my siller. Aye, and I am--and glad I am that's so. I've worked hard for what I have, and I ken the value of it. That's mair than some do that talk against me, and crack jokes about Harry Lauder and his meanness. Are they so free wi' their siller? I'll imagine myself talking wi' ane of them the noo.

"You call me mean," I'll be saying to him. "How much did you give away yesterday, just to be talking? There was that friend came to you for the loan of a five-pound note because his bairn was sick? Of coorse ye let him have it--and told him not to think of it as a loan, syne he was in such trouble?"

"Well--I would have, of course, if I'd had it," he'll say, changing color a wee bit. "But the fact is, Harry, I didn't have the money--"

"Oh, aye, I see," I'll answer him. "I suppose you've let sae many of your friends have money lately that you're a bit pinched for cash? That'll be the way of it, nae doot?"

"Well--I've a pound or two outstanding," he'll say. "But--I suppose I owe more than there is owing to me."

There's one, ye'll see, who's not mean, not close fisted. He's easy wi' his money; he'd as soon spend his siller as no. And where is he when the pinch comes--to himself or to a friend? He can do nothing, d'ye ken, to help, because he's not saved his siller and been carefu' with it.

I've helped friends and strangers, when I could. But I've always tried to do it in such a way that they would help themselves the while. When there's real distress it's time to stint yourself, if need be, to help another. That's charity--real charity. But is it charity to do as some would do in sich a case as this?

Here'll be a man I know coming tae me.

"Harry," he'll say, "you're rich--it won't matter to you. Lend me the loan of a ten-pound note for a few weeks. I'd like to be putting oot some siller for new claes."

And when I refuse he'll call me mean. He'll say the ten pounds wouldn't matter to me--that I'd never miss them if he never did return the siller. Aye, and that's true enough. But if I did it for him why would I not be doing it for Tom and Dick and Harry, too? No! I'll let them call me mean and close fisted and every other dour thing it pleases them to fancy me. But I'll gae my ain gait wi' my ain siller.

I see too much real suffering to care about helping those that can help themselves--or maun do without things that aren't vital. In Scotland, during the war, there was the maist terrible distress. It's a puir country, is Scotland. Folk there work hard for their living. And the war made it maist impossible for some, who'd sent their men to fight. Bairns needed shoes and warm stockings in the cold winters, that they micht be warm as they went to school. And they needed parritch in their wee stomachs against the morning's chill.

Noo, I'll not be saying what Mrs. Lauder and I did. We did what we could. It may have been a little--it may have been mair. She and I are the only ones who ken the truth, and the only ones who wull ever ken it--that much I'll say. But whenever we gave help she knew where the siller was going, and how it was to be spent. She knew that it would do real good, and not be wasted, as it would have been had I written a check for maist of those who came to me for aid.

When you talk o' charity, Mrs. Lauder and I think we know it when we see it. We've handled a goodly share of siller, of our own, and of gude friends, since the war began, that's gone to mak' life a bit easier for the unfortunate and the distressed.

I've talked a deal of the Fund for Scottish Wounded that I raised-- raised with Mrs. Lauder's help. We've collected money for that wherever we've gone, and the money has been spent, every penny of it, to make life brighter and more worth living for the laddies who fought and suffered that we micht all live in a world fit for us and our bairns.

It wasna charity those laddies sought or needed. It was help--aye. And it took charity, in the hearts of those who helped, to do anything for them. But there is an ugly ring to that word charity as too many use it the noo. I've no word to say against the charitable institutions. They do a grand work. But it is only a certain sort of case that they can reach. And they couldna help a boy who'd come home frae Flanders with both legs gone.

A boy like that didna want charity to care for him and tend him all his days, keeping him helpless and dependent. He wanted help--help to make his own way in the world and earn his own living. And that's what the Fund has given him. It's looked into his case, and found out what he could do.

Maybe he was a miner before the war. Almost surely, he was doing some sort of work that he could do no longer, with both legs left behind him in France. But there was some sort of work he could do. Maybe the Fund would set him up in a wee shop of his ain, provide him with the capital to buy his first stock, and pay his first year's rent. There are men all over Scotland who are well able, the noo, to tak' care of themselves, thanks to the Fund--men who'd be beggars, practically, if nothing of the sort had existed to lend them a hand when their hour of need had come.

But it's the bairns that have aye been closest to our hearts--Mrs. Lauder's and mine. Charity can never hurt a child--can only help and improve it, when help is needed. And we've seen them, all about our hoose at Dunoon. We've known what their needs were, and the way to supply them. What we could do we've done.

Oh, it's not the siller that counts! If I could but mak' those who have it understand that! It's not charity to sit doon and write a check, no matter what the figures upon it may be. It's not charity, even when giving the siller is hard--even when it means doing without something yourself. That's fine--oh, aye! But it's the thought that goes wi' the giving that makes it worth while--that makes it do real good. Thoughtless giving is almost worse than not giving at all-- indeed, I think it's always really worse, not just almost worse.

When you just yield to requests without looking into them, without seeing what your siller is going to do, you may be ruining the one you're trying to help. There are times when a man must meet adversity and overcome it by his lane, if he's ever to amount to anything in this world. It's hard to decide such things. It's easier just to give, and sit back in the glow of virtue that comes with doing that. But wall your conscience let you do sae? Mine wull not--nor Mrs. Lauder's.

We've tried aimless charity too lang in Britain, as a nation. We did in other times, after other wars than this one. We've let the men who fought for us, and were wounded, depend on charity. And then, we've forgotten the way they served us, and we've become impatient with them. We've seen them begging, almost, in the street. And we've seen that because sentimentalists, in the beginning, when there was still time and chance to give them real help, said it was a black shame to ask such men to do anything in return for what was given to them.

"A grateful country must care for our heroes," they'd say. "What-- teach a man blinded in his country's service a trade that he can work at without his sight? Never! Give him money enough to keep him!"

And then, as time goes on, they forget his service--and he becomes just another blind beggar!

Is it no better to do as my Fund does? Through it the blind man learns to read. He learns to do something useful--something that will enable him to *earn* his living. He gets all the help he needs while he is learning, and, maybe, an allowance, for a while, after he has learnt his new trade. But he maun always be working to help himself.

I've talked to hundreds and hundreds of such laddies--blind and maimed. And they all feel the same way. They know they need help, and they feel they've earned it. But it's help they want not coddling and alms. They're ashamed of those that don't understand them better than the folk who talk of being ashamed to make them work.

CHAPTER XXVI

In all the talk and thought about what's to be, noo that the war's over with and done, I hear a muckle of different opinions aboot what the women wull be doing. They're telling me that women wull ne'er be the same again; that the war has changed them for good--or for bad!-- and that they'll stay the way the war has made them.

Weel, noo, let's be talking that over, and thinking about it a wee bit. It's true that with the war taking the men richt and left, women were called on to do new things; things they'd ne'er thought about before 1914. In Britain it was when the shells ran short that we first saw women going to work in great numbers. It was only richt that they should. The munitions works were there; the laddies across the Channel had to have guns and shells. And there were not men enough left in Britain to mak' all that were needed.

I ken fine that all that has brocht aboot a great change. When a lassie's grown used to the feel of her ain siller, that's she's earned by the sweat of her brow, it's not in reason that she should be the same as one that has never been awa' frae hame. She'll be more independent. She'll ken mair of the value of siller, and the work that goes to earning it. And she'll know that she's got it in her to do real work, and be really paid for doing it.

In Britain our women have the vote noo' they got so soon as the war showed that it was impossible and unfair to keep it frae them longer. It wasna smashing windows and pouring treacle into letter boxes that won it for them, though. It wasna the militant suffragettes that persuaded Parliament to give women the vote. It was the proof the women gave that in time of war they could play their part, just as men do.

But now, why should we be thinking that, when the war's over, women will be wanting tae go on just as they did while it was on? Would it not be just as sensible to suppose that all the men who crossed the sea to fight for Britain would prefer to stay in uniform the rest of their lives?

Of coorse there'll be cases where women wull be thinking it a fine thing to stay at work and support themselves. A lassie that's earned her siller in the works won't feel like going back to washing dishes and taking orders about the sweeping and the polishing frae a cranky mistress. I grant you that.

Oh, aye--I ken there'll be fine ladies wull be pointing their fingers at me the noo and wondering does Mrs. Lauder no have trouble aboot the maids! Weel, maybe she does, and maybe she doesn't. I'll let her tell aboot a' that in a hook of her own if you'll but persuade her to write one. I wish you could! She'd have mair of interest to tell you than I can.

But I've thocht a little aboot all this complaining I hear about servants. Have we not had too many servants? Were we not, before the war, in the habit of having servants do many things for us we micht weel have done for ourselves? The plain man--and I still feel that it is a plain man's world that we maun live in the noo-- needs few servants. His wife wull do much of the work aboot the hoose herself, and enjoy doing it, as her grandmither did in the days when housework was real work.

I've heard women talking amang themselves, when they didn't know a man was listening tae them, aboot their servants--at hame, and in America. They're aye complaining.

"My dear!" one will say. "Servants are impossible these days! It's perfectly absurd! Here's Maggie asking me for fifteen dollars a week! I've never paid anything like that, and I won't begin now! The idea!"

"I know--isn't it ridiculous? What do they do with their money? They get their board and a place to sleep. Their money is all clear profit --and yet they're never satisfied. During the war, of course, we were at their mercy--they could get work any time they wanted it in a munitions plant----."

And so on. These good ladies think that girls should work for whatever their mistresses are willing to pay. And yet I canna see why a girl should be a servant because some lady needs her. I canna see why a lassie hasna the richt to better herself if she can. And if the ladies cannot pay the wages the servants ask, let them do their own work! But do not let them complain of the ingratitude and the insolence of girls who only ask for wages such as they have learned they can command in other work.

But to gae back to this whole question of what women wull be doing, noo that the war's over. Some seem tae think that Jennie wall never be willing to marry Andy the noon, and live wi' him in the wee hoose he can get for their hame. She got Andy's job, maybe. And she's been making more money than ever Andy did before he went awa'. Here's what they're telling me wull happen.

Andy'll come hame, all eager to see his Jenny, and full of the idea of marrying her at once. He'll have been thinking, whiles he was out there at the front, and in hospital--aye, he'd do mair thinking than usual aboot it when he was in hospital--of the wee hoose he and Jennie wad be living in, when the war was over. He'd see himself kissing Jennie gude-bye in the morn, as he went off to work, and her waiting for him when he came hame at nicht, and waving to him as soon as she recognized him.

And he'd think, too, sometimes, of Jennie wi' a bairn of theirs in her arms, looking like her, but wi' Andy's nose maybe, or his chin. They'd be happy thoughts--they'd be the sort of thoughts that sustained Andy and millions like him, frae Britain, and America, and Canada, and Australia, and everywhere whence men went forth to fight the Hun.

Weel, here'd be Andy, coming hame. And they're telling me Jennie wad be meeting him, and giving him a big, grimy hand to shake.

"Kiss me, lass," Andy wad say, reaching to tak' her in his arms.

And she'd gie a toss of her pretty head. "Oh, I've no time for foolishness like that the noo!" she'd tell him, for answer.

"No time? What d'ye mean, lass?"

"I'll be late at the works if ye dinna let me go--that's what I mean."

"But--dinna ye love me any more'?"

"Oh, aye--I love ye weel enough, Andy. But I canna be late at the works, for a' that!"

"To the de'il wi' the works! Ye'll be marrying be as soon as may be, and then there'll be no more works for ye, lass--"

"That's only a rumor! I'm sticking to my job. Get one for yourself, and then maybe I'll talk o' marrying you--and may be no!"

"Get me a job? I've got one--the one you've been having!"

"Aye--but it's my job the noo, and I'll be keeping it. I like earning my siller, and I'm minded to keep on doing it, Andy."

And off she goes, and Andy after her, to find she's told the truth, and that they'll not turn her off to make way for him.

"We'd like to have you back, Andy," they'll tell him. "But if the women want to stay, stay they can."

Well, I'll be asking you if it's likely Jenny will act so to her boy, that's hame frae the wars? Ye'll never mak' me think so till you've proved it. Here's the picture I see.

I see Jenny getting more and more tired, and waiting more and more eagerly for Andy to come hame. She's a woman, after a', d'ye ken, and a young one. And there are some sorts of work women were not meant or made to do, save when the direst need compels. So, wi' the ending of the war, and its strain, here's puir Jennie, wondering how long she must keep on before her Andy comes to tak' care of her and let her rest.

And--let me whisper something else. We think it shame whiles, to talk o' some things. But here's Nature, the auld mither of all of us. She's a purpose in the world, has that auld mither--and it's that the race shall gae on. And it's in the heart and the soul, the body and the brain, of Jennie that she's planted the desire that her purpose shall be fulfilled.

It's bairns Jenny wants, whether or no she kens that. It's that helps to mak' her so eager for Andy to be coming back to her. And when she sees him, at long last, I see her flinging herself in his arms, and thanking God wi' her tears that he's back safe and sound--her man, the man she's been praying for and working for.

There'll be problems aboot women, dear knows. There are a' the lassies whose men wull no come back, like Andy--whose lads lie buried in a foreign grave. It's not for me to talk of the sad problem of the superfluous woman--the lassie whose life seems to be over when it's but begun. These are affairs the present cannot consider properly. It will tak' time to show what wull be happening and what maun be done.

But I'm sure that no woman wull give up the opportunity to mak' a hame, to bring bairns into the world, for the sake of continuing the sort of freedom she's had during the war. It wad be like cutting off her nose to do that.

Oh, I ken fine that men wull have to be more reasonable than they've been, sometimes, in the past. Women know more than they did before the war opened the gates of industry to them. They'll not be put upon, the way I'm ashamed to admit they sometimes were in the old days. But I think that wull be a fine thing for a' of us. Women and men wull be comrades more; there'll be fewer helpless lassies who canna find their way aboot without a man to guide them. But men wull like that--I can tell ye so, though they may grumble at the first.

The plain man wull have little use for the clinging vine as a wife. He'll want the sort of wife some of us have been lucky enough to have even before the war. I mean a woman who'll tak' a real note of his affairs, and be ready to help him wi' advice and counsel; who'll understand his problems, and demand a share in shaping their twa lives. And that's the effect I'm thinking the war is maist likely to have upon women. It wull have trained them to self-reliance and to the meeting of problems in a new way.

And here's anither thing we maun be remembering. In the auld days a lassie, if she but would, could check up the lad that was courtin' her. She could tell, if she'd tak' the trouble to find oot, what sort he was--how he stud wi' those who knew him. She could be knowing how he did at work, or in business, and what his standing was amang those who knew him in that way. It was different when a man was courtin' a lassie. He could tell little about her save what he could see.

Noo that's been changed. The war's been cruelly hard on women as weel as on men. It's weeded them oot. Only the finest could come through the ordeals untouched--that was true of the women at hame as of the men on the front line. And now, when a lad picks out a lassie he's no longer got the excuses he once had for making a mistake.

He can be finding oot how she did her work while he was awa' at the war. He can be telling what those who worked wi' her thought of her, and whether she was a good, steady worker or not. He can make as many inquiries aboot her as she can aboot him, and sae they'll be on even terms, if they're both sensible bodies, before they start.

And there's this for the lassies who are thinking sae muckle of their independence. They're thinking, perhaps, that they can pick and choose because they've

proved they can earn their livings and keep themselves. Aye, that's true enough.
But the men can do more picking and choosing than before, too!

But doesna it a' come to the same answer i' the end--that it wall tak' more than
even this war to change human nature? I think that's so.

It's unfashionable, I suppose, to talk of love. They'll be saying I'm an auld sen-
timentalist if I remind you of an old saying--that it's love that makes the world go
round. But it's true. And love wall be love until the last trumpet is sounded, and it
wall make men and women, lads and lassies, act i' the same daft way it always has-
-thank God!

Love brings man and woman together--makes them attractive, one to the ither.
Wull some matter of economics keep them apart? Has it no been proved, ever since
the beginning of the world, that when love comes in nothing else matters? To be
sure--to be sure.

It's a strange thing, but it's aye the matters that gie the maist concern to the
prophets of evil that gie me the greatest comfort when I get into an argument or a
discussion aboot the war and its effects upon humanity. They're much concerned
about the bairns. They tell me they've got out of hand these last years, and that
there's no doing anything wi' them any more. Did those folk see the way the Boy
Scouts did, I wonder?

Everywhere those laddies were splendid. In Britain they were messengers;
they helped to guard the coasts; they did all sorts of work frae start to finish. They
released thousands of men who wad have been held at hame except for them.

And it was the same way in America. There I helped, as much as I could, in
selling Liberty Bonds. And I saw there the way the Boy Scouts worked. They sold
more bonds than you would have thought possible. They helped me greatly, I know.
I'd be speaking at some great meeting. I'd urge the people to buy--and before they
could grow cold and forget the mood my words had aroused in them, there'd be a
boy in uniform at their elbows, holding a blank for them to sign.

And the little girls worked at sewing and making bandages. I dinna ken just
what these folk that are so disturbed aboot our boys and girls wad be wanting.
Maybe they're o' the sort who think bairns should be seen and not heard. I'm not
one of those, maself--I like to meet a bairn that's able and willing to stand up and
talk wi' me. And all I can say is that those who are discouraged about the future of

the race because of the degeneration of childhood during the war do not know what they're talking about.

Women and children! Aye, it's well that we've talked of them and thought of them, and fought for them. For the war was fought for them--fought to make it a better world for them. Men did not go out and suffer and die for the sake of any gain that they could make. They fought that the world might be a better one for children yet unborn to live in, and for the bairns they'd left behind to grow up in.

Was there, I wonder, any single thing that told more of the difference between the Germans and the allies than the way both treated women and children? The Germans looked on their women as inferior beings. That was why they could be guilty of such atrocities as disgraced their armies wherever they fought. They were well suited with the Turks for their own allies. The place that women hold in a country tells you much about it; a land in which women are not rated high is not one in which I'd want to live.

And if women wull be better off in Britain and America than they were, even before the war, that's one of the ways in which the war has redeemed itself and helped to pay for itself. I think they wull--but I've no patience wi' those who talk as if men and women had different interests, and maun fight it out to see which shall dominate.

They're equal partners, men and women. The war has shown us that; has proved to us men how we can depend upon our women to tak' over as much of our work as maun be when the need comes. And that's a great thing to have learned. We all pray there need be no more wars; we none of us expect a war again in our time. But if it comes one of the first things we wull do wull be to tak' advantage of what we've learned of late about the value and the splendor of our women.

CHAPTER XXVII

I've been pessimistic, you'll think, maybe, in what I've just been saying to you. And you'll be wondering if I think I kept my promise-- to prove that this can be a better, a bonnier world than it was before yon peacefu' days of 1914 were blotted out. I have'na done sae yet, but I'm in the way of doing it. I've tried to mak' you see that yon days were no sae bonny as we a' thocht them.

But noo! Noo we've come tae a new day. This auld world has seen a great sacrifice--a greater sacrifice than any it has known since Calvary. The brawest, the noblest, the best of our men, have offered themselves, a' they had and were, upon the altar of liberty and of conscience.

And I'll ask you some questions. Gie'n you're asked, the noo, tae do something that's no just for your ain benefit. Whiles you would ha' thought, maybe, and hesitated, and wondered. But the noo? Wull ye no be thinking of some laddie who gave up a' the world held that was dear to him, when his country called? Wull ye no be thinking that, after a', ought that can be asked of you in the way of sacrifice and effort is but a sma' trifle compared to what he had tae do?

I'm thinking that'll be sae. I'm thinking it'll be sae of all of us. I'm thinking that, sae lang as we live, we folk that ken what the war was, what it involved for the laddies who fought it, we'll be comparing any hardship or privation that comes tae us wi' what it was that they went through. And it's no likely, is it, that we'll ha' the heart and the conscience tae be saying 'No!' sae often and sae resolutely as used tae be our wont?

They've put shame into us, those laddies who went awa'. They ha' taught us the real values o' things again. They ha' shown us that i' this world, after a', it's men, not things, that count. They helped to prove that the human spirit was a greater, grander thing than any o' the works o' man. The Germans had all that a body could ask. They had numbers, they had guns, they had their devilish inventions. What beat them, then? What held them back till we could match them in numbers and in a' the other things?

Why, something Krupp could not manufacture at Essen nor the drillmasters of the Kaiser create! The human will--the spirit that is God's creature, and His alone.

I was in France, you'll mind. I remember weel hoo I went ower the ground where the Canadians stood the day the first clouds of poison gas were loosed. There were sae few o' them--sae pitifully few! As it was they were ootmatched; they were hanging on because they were the sort o' men wha wouldna gie in. French Colonials were supporting them on one side.

And across the No Man's Land there came a sort o' greenish yellow cloud. No man there knew what it meant. There was a hissing and a writhing, as of snakes, and like a snake the gas came toward them. It reached them, and men began to cough and choke. And other men fell doon, and their faces grew black, and they deed, in an agony such as the man wha hasna seen it canna imagine--and weel it is, if he would sleep o' nichts, that he canna.

The French Colonials broke and ran. The line was open. The Canadians were dying fast, but not a man gave way. And the Hun came on. His gas had broken the line. It was open. The way was clear to Ypres. That auld, ruined toon, that had gi'en a new glory to British history in November o' the year before, micht ha' been ta'en that day. And, aye, the way was open further than that. The Germans micht ha' gone on. Calais would ha' fallen tae them, and Dunkirk. They micht ha' cut the British army awa' frae it's bases, and crumpled up the whole line along the North Sea.

But they stopped, wi' the greatest victory o' the war within their grasp. They stopped. They waited. And the line was formed again. Somehow, new men were found tae tak' the places of those who had deed. Masks against the gas were invented ower nicht. And the great chance o' the Germans tae win the war was gone.

Why? It was God's will? Aye, it was His will that the Hun should be beaten. But God works wi' human instruments. And His help is aye for they that help themselves--that's an auld saying, but as true a one as ever it was.

I will tell you why the Germans stopped. It was for the same reason that they stopped at Verdun, later in the war. It was for the same reason that they stopped again near Chateau Thierry and gave the Americans time to come up. They stopped because they couldna imagine that men would stand by when they were beaten.

The Canadians were beaten that day at Ypres when the gas came upon them. Any troops i' the world would ha' been beaten. The Germans knew that. They knew just hoo things were. And they knew that, if things had been sae wi' them, they would ha' run or surrendered. And they couldna imagine a race of men that would do otherwise--that would dee rather than admit themselves beaten.

And sae, do you ken hoo it was the German officers reasoned?

"There is something wrong with our information," they decided. "If things were really, over there, as we have believed, those men would be quitting now. They may be making a trap ready for us. We will stop and make sure. It is better to be safe than sorry."

Sae, because the human spirit and its invincibility was a thing beyond their comprehension, the German officers lost the chance they had to win the war.

And it is because of that spirit that remains, that survives, in the world, that I am so sure we can mak' it a world worthy of those who died to save it. I would no want to live anither day myself if I didna believe that. I would want to dee, that I micht see my boy again. But there is work for us all tae do that are left and we have no richt to want, even, to lay doon our burdens until the time comes when God wills that we maun.

Noo--what are the things we ha' tae do? They are no just to talk, you'll be saying. 'Deed, and you're richt!

Wull you let me touch again on a thing I've spoken of already?

We ken the way the world's been impoverished. We've seen tae many of our best laddies dee these last years. They were the husbands the wee lassies were waiting for--the faithers of bairns that will never be born the noo. Are those that are left doing a' that they should to mak' up that loss?

There's selfishness amang those who'll no ha' the weans they should. And it's a selfishness that brings its ain punishment--be sure of that. I've said before, and I'll say again, the childless married pair are traitors to their country, to the world, to humanity. Is it that folk wi' children find it harder to live? Weel, there's truth i' that, and it's for us a' tae see that that shall no be so.

I ken there are things that discourage them that would bring up a family o' bairns. Landlords wull ask if there are bairns, and if there are they'll seek anither tenant. It's no richt. The law maun step in and reach them. Oh, I mind a story I heard frae a friend o' mine on that score.

He's a decent body, wi' six o' the finest weans e'er you saw. He'd to find a bigger hoose, and he went a' aboot, and everywhere, when he told the landlords he had six bairns, they'd no have him. Else they'd put up the rent to sic a figure he couldna pay it. In the end, though, he hit upon a plan. Ane day he went tae see an agent aboot a hoose that was just the yin to suit him. He liked it fine; the agent saw he was a solid man, and like tae be a gude tenant. Sae they were well along when the inevitable question came.

"How many children have you?" asked the agent.

"Six," said my friend.

"Oh," said the agent. "Well--let's see! Six is a great many. My principal is a little afraid of a family with so many children. They damage the houses a good deal, you know. I'll have to see. I'm sorry. I'd have liked to let the house to you. H'm! Are all the children at home?" "No," said my friend, and pulled a lang face. "They're a' in the kirkyard."

"Oh--but that's very different," said the agent, growing brichter at once. "That's a very different case. You've my most sincere sympathy. And I'll be glad to let you the house."

Sae the lease was signed. And my friend went hame, rejoicing. On the way he stopped at the kirkyard, and called the bairns, whom he'd left there to play as he went by!

But this is a serious matter, this one o' bairns. Folk must have them, or the country will gae to ruin. And it maun be made possible for people to bring up their weans wi'oot sae much trouble and difficulty as there is for them the noo.

Profiteering we canna endure--and will'na, I'm telling you. Let the profiteer talk o' vested richts and interests--or whine o' them, since he whines mair than he talks. It was tae muckle talk o' that sort we were hearing before the war and in its early days. It was one of the things that was wrang wi' the world. Is there any richt i' the world that's as precious as that tae life and liberty and love? And didna our young men gie that up at the first word?

Then dinna let your profiteer talk to me of the richts of his money. He has duties and obligations as well as richts, and when he's lived up to a' o' them, it'll be time for him tae talk o' his richts again, and we'll maybe be in a mood tae listen. It's the same wi' the workingman. We maun produce, i' this day. We maun mak' up for a' the waste and the loss o' these last years. And the workingman kens as weel as do I that after a fire the first thing a man does is tae mak' the hoose habitable again.

He mends the roof. He patches the holes i' the walls. Wad he be painting the veranda before he did those things? Not unless he was a fule--no, nor building a new bay window for the parlor. Sae let us a' be thinking of what's necessary before we come to thought of luxuries.

CHAPTER XXVIII

Weel, I'm near the end o' my tether. It's been grand tae sit doon and talk things ower wi' you. We're a' friends together, are we no? Whiles I'll ha' said things wi' which you'll no agree; whiles, perhaps, we've been o' the same way o' thinking. And what I'm surest of is that there's no a question in this world aboot which reasonable men canna agree.

We maun get together. We maun talk things over. Here and noo there's ane great trouble threatening us. The man who works isna satisfied. Nor is the man who pays him. I'll no speak of maister and man, for the day when that was true of employer and workman has gone for aye. They're partners the noo. They maun work together, produce together, for the common gude.

We've seen strikes on a' sides, and in a' lands. In Britain and in America I've seen them.

I deplore a strike. And that's because a strike is like a war, and there's no need for either. One side can force a war--as the Hun did. But if the Hun had been a reasonable, decent body--and I'm praying we've taught him, all we Allies, that he maun become such if he's tae be allowed tae go on living in the world at a'!--he could ha' found the rest o' the world ready to talk ower things wi' him.

And when it comes tae a strike need ane side or the other act like the Hun? Is it no always sae that i' the end a strike is settled, wi' both sides giving in something to the other? How often maun one or the other be beaten flat and crushed? Seldom, indeed. Then why canna we get together i' the beginning, and avoid the bitterness, and the cost of the struggle?

The thing we've a' seen maist often i' the war was the fineness of humanity. Men who hadna seemed tae be o' much account proved themselves true i' the great test. It turned oot, when the strain was put upon them, that maist men were fine and brave and full of the spirit of self sacrifice. Men learned that i' the trenches. Women proved it at hame. It was one for a', and a' for one.

Shall we drop a' that noo that peace has come again? Shall we gie up a' we ha' learned of how men of different minds can pull together for a common end? I'm thinking we'll no be such fools. We had to pull together i' the war to keep frae being destroyed. But noo we've a chance to get something positive--to mak' something profitable and worth while oot of pulling together. Before it was just a negative thing that made us do it. It was fear, in a way. It was the threat that the Hun made against all we held most dear and sacred.

Noo it's sae different. We worked miracles i' the war. We did things the world had thought impossible. They've aye said that it was necessity that was the mither of invention, and the war helped again tae prove hoo true a saying that was. Weel, canna we make the necessity for a better world the mother of new and greater inventions than any we ha' yet seen? Can we no accomplish miracles still, e'en though the desperate need for them has passed?

That's the thing I think of maist these days--that it would be a sair thing and a tragic thing if the spirit that filled the world during the war should falter the noo. We've suffered sae much--we've given sae much of our best. We maun gain a' that we can in return. And the way has been pointed tae us. It is but for us to follow it.

Things have aye been done in certain ways. Weel, they seemed ways gude enow. But when the war came we found they were no gude enow, for all we'd thocht. And because it was a case of must, we changed them. There's many would gae back. They say that wi' the end o' the war there maun be an end o' all the changes that it brought. But we could do more, we could accomplish more, through those changes. I say it would be a foolish thing and a wicked thing to go back.

It was each man for himself before the war. It couldna be sae when the bad times came upon us. We had to draw together. Had we no done so we should have perished. Men drew together in each country; nations approached one another and stood together in the face of the common peril. They have a choice now. They can draw apart again. Or they can stay together and advance wi' a resistless force toward a better life for a' mankind.

I've the richt to say a' this. I made my sacrifice. I maun wait, the noo, until I dee before I see my bairn again. When I talk o' suffering it's as ane who has suffered. When I speak of grief it's as ane who has known it, and when I think of the tears that have been shed it is as ane who has shed his share. When I speak of a mother's grief for her son that is gone, and her hope that he has not deed in vain, it is as one who has sought to comfort the mither of his ain son.

So it's no frae the ootside that auld Harry Lauder is looking on. It's no just talk he's making when he speers sae wi' you. He kens what his words mean, does Harry.

I ken weel what it means for men to pull together. I've seen them doing sae wi' the shadow of death i' the morn upon their faces. I've sung, do you mind, at nicht, for men who were to dee next day, and knew it. And they were glad, for they knew that they were to dee sae that the world micht have a better, fuller life. I'd think I was cheating men who could no longer help themselves or defend themselves against my cheating were I to gie up the task undone that they ha' left tae me and tae the rest of us.

Aye, it's a bonny world they've saved for us. But it's no sae bonny yet as it maun be--and as, God helping us, we'll mak' it!

The Codes Of Hammurabi And Moses
W. W. Davies

QTY

The discovery of the Hammurabi Code is one of the greatest achievements of archaeology, and is of paramount interest, not only to the student of the Bible, but also to all those interested in ancient history...

Religion   **ISBN:** *1-59462-338-4*   **Pages:132**
MSRP $12.95

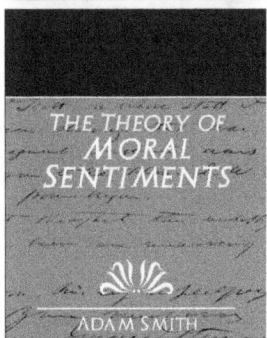

The Theory of Moral Sentiments
Adam Smith

QTY

This work from 1749. contains original theories of conscience amd moral judgment and it is the foundation for systemof morals.

Philosophy   **ISBN:** *1-59462-777-0*   **Pages:536**
MSRP $19.95

Jessica's First Prayer
Hesba Stretton

QTY

In a screened and secluded corner of one of the many railway-bridges which span the streets of London there could be seen a few years ago, from five o'clock every morning until half past eight, a tidily set-out coffee-stall, consisting of a trestle and board, upon which stood two large tin cans, with a small fire of charcoal burning under each so as to keep the coffee boiling during the early hours of the morning when the work-people were thronging into the city on their way to their daily toil...

Pages:84

Childrens   **ISBN:** *1-59462-373-2*   *MSRP $9.95*

My Life and Work
Henry Ford

QTY

Henry Ford revolutionized the world with his implementation of mass production for the Model T automobile. Gain valuable business insight into his life and work with his own auto-biography... "We have only started on our development of our country we have not as yet, with all our talk of wonderful progress, done more than scratch the surface. The progress has been wonderful enough but..."

Pages:300

Biographies/   **ISBN:** *1-59462-198-5*   *MSRP $21.95*

www.bookjungle.com *email: sales@bookjungle.com fax: 630-214-0564 mail: Book Jungle PO Box 2226 Champaign, IL 61825*

The Art of Cross-Examination
Francis Wellman

QTY

I presume it is the experience of every author, after his first book is published upon an important subject, to be almost overwhelmed with a wealth of ideas and illustrations which could readily have been included in his book, and which to his own mind, at least, seem to make a second edition inevitable. Such certainly was the case with me; and when the first edition had reached its sixth impression in five months, I rejoiced to learn that it seemed to my publishers that the book had met with a sufficiently favorable reception to justify a second and considerably enlarged edition. ..

Reference **ISBN:** *1-59462-647-2*   **Pages:412**
MSRP $19.95

On the Duty of Civil Disobedience
Henry David Thoreau

QTY

Thoreau wrote his famous essay, On the Duty of Civil Disobedience, as a protest against an unjust but popular war and the immoral but popular institution of slave-owning. He did more than write—he declined to pay his taxes, and was hauled off to gaol in consequence. Who can say how much this refusal of his hastened the end of the war and of slavery ?

Law   **ISBN:** *1-59462-747-9*   **Pages:48**
MSRP $7.45

Dream Psychology Psychoanalysis for Beginners
Sigmund Freud

QTY

Sigmund Freud, born Sigismund Schlomo Freud (May 6, 1856 - September 23, 1939), was a Jewish-Austrian neurologist and psychiatrist who co-founded the psychoanalytic school of psychology. Freud is best known for his theories of the unconscious mind, especially involving the mechanism of repression; his redefinition of sexual desire as mobile and directed towards a wide variety of objects; and his therapeutic techniques, especially his understanding of transference in the therapeutic relationship and the presumed value of dreams as sources of insight into unconscious desires.

Psychology   **ISBN:** *1-59462-905-6*   **Pages:196**
MSRP $15.45

The Miracle of Right Thought
Orison Swett Marden

QTY

Believe with all of your heart that you will do what you were made to do. When the mind has once formed the habit of holding cheerful, happy, prosperous pictures, it will not be easy to form the opposite habit. It does not matter how improbable or how far away this realization may see, or how dark the prospects may be, if we visualize them as best we can, as vividly as possible, hold tenaciously to them and vigorously struggle to attain them, they will gradually become actualized, realized in the life. But a desire, a longing without endeavor, a yearning abandoned or held indifferently will vanish without realization.

Self Help   **ISBN:** *1-59462-644-8*   **Pages:360**
MSRP $25.45

www.bookjungle.com *email: sales@bookjungle.com fax: 630-214-0564 mail: Book Jungle PO Box 2226 Champaign, IL 61825*

QTY

The Rosicrucian Cosmo-Conception Mystic Christianity by *Max Heindel* ISBN: *1-59462-188-8* **$38.95**
The Rosicrucian Cosmo-conception is not dogmatic, neither does it appeal to any other authority than the reason of the student. It is: not controversial, but is: sent forth in the, hope that it may help to clear... New Age/Religion Pages 646

Abandonment To Divine Providence by *Jean-Pierre de Caussade* ISBN: *1-59462-228-0* **$25.95**
"The Rev. Jean Pierre de Caussade was one of the most remarkable spiritual writers of the Society of Jesus in France in the 18th Century. His death took place at Toulouse in 1751. His works have gone through many editions and have been republished... Inspirational/Religion Pages 400

Mental Chemistry by *Charles Haanel* ISBN: *1-59462-192-6* **$23.95**
Mental Chemistry allows the change of material conditions by combining and appropriately utilizing the power of the mind. Much like applied chemistry creates something new and unique out of careful combinations of chemicals the mastery of mental chemistry... New Age Pages 354

The Letters of Robert Browning and Elizabeth Barret Barrett 1845-1846 vol II ISBN: *1-59462-193-4* **$35.95**
by *Robert Browning* and *Elizabeth Barrett* Biographies Pages 596

Gleanings In Genesis (volume I) by *Arthur W. Pink* ISBN: *1-59462-130-6* **$27.45**
Appropriately has Genesis been termed "the seed plot of the Bible" for in it we have, in germ form, almost all of the great doctrines which are afterwards fully developed in the books of Scripture which follow... Religion/Inspirational Pages 420

The Master Key by *L. W. de Laurence* ISBN: *1-59462-001-6* **$30.95**
In no branch of human knowledge has there been a more lively increase of the spirit of research during the past few years than in the study of Psychology, Concentration and Mental Discipline. The requests for authentic lessons in Thought Control, Mental Discipline and... New Age/Business Pages 422

The Lesser Key Of Solomon Goetia by *L. W. de Laurence* ISBN: *1-59462-092-X* **$9.95**
This translation of the first book of the "Lernegton" which is now for the first time made accessible to students of Talismanic Magic was done, after careful collation and edition, from numerous Ancient Manuscripts in Hebrew, Latin, and French... New Age/Occult Pages 92

Rubaiyat Of Omar Khayyam by *Edward Fitzgerald* ISBN:*1-59462-332-5* **$13.95**
Edward Fitzgerald, whom the world has already learned, in spite of his own efforts to remain within the shadow of anonymity, to look upon as one of the rarest poets of the century, was born at Bredfield, in Suffolk, on the 31st of March, 1809. He was the third son of John Purcell... Music Pages 172

Ancient Law by *Henry Maine* ISBN: *1-59462-128-4* **$29.95**
The chief object of the following pages is to indicate some of the earliest ideas of mankind, as they are reflected in Ancient Law, and to point out the relation of those ideas to modern thought. Religion History Pages 452

Far-Away Stories by *William J. Locke* ISBN: *1-59462-129-2* **$19.45**
"Good wine needs no bush, but a collection of mixed vintages does. And this book is just such a collection. Some of the stories I do not want to remain buried for ever in the museum files of dead magazine-numbers an author's not unpardonable vanity..." Fiction Pages 272

Life of David Crockett by *David Crockett* ISBN: *1-59462-250-7* **$27.45**
"Colonel David Crockett was one of the most remarkable men of the times in which he lived. Born in humble life, but gifted with a strong will, an indomitable courage, and unremitting perseverance... Biographies/New Age Pages 424

Lip-Reading by *Edward Nitchie* ISBN: *1-59462-206-X* **$25.95**
Edward B. Nitchie, founder of the New York School for the Hard of Hearing, now the Nitchie School of Lip-Reading, Inc, wrote "LIP-READING Principles and Practice". The development and perfecting of this meritorious work on lip-reading was an undertaking... How-to Pages 400

A Handbook of Suggestive Therapeutics, Applied Hypnotism, Psychic Science ISBN: *1-59462-214-0* **$24.95**
by *Henry Munro* Health/New Age/Health/Self-help Pages 376

A Doll's House: and Two Other Plays by *Henrik Ibsen* ISBN: *1-59462-112-8* **$19.95**
Henrik Ibsen created this classic when in revolutionary 1848 Rome. Introducing some striking concepts in playwriting for the realist genre, this play has been studied the world over. Fiction/Classics/Plays 308

The Light of Asia by *sir Edwin Arnold* ISBN: *1-59462-204-3* **$13.95**
In this poetic masterpiece, Edwin Arnold describes the life and teachings of Buddha. The man who was to become known as Buddha to the world was born as Prince Gautama of India but he rejected the worldly riches and abandoned the reigns of power when... Religion/History/Biographies Pages 170

The Complete Works of Guy de Maupassant by *Guy de Maupassant* ISBN: *1-59462-157-8* **$16.95**
"For days and days, nights and nights, I had dreamed of that first kiss which was to consecrate our engagement, and I knew not on what spot I should put my lips..." Fiction/Classics Pages 240

The Art of Cross-Examination by *Francis L. Wellman* ISBN: *1-59462-309-0* **$26.95**
Written by a renowned trial lawyer, Wellman imparts his experience and uses case studies to explain how to use psychology to extract desired information through questioning. How-to/Science/Reference Pages 408

Answered or Unanswered? by *Louisa Vaughan* ISBN: *1-59462-248-5* **$10.95**
Miracles of Faith in China Religion Pages 112

The Edinburgh Lectures on Mental Science (1909) by *Thomas* ISBN: *1-59462-008-3* **$11.95**
This book contains the substance of a course of lectures recently given by the writer in the Queen Street Hall, Edinburgh. Its purpose is to indicate the Natural Principles governing the relation between Mental Action and Material Conditions... New Age/Psychology Pages 148

Ayesha by *H. Rider Haggard* ISBN: *1-59462-301-5* **$24.95**
Verily and indeed it is the unexpected that happens! Probably if there was one person upon the earth from whom the Editor of this, and of a certain previous history, did not expect to hear again... Classics Pages 380

Ayala's Angel by *Anthony Trollope* ISBN: *1-59462-352-X* **$29.95**
The two girls were both pretty, but Lucy who was twenty-one who supposed to be simple and comparatively unattractive, whereas Ayala was credited, as her Bombwhat romantic name might show, with poetic charm and a taste for romance. Ayala when her father died was nineteen... Fiction Pages 484

The American Commonwealth by *James Bryce* ISBN: *1-59462-286-8* **$34.45**
An interpretation of American democratic political theory. It examines political mechanics and society from the perspective of Scotsman James Bryce Politics Pages 572

Stories of the Pilgrims by *Margaret P. Pumphrey* ISBN: *1-59462-116-0* **$17.95**
This book explores pilgrims religious oppression in England as well as their escape to Holland and eventual crossing to America on the Mayflower, and their early days in New England... History Pages 268

QTY

The Fasting Cure *by Sinclair Upton*　　　　　　ISBN: *1-59462-222-1*　**$13.95**
In the Cosmopolitan Magazine for May, 1910, and in the Contemporary Review (London) for April, 1910, I published an article dealing with my experiences in fasting. I have written a great many magazine articles, but never one which attracted so much attention... New Age/Self Help/Health Pages 164

Hebrew Astrology *by Sepharial*　　　　　　　ISBN: *1-59462-308-2*　**$13.45**
In these days of advanced thinking it is a matter of common observation that we have left many of the old landmarks behind and that we are now pressing forward to greater heights and to a wider horizon than that which represented the mind-content of our progenitors...　Astrology Pages 144

Thought Vibration or The Law of Attraction in the Thought World　ISBN: *1-59462-127-6*　**$12.95**
by William Walker Atkinson　　　　　　　　　　　　　　　　　*Psychology/Religion Pages 144*

Optimism *by Helen Keller*　　　　　　　　　ISBN: *1-59462-108-X*　**$15.95**
Helen Keller was blind, deaf, and mute since 19 months old, yet famously learned how to overcome these handicaps, communicate with the world, and spread her lectures promoting optimism. An inspiring read for everyone...　Biographies/Inspirational Pages 84

Sara Crewe *by Frances Burnett*　　　　　　　ISBN: *1-59462-360-0*　**$9.45**
In the first place, Miss Minchin lived in London. Her home was a large, dull, tall one, in a large, dull square, where all the houses were alike, and all the sparrows were alike, and where all the door-knockers made the same heavy sound...　Childrens/Classic Pages 88

The Autobiography of Benjamin Franklin *by Benjamin Franklin*　　ISBN: *1-59462-135-7*　**$24.95**
The Autobiography of Benjamin Franklin has probably been more extensively read than any other American historical work, and no other book of its kind has had such ups and downs of fortune. Franklin lived for many years in England, where he was agent...　Biographies/History Pages 332

Name	
Email	
Telephone	
Address	
City, State ZIP	

☐ **Credit Card**　　　　　☐ **Check / Money Order**

Credit Card Number	
Expiration Date	
Signature	

Please Mail to:　Book Jungle
PO Box 2226
Champaign, IL 61825
or Fax to:　　　630-214-0564

ORDERING INFORMATION

web: *www.bookjungle.com*
email: *sales@bookjungle.com*
fax: *630-214-0564*
mail: *Book Jungle PO Box 2226 Champaign, IL 61825*
or PayPal *to sales@bookjungle.com*

Please contact us for bulk discounts

DIRECT-ORDER TERMS

**20% Discount if You Order
Two or More Books**
Free Domestic Shipping!
Accepted: Master Card, Visa,
Discover, American Express